EMBERS

By

David Atherall

ISBN: 978-1-917778-12-1

Sometimes, your feet are weary,
Sometimes, the way is long,
Sometimes, the day is dreary,
Sometimes, the world goes wrong,
But if you let your voices ring,
Your hope will soar up high,
So, we'll sing a song as we march along,
Of Sussex by the Sea.

Oh Sussex, Sussex by the Sea!
Good old Sussex by the Sea!
You may tell them all that we stand or fall
For Sussex by the Sea.

Adapted from William Ward-Higgs' original

Steve Gritt

Foreword

When I joined Brighton and Hove Albion in December of the 1996/97 season, little did I know what effect my decision would have on that season, on my own career and, ultimately, my long-term relationship with the Brighton supporters. I am pleased and proud to say that I have never been allowed to forget that incredible season by supporters who I meet at various locations around the country. Over the years, the club have always invited me back for dinners, presentations and anniversaries of that memorable season. Another journey back into the past came when I received a message from Brighton and Hove Albion supporter, David Atherall telling me about a project that he was embarking on.

He told me that he was going to write a novel, not just relating to that season, but also about the life of a 16-year-old lad at the time, the boys' own personal ups and downs throughout those turbulent times as a Brighton supporter, about his family, friends and others involved in his life during that intriguing time.

On reading *Embers* for the first time, I was absorbed as it conveyed the emotions of Danny - a lad going through his formative years, having to deal with many obstacles that would suddenly come his way, many of which, I'm sure, will resonate with people reading this book. Alongside his personal challenges, he was also going through what was happening to his beloved Brighton, coping with the highs and lows of life on the terraces, along with the other supporters at the time.

Before arriving at Brighton, I'd been looking for an opportunity to get back into football, having left Charlton Athletic in the summer of 1995. There are only ninety-two manager jobs in the football league and there is always a lot of competition for every job; I feared that I might not be able to get back involved with football in the way I wanted to. I'd been turned down by Gravesend and Northfleet for being over-qualified and I didn't know where my next opportunity would come. And then, along came Brighton. I met with David Bellotti at Gatwick Airport before travelling up to Crewe for an interview with Bill Archer. I don't know if I was their first choice or whether they even thought it was realistic that we would survive relegation, but they gave me the job.

I could see immediately that Brighton had good players and that if I could get them playing as a team, to their potential, we would get results. The front four of Craig Maskell, Ian Baird, Stuart Storer and Paul McDonald would provide goals and so I built the rest of the team around players I could trust to run their hearts out, put a tackle in and give the ball to one of the front four. We needed defensive stability and at home, we achieved that, keeping eight clean sheets out of the twelve games I oversaw at the Goldstone. I knew that work-rate was crucial to winning football games and I made that central to my coaching as well as trying to bring positivity to a group of players who hadn't had much success in recent matches.

One thing that I realised while reading *Embers* was that a lot, if not all, of the supporters were equally mystified, as indeed I am, that the team were unable to win a game away from the Goldstone when we seemed unbeatable at home during my time at the club that season. There was clearly something very special about the Goldstone! The crowd were a massive influence and as the results improved, the crowds grew and the atmosphere changed, driving us onto victory.

There was barely any money to bring players into the club, so I had to look at the players and the squad and consider how to build a team. Kerry Mayo hadn't had much game-time before I came and looked like he was about to leave the club, but I saw that he had the energy we needed in central midfield. I'm proud that he went on to be a club legend and make over four-hundred appearances for the club.

I brought in John Humphrey on a free transfer. He was thirty-six and coming to the end of his career, but I knew that he could defend and that he would also offer us an option going forward. The only money I managed to convince the board to spend was on Robbie Reinelt and I'm sure every Brighton fan will agree, he was worth every penny. I knew what he was capable of, knew he had goals in him and he had one very special goal just when we needed it.

Embers also made me realise, even more so than at the time, the feelings and actions of the supporters during this period, which was something I never always saw, or experienced enough of. I was busy preparing the team for each game and time has allowed me to reflect on the wider picture that *Embers* explores. It also gave me an insight into what happened before I arrived at the club. As a manager, I had to be focused on the football and getting the best out of the team and while I think what we achieved on the pitch was special, I also recognise that what the fans achieved off the pitch was special and is the foundation of what the club are today.

Before Brighton, I was at Charlton Athletic and my time there coincided with one of the most turbulent times of their history during the 1985/86 season when they suddenly left The Valley after playing against Stoke City in September of that season, with the fans only really being told in a note inserted into the programme for that day. As you can imagine, the supporters, like the Brighton fans, were not happy, especially when they were informed that they would have to watch their team playing 'home' games at their local rivals, Crystal Palace. A protest ensued at half-time of that game, which was the start of many campaigns by the supporters to get the club back to The Valley, which would not happen for another eight years!

A decade later, I was at another club facing similar troubles and *Embers* highlights the lengths fans go to when they want to make their point about how their clubs are treated, and what steps they are prepared to take. Charlton brought several coaches of fans to Brighton's fabulous victory over Hartlepool for the Fans United Day and they were there because they knew how important a club's home is to them. They were always a massive support to me and that day, they led the Brighton fans in singing my name for the very first time. It was a special moment after a frosty welcome at the start. Undoubtedly, the fans saved Brighton during that season and look at the heights they've climbed to now.

The combination of the stories, trials and tribulations that Danny goes through in this novel alongside the memories of each game made this book even more interesting for me, and it is put together wonderfully well. That fateful, yet wonderful season can be relived again through these pages, enjoyed by not just Brighton fans but all football fans. I found it absorbing and enjoyable to read, and I'm sure you will too.

Forever, COME ON YOU SEAGULLS!

27th April 1996

Brighton & Hove Albion vs York City

"Which one do you want? You can have any one of them for four quid."

Ethan flipped through Danny's CD collection - all five of them. He already knew what would be there, knew the soundtrack to Danny's life: *Nevermind* by Nirvana, *Replenish* by Reef, *I Should Coco* by Supergrass and Oasis' first two albums, *Definitely Maybe* and *What's the Story Morning Glory?* Danny played these albums on a loop, at a distorted top volume in his tiny box-bedroom, that he shared with his nine-year-old brother, Simon, until his mum wearily battled through the piles of dirty clothes that were clogging up the door to tell him that the music was depressing her. The tracks also accompanied him on his paper-round route, blasting out of the headphones until the batteries sent Kurt/Gary/Gaz/Liam into a slow-motion drawl and then, into nothingness. Each of them felt like part of his soul - melodramatic (of course) but what sixteen-year-old doesn't feel every emotion like it's the nadir or zenith of existence? *Nevermind* was his impotent fury; *Replenish* was the late-night longing for something more, the album he put on just before he got into bed; *I Should Coco* was his optimism and Oasis was the hopeless euphoria - their songs captured his love of life whilst at the same time, a frustrating futility: "Is it worth the aggravation to find yourself a job when there's nothing worth working for?" he sang at the top of his voice as he walked down the stairs in just his boxer shorts every morning. The rousing battle-cry, a line from Oasis' 'Cigarettes and Alcohol,' made his mum wince, knowing that the best she could hope for from his GCSEs next month was that he would actually turn up.

Study leave had been granted to the students of Hove High School - shortened to HoHi by the students - but Danny had not used the 'study leave' to dedicate himself to mastering algebra, contemplating Macbeth's hamartia or getting his head around electrolysis. Instead, it had simply given him the freedom to develop the slothful routine of sleeping until the *Neighbours* theme-tune woke him up at 1.35pm; an hour or so of *Sensible World of Soccer* accompanied by the album that most matched his mood; exercise for the day: a thirty-minute paper-round route and then back to Ethan's house to see what Ethan's mum had on the menu that evening. Ethan's parents had come to accept that their weekly food-shop needed to include Danny. They'd gently suggested that Danny's family might want to have dinner with him some nights of the week, but Danny knew that his absence made life simpler and cheaper for his family and he tactically pretended to ignore the implied meaning which was something along the lines of: *We like you and feel sorry for you and we do want to show you kindness by welcoming you to our dinner table... but not every bloody day.* They were too nice to say this though and so, every single day, Danny was there, sat around the small circular table in the Brown family kitchen enjoying Mrs Brown's, occasionally Mr Brown's, delicious food. Every now and then, they even ordered an Indian takeaway, something Danny's family were never able to extend their budget to and he was introduced to the wonders of chicken bhunas, rogan joshes, lamb pathias, onion bhajis and peshwari naans.

"Come on, these cost me double that - it's a bargain," implored Danny, desperate to get the four quid from his friend.

His desperation came from the fact that there was one home game of the football season remaining and it was unthinkable that Danny would not be at the Goldstone Ground, stood two-thirds of the way up the North Stand terrace in line with the left goalpost. He had to be there to witness his beloved and already relegated Brighton and Hove Albion finish the season against York City, perhaps finish altogether.

"I'll take *Nevermind* and *I Should Coco* for four quid," said Ethan, "and I don't even really want them, but I know you're desperate to be at the game."

He was desperate to be at the game. He would have sold all five albums, purchased for close to £40 with his birthday money the previous month, for the entrance fee. The thought of not being there felt tortuous. Even an average game, even an Auto Windscreens Shield match felt unmissable, so whatever possession he had to part with, he would part with if it got him through those blue, rusty turnstiles.

The final home game of the season almost always promised the treat of a pitch invasion. Usually, this was a once-a-season moment - a thrilling spilling onto the turf at every goal, regardless of its meaninglessness in the grand scheme of the league table. This season, however, was different. The football had been, mostly, terrible and Brighton were 23rd out of twenty-four and could not move up or down in the league table, regardless of the result. But, the football hadn't felt like the thing that had mattered most that year. The thing that mattered deeply to every fan was the betrayal by the board which came down to the selling of the Goldstone Ground with no replacement or plans for the future. There were regular articles in the local paper, *The Argus*, that explained the board's lack of scruples, in particular their removal of a non-profit clause in the club's paperwork that meant that individuals could now use the club to boost their own personal funds. The paper explained how Bill Archer had acquired the club for a tiny £56.25 investment and was now negotiating the multi-million-pound sale of the one asset the club had (the ground was worth around £7.4 million pounds, the players worth nothing). Danny understood little of the financial foul play. What he did understand at a visceral level was that he loved Saturday afternoons on the crumbling terraces, being knocked off his feet every time a goal went in but some blokes in suits that reminded him of his dad were taking that away.

Doors were shutting everywhere. His dad had walked out four months ago. On Boxing Day, his dad had sat him down and told him that he was old enough to understand that relationships don't always work out and that he'd always be his dad, but that he wasn't going to live with him anymore. He told him that he needed to be the "man of the house," to look after his brother for him. Three weeks later, on a cold January morning, he'd left in his creased suit and had never returned, gone to Wales or somewhere near Wales to be with a woman called Sharon. It had been obvious that his mum and dad were unhappy, but Danny had thought that everyone was unhappy, that it was just the way things were, particularly for adults with kids and jobs and bills. His dad had called every Friday and spoken with his brother, Simon, but Danny had decided that his dad needed punishing and his silence, his refusal to come to the phone was the mildest of punishments for his dad's departure.

The school door had pretty much closed too. He didn't care about that, was glad in fact. On the last day of Year 11, everyone was getting their shirts signed by each other, but he didn't see the point. While the rest of the school strolled around, names of classmates, hastily drawn genitalia and swear words scrawled across their shirts, Danny ambled through his final few hours of education with a pristine, untouched white shirt. He'd enjoyed the moment at the end of the day when two boys had whipped all their clothes off and sprinted round the field and he'd enjoyed it even more when their mates had stolen the pile of abandoned clothes and chucked them onto the roof of the school gym. School though was a place of vindictive cruelty most of the time, lads who rode mopeds stalking the corridors dishing out dead arms and sometimes, gobs of phlegm. The shutting of that door was an utter relief.

Now, these men in suits seemed to be shutting the door to his football club too, robbing him of his Saturdays. Whilst the football had been repeatedly drab, off the pitch, the righteous anger of the crowd had created an unpredictable, chaotic and exciting atmosphere on the terraces. Thoughtful men and women sought solutions: wrote letters, created petitions, tried to pull in local politicians, but the young men of the North Stand just wanted to lash out: invading pitches, singing songs of defiance and violence, and burning papier-mâché effigies of the Chairman, Bill Archer. The anger was a bubbling river of lava that poured from the stands onto the pitch every game; it was the anger of a lover who knows that their relationship is dying. For Danny, the thought of Brighton not existing was unthinkable, but when he artificially lowered his voice to a more masculine twang and launched into a furious rendition of "Sack the board," his cry of anger was an expression of all that he had lost: childish exuberance, certainty of what life was all about, purpose, his dad… and his football club.

He just had to be at what was potentially the funeral of the club. There was no certainty of what the next season held. There were talks of ground-sharing with Portsmouth, but Danny had joined with the chant, "We'll never go to Pompey," and to travel forty-seven miles to the home of one of their rivals each week would feel like supporting a different club and Danny's reason for not going to Portsmouth was not simply a gesture of protest, but a recognition of the fact that he did not have enough CDs to sell to make that journey regularly.

Ethan dropped the four pound coins into Danny's hand and the hand-to-mouth scrambling for enough money to attend matches had worked once again as it had done for every previous game that season. The £8 wages for his paper-round usually did the trick, but sometimes, games piled up in quick succession and budgeting for expanding his CD collection and never missing a home game was something that stretched his budget too thin.

Danny knew, though, that he would get the money. Ethan wouldn't leave him hanging. A quick raid of the Brown fridge yielded two scotch eggs, four sausage rolls and a quick gobble-down of some leftover rhubarb crumble. This match demanded super-early arrival and so, with still two and a half hours until kick-off, Danny and Ethan knocked on Ethan's neighbour, James' door. There were two years between Danny and Ethan and another two years down to the squeaky-voiced James. James' parents were entirely ignorant of the frenzied atmosphere at the Goldstone Ground. They'd taken James to a sedate 0-0 draw two years earlier in better and calmer times for his birthday and sat in the family-friendly South Stand. They thought him well looked after by Danny and Ethan, but the reality was that if James wanted to go the game with these older boys, and he desperately did, he simply had to survive the riotous mosh-pit every time Brighton scored and to be fair to him, although there were occasional tears, he did pretty well.

James emerged in his Brighton goalkeeper shirt, completing the look with goalie gloves. His toothy eager grin was an almost constant feature on his face - at twelve-years-old, he hadn't yet developed the teenage cynicism that Danny and Ethan carried with them. He still ran rather than walked, always eager like a dog chasing a ball, his thick black mop of hair bouncing as he approached the boys.

Ethan had gone for the more straightforward XL men's home shirt; Danny wore an XXXL blue and black striped third kit which had been on sale for fiver in the club shop when the shirt ceased to be used, the only size remaining, a shirt that

Danny could camp in. The sleeves would have taken the biceps of Jeff Capes with room to spare and on Danny's spindly arms, they flapped in the breeze. Ethan added his dad's 1983 FA Cup Final bucket hat, an object of awe, a connection with the successful Brighton of the past that neither Danny nor James had. When Danny was three, unbeknownst to him at the time, Brighton had their most glorious moment, an FA Cup final against Manchester United: a 2-2 draw with a chance to win it at the death - *and Smith must score!* but he didn't - and they lost the replay 4-0 and they'd never had it so good since and now, they'd never had it so bad. This hat, that had perched on top of Mr Brown's head as he walked Wembley Way, spoke of better times when football was what people talked about at Brighton. Thirteen years on, those days felt like they would never return.

The walk to the ground took the boys through Hove Park where families strolled with their young children; a cluster of teenagers sat around the basketball court and elderly people tottered past, slowly circling the paved path that surrounded football pitches, ancient trees and youthful saplings, tennis courts and a fenced-off children's playground. Alongside the path, a miniature train, families perched on top, clattered along a raised track, hiccupping a discordant whistle as it passed the boys who paid it no attention. In amongst the purposeless people whiling away their Saturdays, there were flashes of blue and white stripes, Brighton shirts appearing from behind trees, people on a mission, and as eyes met, a greeting of 'Seeeeeagulls' erupted, startling toddlers and grannies alike.

"It's got to be Nicky Rust for Player of the Season," chirped James.

Ever since he'd got the goalkeeper's shirt for his birthday, he'd been obsessed with playing in goal and the Brighton keeper.

"Nicky, can I have your gloves?" chimed Danny and Ethan as high-pitched as they could muster, before laughing hysterically at James.

This had become James' mantra from behind the goal every time Rust had come to collect a ball that hit the advertising hoardings during the warm-up. Rust had probably never heard James' ridiculous request that he part with his gloves before the game had even started and if he had heard, he simply ignored the squeaked request.

"There is no chance it's going to Rust. It will be Sneaky George or da-na-na-na" - Ethan joined Danny in the build-up to the *Batman* theme tune - "na-na-na-na-na, CHAPMAN!" said-sung the boys.

"It'll be Chapman. Sneaky George has only scored *that* goal. He can't get around the pitch. Chapman has been solid," said Ethan.

The goal that had endeared the Brighton fans to Sneaky George Parris was a moment of a quick-thinking, where he'd hidden behind the goalpost until the goalkeeper had thrown the ball in front of him to launch it up-field. Parris had burst from behind the goal, nudged the ball away from the keeper and rolled the ball into the empty net, a glorious high-point in an otherwise terrible season. Ian Chapman, Brighton's left-back, was popular for the more obvious reason of being a tough-tackling defender who left opposition wingers in crumpled heaps (much to the fans' delight).

The boys approached the huge rock - the Goldstone - that Brighton's ground had been named after. The legend went that the devil had been excavating a valley on the South Downs - Devil's Dyke - and had stubbed his toe on this boulder and in anger, had booted it, like one of Nicky Rust's goal-kicks, high into the sky and it had landed in this spot in Hove Park. A small iron fence surrounded it now and the smell of cheap fried sausages and cigarette smoke flowed over it as fans milled around, the normal end-of-season's careless frivolity replaced with angst and uncertainty.

Danny, Ethan and James walked to the turnstiles, squeezing themselves into the small gap in the brickwork and, after handing their money over, gave the barrier a hefty jolt to send it clunking forward to admit them. The boys loved to arrive early for games, to be one of the first people through the gates, and they had expected to walk onto an empty terrace when they climbed the steps to its summit, but it was an important day for all the wrong reasons and the urgency of the situation had brought the fans into the ground far earlier than they would usually arrive.

The boys' regular spot in the stand was 'The Box' - with

harsh metal barriers every ten steps of the terracing, this created sections of supporters and 'The Box' was the square of the North Stand that was the loudest and most tempestuous. It was the place from which songs started and then spread around the ground, the place where you were rocked back and forth, lifted off your feet. If you were directly in front of the barrier when a goal went in, your chest was slammed against it and you were pinned there until all the celebrations subsided. Danny and Ethan loved it there - James, not so much. Mostly, he braved it, but occasionally, he sidled across the gangway to a calmer spot or went down the front to bother Nicky Rust. On this day though, even Danny and Ethan couldn't handle 'The Box.' They spent five minutes there and before the game had even kicked off, the violent jostling had knocked them repeatedly off their feet. As they fell, hands reached out to pull them back up, but on the sixth time, they reluctantly left their spot behind and wrestled their way through the crowd, emerging into the bright sunlight that lit up the front few rows.

Overnight, someone had broken into the ground and sprayed, 'SACK THE BOARD' in giant letters on the pitch and at the front of the Directors' Box, the same artist had been at work, but with slightly less accuracy: 'WE HAT PALACE.' There was an edge, an aggression to the crowd, a sense of anarchy in the air. It had seemed that every week, there had been a meeting, a discussion, an effort to find a solution to what was going to happen to this football club, but here they were, at the end of the season and there was no answer and everywhere you looked, there weren't faces of people coming to be entertained and distracted by football, but faces of fury.

Shortly before kick-off, Ethan's Player of the Season prediction was confirmed as Ian Chapman was announced in a brief and perfunctory manner. By this time, the ground was absolutely heaving and in particular, the North Stand.

The match kicked off, but even outside of 'The Box,' bodies were crammed up against each other and it was impossible to focus in the stifling and claustrophobic jumble of bodies. Every now and then, York City scurried forwards before sending tame shots into Nicky Rust's arms. Minutes of the game ticked by, but none of it was taken in by the boys. Then, from the West Stand, a group of men calmly walked onto the pitch, arms aloft and all around, hordes charged forward, leaping the three-foot wall that separated the fans from the pitch while others forced open the two emergency gates at the front of the North Stand. Rust grabbed his bag from the back of the goal and legged it for the dressing room along with the rest of the players as the pitch filled. One fan jumped for the crossbar and hung there, grinning at the fans that remained in the stand behind and then he was joined by five, ten, fifteen fans bouncing up and down until the crossbar cracked and came tumbling down, turning the rectangle into an M-shape.

It was perhaps obvious that the game wasn't going to go ahead as soon as the fans entered the pitch, but the crossbars coming down - and they had now come down in front of the South Stand too - brought an utter finality to proceedings. Danny, Ethan and James just stood there silently staring out. Pitch invasions often felt playful and celebratory and the boys longed for those exciting moments where the rules could be broken with joyful abandon, but this moment felt different. The boys walked through the emergency gates more out of obligation than excitement. People were furious that the Goldstone Ground, their home, was being ripped away from them and they were ripping up hunks of turf, smashing up the thin plastic of the players' tunnel and lobbing the debris around.

"Ladies and gentlemen," announced the Tannoy, "you aren't doing anyone any favours."

It was such a strange announcement. The game was over, the goals destroyed. There was no coming back from this moment, not today. Did the announcer think that the crowd would pause and consider their actions, perhaps gaffer-tape the crossbar back together?

Danny knelt on the ground and dug his hands as deep into the turf as he could manage and pulled free a large clod. He'd lost *Nevermind* and *I Should Coco* to be at this game, so he was going to get something out of it. Ethan and James knelt down and did the same. Strolling the pitch was a novelty, treading the same turf as Nicky Rust, Sneaky George and Ian Chapman.

They walked past a group of men wearing smart shirts and sunglasses who were shouting abuse at a fan who had chosen to stay in the stands. Later, a rumour went around that a load of Millwall fans had turned up for the game just to enjoy the crazy chaos and Danny thought back to these pugnacious men who didn't seem sad in the slightest, just angry and confrontational. But others sat on the grass or in the stands and wept, men and women whose lives had been bookmarked by coming to this place every fortnight. A few went over to the York City fans who applauded enthusiastically and some swapped shirts and scarves with the away fans in a gesture of solidarity.

Songs were sung on repeat. A beach ball emerged and a game of football of sorts took place and the crowd slowly dispersed. No one from the Brighton board had been present at the game, knowing the potential for unrest. The police gradually advanced onto the pitch, slowly herding the pitch encroachers back to the stands and while they received chants of abuse, the fans knew that the police weren't the enemy. The board were the absent recipients of their anger, but the police represented authority and their attempts to bring order when the fans wanted chaos aligned them with the board.

Danny, Ethan and James walked out of the ground, back through Hove Park and back to the Browns' house where they switched on the TV, loaded up Ceefax, and watched the Saturday scores scroll by, but none of them cared that Andrei Kanchelskis had scored a hat-trick for Everton at Hillsborough. They all just sat there, grieving, wondering if they would ever see their beloved Brighton play football again.

An hour of silence slipped by, and Danny trudged to the door - he wasn't staying for dinner tonight. Ethan pushed *Nevermind* and *I Should Coco* into his hands: "We didn't get to see a game today."

That evening, the abandonment of the game was featured on *Match of the Day*, described by Des Lynam, a man who sat in the West Stand to watch Brighton most home games, as "terrible scenes." Even though the fans' actions were criticised, it felt special that they'd been included in this show that only showed the elite teams of the Premiership. When a ten-second snapshot of the trouble was shown without context, the fans looked like hooligans, but Danny knew that in their desperation, they'd become reckless, the snapping of the crossbars a desperate cry for help because no one was listening.

27/04/96: Brighton and Hove Albion A-A York City

17th August 1996

Brighton & Hove Albion vs Chester City

The turnstiles at the Goldstone Ground were mercifully open once again. The deal to sell the ground had been sealed, but a one-year delay to it being turned into a bunch of shops had been agreed upon just three days after the abandonment against York: £480,000 to rent the ground for one more season. Years ago, Brighton had spent that sort on money on players, parting with half a million pounds for Andy Ritchie from Manchester United back in 1980, but now Brighton were scrambling for cheap players, free transfers and loan deals to bulk out a squad.

A year opened up in front of Danny, Ethan and James, and in August, that felt like an eternity. When the year was up, Brighton would have no permanent home and the stopgap was that they would be playing their home games forty-seven miles away in Portsmouth, a hideous and unaffordable prospect for Danny.

Over the summer, Ethan had perfected the curtained fringe hoping that he might appeal to the girls as much as Joe Wicks from *Eastenders*. Each morning, he would meticulously find his centre parting before spraying half a can of hairspray around the bathroom so that it stuck rigidly in place for the day. Danny had let Ethan shave and then Bic-razor his head at the end of the previous season and had since let it grow out into the shaggy mess it now was. He imagined that it made him look like Liam Gallagher and he tried to mimic the swagger as well but was entirely unsuccessful. James was still getting a short back and sides from his mum and cared nothing for his appearance. The boys had been so starved of football for the last few weeks that they turned up two hours early for the opening day fixture and were the first in the ground, perched in position on the North Stand, watching the crowd gradually fill the stands, the gaps in the terracing disappearing and replaced with blue and white shirts and scarves. The east terrace was now largely unused except for a small square of it designated to the away fans. It had been condemned as unsafe and with demolition on the horizon, there would be no repairs. Weeds had found their way through cracks, standing as tall as three feet high. The chasm to the east gave the ground an unbalanced feel and revealed the front gardens of Goldstone Lane where residents gathered each game, getting a view of the action for free. Danny always gazed at them with envy, wishing that he lived there.

A disorientating limbo of a season was about to begin - the joy the fans felt at being back at the place they loved was in the shadow of the dread that as every game went by, this familiar comforting rhythm, this place of escape where everything mattered for ninety minutes in a bubble outside the rest of your life, this community where men who found relationships difficult would bewilderingly hug and kiss with abandon if the boys in blue and white scored… this was all being slowly wrenched away, bricks being torn from a wall that had stood for ninety-six years. Each team that visited was visiting for the last ever time. Every moment that happened was happening for the last ever time, but that was true of every moment in life. Football offered a routine, a repetition, a revisiting week in, week out, season in, season out that gave a structure to life, but no moment was really the same, each goal, each celebration an echo of the past relived again, but also unique.

Nothing at the club had really been solved. The end had just been delayed, but the mood at the ground felt lighter and more optimistic in the August sunshine - it could hardly have felt as bleak as the York game - as Danny, Ethan and James gazed out onto the sparkling green pitch. They'd strolled down to the ground earlier in the week, bored by the long summer days, desperate for Saturday to come. They'd found a set of gates open and walked in and looked out onto the pitch where a fire engine stood; a group of firefighters were hosing the pitch, trying to soften the rock-hard surface ready for the start of the season. With no one paying any attention to them, the boys crept into the dugout and sat where the manager, Jimmy Case would sit in just a few days' time.

Jimmy had been seeing out the end of his playing career at Brighton, still making occasional appearances when the team needed him in his forties. Last season, he'd been the oldest player in the football league - a statistic often repeated by Brighton fans but also a sign of the club's desperation. One of his last games had seen him get a red card for time-wasting which he'd blamed on the fact that he wasn't wearing his hearing aid and couldn't hear the referee telling him to hurry up. "I got sent off for being deaf," he told the press.

When manager, Liam Brady got fed up with having to work with the club's owners and quit last November, Case took on the reins. The form was patchy for the rest of the season, mildly better than it had been under Brady, but Case lost double the games he won and finished his first season in charge overseeing a relegation. No one blamed him - he was a club legend who had been a part of the greatest era in the club's history, their brief two seasons in the top flight in the early 1980s while Danny was saying his first words, unaware that he was missing the glory years, watching *Playschool* instead. Jimmy had arrived from Liverpool, having been a part of Bob Paisley's team that had won the European Cup twice, but heavy drinking and a propensity to give someone a wallop, including team-mates, meant that he was deemed to be too much of a loose cannon and Brighton benefited by getting one of the greatest players to ever wear the Brighton blue. He was a key part of the Brighton team that took the field at Wembley in 1983 and almost brought Brighton their first major trophy. No, he wasn't to blame for the current slump. The crowd had immense affection for him and poured all their frustration on the board. Results had started to become irrelevant to the fans anyway when their very existence was in doubt. Relegation was nothing compared to extinction.

The firefighters spotted the boys as they turned to water a new patch of turf and decided to have some fun, turning their hoses on them. Each boy was pinned by the fierce jet of water to the back wall of the dugout. In between bursts, the boys attempted to scamper out of the line of fire but were repeatedly pinioned until the firefighters eventually showed some mercy, although they laughed hysterically as the boys made their exit, leaving puddles behind them on the terracing. Utterly drenched, but thrilled at the access they'd gained, the boys made their way back to Ethan's house, Danny with a stud from a football boot, that he had found in the dugout, in his pocket. Later that night, he added it to a shoebox that contained the shrivelled and dead clump of grass that he'd ripped from the pitch four months earlier and newspaper cuttings from the previous season.

Now, the fans were back on North Stand terrace, preparing for another year of football and protest. They had a year to force the board to find a solution that made sense, or more importantly, to force the board to leave the club to better hands. The animosity towards the owners was so strong, so primal, that it was difficult to see anything but their departure being the next step, but that wasn't simple. They weren't philanthropists who would walk away for the good of the club, but businessmen who would make financial decisions with their heads and not their hearts. They would only part with the club for the right money. Football fans were all heart and neither would compromise, hard-headed business facts versus unconditional loyalty to a group of men who carried the fans' dreams forth every Saturday afternoon. Up in the Premiership, television money, sponsorship deals and wealthy chairmen were flooding the game with cash. In a summer where Brighton struggled to placate their creditors, Alan Shearer had moved from Blackburn Rovers to Newcastle United for a record fee of £15,000,000, double the cost of the Goldstone Ground. If only Brighton had a striker that was so coveted by other teams that they demanded a fee that would save them, but none of the departures from last season had even demanded a fee. Fan-favourite, John Byrne had only managed four goals in the previous campaign and was off to play County League football for Shoreham, not quite the transfer that was required. Not one player who left brought a single penny to Brighton and no one in the squad was tempting any offers Albion's way.

The previous evening, during a game of *Mariokart*, Simon told Danny that their dad had said that it didn't matter that they no longer lived in the same town; he was still their dad. Danny had kept to his word and ignored the 6pm phone-call from his dad and had just shaken his head when his brother had offered him the phone. Danny hadn't been in the mood to accept anything his dad said. He still hadn't exchanged a word with his father since his departure. Danny knew the hollowness of his dad's words, knew that his dad's absence was a gaping abyss in his family, that not being there mattered and that these men in suits were doing the same thing to Brighton, tearing something he loved out of his reach. Why couldn't things just stay the same:

his dad telling him to tidy his room and asking him if he'd done his homework and his football team playing down the road? He just ignored Simon while tumbling off Rainbow Road for the eighteenth time that race.

Danny's summer had been one in which he'd slept right through into the afternoons. Other than the Friday phone-calls from his dad to avoid, there had been regular dinner at the Browns', his paper-round, games of football at the Rec and *Neighbours*. The highlight of his paper-round was whether he would see Brighton midfielder, Denny Mundee sitting in his front room when he delivered him his copy of *The Argus*, but sightings were rare; he had seen him once watching *Going for Gold* which was a story Danny had now told more than a hundred times. Once, he had noticed that Mundee had only got five out of ten in a match performance rating and Danny had taken a biro out of his bag and doctored the rating, changing the five to an eight. When he'd scored the next game, Danny credited himself with building his confidence with his editorial decision. He just hoped Mundee hadn't read the comment next to the rating saying that he'd lost his man at a corner.

There was also one last trip to HoHi to collect his GCSE results: middling to poor results to match his lacklustre effort. He laughed as he exited the school with Bryan, the boy who'd sat next to him in Art. Danny had made a cardboard-box replica of the Goldstone Ground for his final piece to demonstrate his artistic flair while Wolves fan, Bryan had constructed a pretty much identical piece, but covered in lurid yellow paint to match the exterior of Molineux. Neither piece had impressed the examiners, but Bryan had narrowly beaten Danny, achieving a D-grade to Danny's E. He'd done okay in English - he'd enjoyed writing, had kept a diary for the last five years, a place where he poured out his angst in a highly-charged, sometimes incoherent poetic fashion. Finding expression for his frustration had meant that, whilst lacking any exam technique, he'd been able to impress the examiner enough with his ability to express himself, enough to cover for his patchy knowledge of *Macbeth*. He'd just about passed Maths as well, being able to do the stuff that required logic and intuition, but as soon as a formula was required, he didn't know what to do. Those were the only passes though. Every other subject required dedicated revision and that was something he'd been unwilling, or more accurately, unmotivated to do.

The menacing atmosphere of the corridors eroded away any desire Danny had to do well at school. He'd started in Year 7 with enthusiasm and excitement, his hand waving eagerly in the air when he knew an answer, but the unrelenting cruelty of the place wore him down, made him care less and less by the day until the results that he received in the summer of 1996 meant nothing to him. His final days at school had been merely a countdown to freedom.

Of far more importance to him had been the Three Lions and their attempt to bring football home. The boys had got together for every game, played Baddiel and Skinner's anthem at top volume and celebrated each goal by piling on top of each other. Paul Gascoigne flicking the ball over Colin Hendry, volleying the ball past Andy Goram and the dentist-chair celebration had felt like the perfect moment. When Shearer had put England ahead against Germany in the semi-final, they'd celebrated so violently that James had his head rammed against the television so hard that it emitted a loud pop and then went blank. The boys sprinted to the nearest pub and sat on the floor below a large screen, looking on as Gascoigne came so close to connecting with a cross and sending England into the final. The penalty shoot-out against West Germany in 1990 had been one of Danny's earliest footballing memories. He remembered sitting with his dad, too nervous to even breathe as Stuart Pearce's penalty cannoned back off of the goalkeeper and then, Chris Waddle blazed the ball over the bar, and now it was happening again. When Gareth Southgate's tame penalty was saved, the silent misery of defeat descended upon the pub. Danny was wearing the giant blue and black Brighton third shirt, and as the grumbles and swearing emerged from the gloom, a man put his hand on Danny's shoulder and said, "Don't worry. We've got football back at the Goldstone again this year."

That's the good thing about football. As the devastation of defeat settles, an opportunity for triumph in the future emerges, but was that true for Brighton? Today, the boys could pretend and believe it was because they were at a match, ready to watch a cheaply assembled squad of ageing players past their best, and discarded individuals that other clubs had dispensed with.

And the boys were back - back in 'The Box' which, whilst being a jostling mass of men, was nothing like the violent storm of York City. The good news was that they still had a football club to support and that was a silver lining to the horrible cloud that was the future. The chants were split between criticisms of the board, mainly suggestions that they should be thrown onto a bonfire, and support for the team that just might have a good season. A pitch invasion seemed unlikely although one excitable bloke stripped off all of his clothes and had a brief cavort around the corner flag before leaping back into the stands. Surely, Division 3 was such a low level of football, that Brighton should walk this league. That had been the boys' conclusion as they'd marched to the match. Jimmy Case had written a letter to fans that appeared in the local paper, *The Argus* and he was optimistic: "I'd like to think we'll be up there," he wrote, telling fans that Brighton should expect to be in and around the promotion places. There was a three-point deduction hanging over the side, should there be any repeat of the pitch invasions at the end of the previous season, and it seemed unlikely that the season would pass without fans venting their frustration by invading the playing surface, but nevertheless, winning the league and a good FA Cup run felt like an achievable aim.

Chester were the opening day opponents and it was they that opened the scoring, bringing those dreaming of glory down to earth, their centre-forward manoeuvring the ball away from James' favourite, Nicky Rust to sweep into an empty net. But, Brighton came back. Ian Baird had arrived over the summer, a brute of a forward who had already scored for nine different clubs. Slowed down by his advancing years, he had dropped down the leagues, finding himself at the Goldstone, but he could still outmuscle a hapless centre-back and he did just that, arriving at the back post to power a header past the keeper to equalise and score for his tenth club, immediately endearing himself to the fans. Sneaky George, another player not quite what he once was but who'd had a successful career at a higher level, particularly for West Ham United, then took advantage of some horrific defending. After the ball was sliced into his path, he smashed the ball into the roof of the net in front of the North Stand. What a joy it was for Danny to be crushed in an ecstatic mass of bodies once again. Danny had both feet off the floor and was being carried by the mass of bodies; Ethan's chest was rammed against the barrier - he roared with glee through the gasps for breath - and James had his face trapped in the armpit of a large gentlemen who was struggling to keep his balance. Trapped, with his hair sponging up the man's stale sweat, he was the happiest he'd been in months.

From depression and destruction four months earlier, the fans launched into, "We're gonna win the league" - the euphoria and optimism that an opening day victory can bring.

"This league is gonna be so easy," said Danny as they walked back through Hove Park at the end of the game.

"We could have won 9-1 today," replied James.

And then once again, but just three chirpy voices this time, "We're gonna win the league…"

17/08/96: Brighton 2-1 Chester City (Baird, Parris)
24/08/96: Cardiff City 1-0 Brighton
27/08/96: Barnet 3-0 Brighton

31st August 1996

Brighton & Hove Albion vs Scunthorpe United

Simon had just smashed Danny with a red shell and snatched victory on Bowser's Castle, a source of intense irritation to Danny. For years, his little brother had been close to hopeless at computer games and he had always won, but in the last few months, his brother had become more adept, honing his craft while Danny was sleeping or out watching football and now, he'd beaten him for the third race running on *Mariokart*.

"Why won't you talk to Dad?" Simon asked as he selected the next race.

"No, not Rainbow Road, you know I can't stay on the track," said Danny, ignoring his brother's question.

Simon grumpily chose another track and repeated his question. Danny looked at his brother, wearing a yellow and purple striped t-shirt, a hand-me-down that he'd worn five years earlier. How could he make his brother understand? Simon had cried when their dad left. Danny had felt guilty when he heard the snuffles coming from the lower bunk and felt like he should say something, but he was too busy burying his own pain and couldn't bring himself to say a word. When he'd been younger, he'd started digging a hole in his back garden. Every day, he'd gone out and used the garden spade to shift soil until he got tired and bored, distracted by the plastic orange football that he would belt against the house, pretending to be John Byrne, back when he scored for fun in the early nineties.

His intention was that he'd dig a hole big enough to create a room that he would use as a hideout, but his digging was barely making a dent until his dad had joined him and together, they created a huge hole, although not room-sized. It had remained in his back garden ever since, a reminder of what they had achieved together. Now, Danny wanted to throw all the pain and confusion he felt into this hole and cover it over, make it all disappear, but it was never going to disappear when every Friday, he had to go through the painful procedure of refusing to talk to his dad. And then there was his brother who asked him two questions on repeat: "Do you want to play *Mariokart*?" and, "Why won't you talk to Dad?"

Danny drove Yoshi round the track silently, choosing his words and lobbing pixelated bananas at Luigi.

"He left us, Simon. He chose to go off with Sharon. I can't stand that he did that, and I don't want to hear him try and tell me that he still loves me."

"He does love me," said Simon, reassuring himself.

"Love is a verb," said Danny, plagiarising Toadfish from *Neighbours.*

"What?"

"Love is a verb. It's a doing word. It's something you do. You can't just say it and make it true. It's something you have to do."

Simon didn't really understand. He'd found his dad's departure upsetting. He'd cried each night for a week and then, one day, he'd woken up and felt okay about it and had just got on with being a nine-year-old. When he spoke to his dad on the phone, he chatted away excitedly and Danny couldn't stand it. He'd leave the room and lie on his bed, staring at the George Parris poster on his ceiling.

Simon and Danny's mum came in and put plates of sausage, chips and beans down in front of the boys. They'd clocked that food had been delivered, but they were so engrossed in their race that they didn't acknowledge her and only when Simon had made it four wins in a row did they stop and pick up their plates.

"Danny, would you go to supermarket after dinner and do a bit of shopping for me?" his mum asked.

Danny did not want to do this, but he also knew that without his dad around, his mum was doing everything for her boys, so he ungraciously agreed.

"Thanks, love. Here's a list and twenty quid. Get own brand everything, none of the expensive stuff."

Danny went up to his bedroom to get his Walkman. His clothes littered the floor to the point where the carpet wasn't visible at all. His wall was plastered with last year's team poster. At the end of the previous season, he'd gone down to the ground and found a stash of them in a tip and then come home and wall-papered his room with the same poster over and over again. His

Walkman was perched on top of a pile of books on his shelves. Simon's toys took up most of the space on the shelves, chaotically tangled together so that removing one would bring the whole lot crashing down, but Danny had half a shelf that was his: the modest CD collection, a few books that had rarely been picked up in the last couple of years, and a few football programmes on the infrequent occasion when his finances stretched beyond the entrance fee. He grabbed the Walkman and turned Reef up to top volume, 'Naked' blasting out through the earphones as he left the house.

Danny's family had moved into a semi-detached house on the Knoll Estate, a collection of weaving roads and crescents, a few months after Simon was born. They'd been on the waiting list for a council property for a few years and the growth of the family from three to four had propelled them into a category of greater need. Their nomadic existence, in and out of tiny living spaces, was finally over when they were granted a two-bedroom house in the heart of the small estate in the north-west of Hove. Danny had been seven when they'd moved in and he remembered waking up on his first night at the new house and noticing an orange glow outside. When he'd walked to the window, he'd seen a car on fire, flames leaping high into the sky and then a fire engine had roared into the road and extinguished the blaze; his new house felt like a place of danger and excitement. The neighbours were all out on the street in their dressing gowns: the man at the top of the road who Danny would see walking his goat around the estate; the couple next door who over the next few years would regularly wake Danny up by screaming at each other and the lady who lived in the house opposite who had hundreds of guinea pigs in individual hutches in her back garden.

The scorch marks from the car-fire that first night were still dimly visible in the road nine years on as Danny walked south out of the estate and towards Boundary Road where he would find Tesco once he'd crossed the level crossing at Portslade Station. He'd been to the supermarket a couple of times for his mum, but still had no sense of the way things were organised, so he inefficiently walked back and forth, collecting one thing at a time and pausing to make sure that he was buying the cheapest possible version of each item. He was unsure whether he should buy two loaves of bread for £1 or just the one for 65p. He decided on just the one. If he stuck to the list, he couldn't get it wrong.

Finally, having found everything on the list and taking it through the checkout, he was on his way out when a security guard, dressed to look like a policeman stepped in front of him.

"Excuse me, may I see your receipt."

At first Danny didn't hear him, having to first extract his headphones.

"What?"

"May I see your receipt?"

"Why?" asked Danny, genuinely confused at the request.

"Don't be awkward. Show me the receipt."

There was a threatening edge to the security guard's voice as he pushed his belly out towards Danny like a cannon ball.

Danny fished in the bag for the receipt and handed it over. The security guard looked at it like he'd handed him some used toilet paper and then started rifling through the bag aggressively. Once he'd checked off each item on the receipt, he handed the bags back although one of the plastic bags was now ripped.

Danny took them back, angry at the assumption that he was a thief. On the walk back up the hill towards home, the four-pint plastic bottle of milk fell from the torn bag and a corner of the bottle sliced open, sending milk squirting out onto the road. Danny rescued the milk and held it upside-down so that no more milk would escape. Once home, he used the almost-empty bottle in the fridge to contain the newly-bought milk. He didn't say a word to his mum about the search, but just handed over the change.

It was the last week of the summer holidays and Ethan and James were being cajoled into getting themselves organised for the first week back at school. They'd both had to go on trips to buy new uniform and stationery and Danny laughed as Ethan tried his new trousers on. Ethan had insisted on a waist-size ten inches bigger than his own so that they would be super-baggy. In Danny's mind, he'd seen the last of education and certainly wasn't going to be seen wearing a school uniform ever again.

"Aren't you going to do A-levels?" asked Ethan.

"What's the point? If I get a job, I can earn some money and start going to away games," replied Danny.

The thought of having enough money to go to away games was a tantalising prospect for Danny.

"What job are you going to get?"

"I don't know. I'll just go to the Job Centre on Monday and see what they've got."

Ethan's parents had helped him to see the value of education, talked to him about how hard graft now could open up opportunities in the future, but Danny couldn't see the value. There were aspects of learning that he'd enjoyed - particularly some of the books he'd read in English, but school had been a bruising experience, physically and mentally, and the idea of choosing to extend that seemed ludicrous when he could earn some money and then spend that money travelling up and down the country following the Albion.

On Monday, when Ethan and James were putting on their new school uniforms, he'd stroll to the Job Centre at midday and take any job that didn't demand Saturdays.

Ethan and James were jealous of the freedom and money that seemed to be coming Danny's way. Grown-ups had all the things the boys wanted at their fingertips and yet they wasted it by sitting around watching TV, but their friend seemed to be fast-forwarding the route to adulthood, taking the leap at sixteen. To Ethan and James, Danny was still a child, kicking a ball around and whiling hours away, playing *Sensible World of* Soccer, except now he could keep being a child but without the tedium of school or the limitation of finances. What a life he was about to embark on!

The boys arrived for Brighton versus Scunthorpe United an hour before kick-off on Saturday, ready to see Nicky Rust going through his warm-up with the coaches before the outfield players emerged to a crowd just about big enough to give a rousing chorus of "Seagulls, seagulls, seagulls…"

The arrogant ebullience of the Chester win had been severely dampened by back-to-back away defeats, 1-0 to Cardiff and 3-0 to Barnet. A tall ginger lad in his late teens arrived in 'The Box' three minutes before kick-off and almost immediately opened his mouth to roar out, "If you all went to Barnet, all went to Barnet, all went to Barnet, clap your hands."

There was a smattering of scattered applause as the few away attendees showed off their loyalty by demonstrating their attendance on the short route up the M23 and then a half-circle of the M25. The ginger lad was a mixture of pride and righteous anger. He was a loyal supporter, who would use his time, money and energy to travel the country for his football team, and what better specimen of a man is there? But, he was angry that the away following was so pitiful, and it was their fault, the non-attendees, that Brighton had been so toothless and had lost so emphatically to such a poor side. How could the side hope to be successful on the road if they were so outnumbered by the home crowd?

"Where were you?" he snarled, casting his eyes around the crowd before bringing his eyes to rest on Danny who had been staring in awe at the man he so wanted to be, well, sort of. His bellicose behaviour was not something Danny desired to emulate, but here was a man who had the confidence to launch into a chant in the North Stand and bellow it out without accompaniment and here was a man who went to Barnet. It was a long-held discussion on the way to the ground that this would be the day that one of them would start a chant. James tried to claim that he'd started 'Seagulls' when the players emerged for their pre-match warm-up, but Danny and Ethan knew that the emergence of the players always prompted the crowd to roar the name of the nuisance-bird in unison; James was certainly not getting away with claiming that he had initiated the chant.

Danny wanted to explain that he would have gone to Barnet if he'd had enough money and that in the near future, he hoped to travel to away games, but what he did reply was garbled and the snarling ginger lad, 'Barnet,' as he was from this moment known to the boys, laughed mockingly at Danny as if he were solely responsible for Brighton's two shameful away results.

Barnet continued to rouse 'The Box' from the slumber of a dull goalless first half with less elitist chants: "We've got no home, we've got no home, we've got no… Brighton's got no home." The anthemic *Three Lions* had been transformed into a depressive acceptance that in a year's time, the spot where they stood would be a Toys 'R' Us. The crowd came together in their suffering in a way they never would have done had the team been successful. They were homeless, huddling together for warmth, singing a collective lament and all around, there was raw emotion. Danny looked around and caught the eye of an elderly man whose eyes were welling with tears. The boys had only been coming to watch Brighton regularly for two years and it felt wretched for them to be losing what they'd so quickly come to love, but how must it feel for people who had poured decades of their life into standing on these grey concrete steps, shouting the name of a bird to inspire a bunch of men to score a goal?

In the second half, the melancholy really set in when a Scunthorpe player half-volleyed them into the lead, but it wasn't going to be three league defeats in a row. Brighton would rescue a point, their fourth point in four games when the beautiful Baird, his jowls scarlet with exertion, stretched an ageing leg out to connect with a header across goal to divert the ball into the net, salvaging a point that Brighton's football really hadn't deserved.

That evening, the boys played a game of street football, two driveways diagonal to each other being the goals. Other boys from James' close, a little cul-de-sac that had never seen a car-fire, joined in, and James took up his normal position in goal, imagining that he was Nicky Rust. It was a tetchy affair with constant arguing about whether goals had actually gone in or not and the game had to pause every time a resident drove into the close to park their car. The game finally came to an end when Danny challenged James heavily for a ball that James had already caught. James clattered to the floor and rather than release the ball to break the fall with his hands, he clutched it tightly and his teeth clattered into the kerb. He huddled into the ball on the kerb and cried and Danny felt terrible, apologising repeatedly and then helping James into his house. His mum wasn't happy and wanted to know what had happened, but all that she was told was that they had been "playing football."

Danny walked home feeling terrible. This weekend marked the end of the summer holiday and he was scared about the future, scared to become an adult and enter the world of work, but it was what he had committed to and he felt that although there were so many routes that he could take at this junction in his life, he could only see the one he was on.

When he got home, he phoned James, "Are you okay?" he asked, "I'm really sorry."

"Yeah, I'm alright," said James at the other end. His teeth still ached and one of them was wobbly, but there was no point saying that. He wanted to be tough with his older friend and he also wanted to make him feel better.

Danny apologised again and put the phone down.

31/08/96: Brighton 1-1 Scunthorpe United (Baird)

7th September 1996

Brighton & Hove Albion vs Scarborough

On Monday morning, as Ethan and James awoke early and put on their school uniforms, Danny stayed in bed. He'd been woken briefly by Simon who had switched the light on to try and find his school tie. Simon was supremely jealous that Danny didn't have to go to school anymore and he deliberately left the light on as a punishment when he finally found his tie underneath the bed and left the room.

Danny didn't make it to the Job Centre that day. He had half-intended to, but it felt luxuriant to be able to relax and please himself for the day while his friends were at school. He had planned to go after *Neighbours*, but then he reasoned that there wasn't really enough time before he needed to do his paper-round and there wasn't really enough time after his paper-round, so when he sat down for dinner - a spaghetti Bolognese - at the Browns' that evening, he replied rather sheepishly that he hadn't had time to go to the Job Centre.

Mr Brown had asked him what he had done and Danny did not want to be dishonest or in fact, honest, so was cryptically vague about having had things to do - the two tasks of the day being to watch in shock when Doctor Karl Kennedy had been unfaithful to Susan with one of his patients, Kate Cornwall, and to do his paper-round. Karl's infidelity had been a painful moment as Danny replaced Karl and Kate in his mind with his dad and Sharon. The Kennedy family had seemed like a solid, happy unit when they'd arrived on Ramsey Street, but now Karl was destroying this. The moment had cemented Danny's determination that he would continue to ignore his dad's phone-calls.

"What job do you think you'd like to do?" asked Mr Brown.

"Er, I don't know really. Maybe work in a shop or something," Danny replied.

"Hmm," Mr Brown ruminated. "You used to be interested in writing, doing journalism or something like that, didn't you?"

"Yeah, well, I'd still like to do that. I'd like to be a football reporter."

"You should keep going with that dream, Danny," Mr Brown responded.

The next morning, Danny managed to get up at 11am and so, his no-show at the Job Centre from the day before was not repeated. He paused as he reached the entrance, a sense of trepidation at entering this very adult world. Four dogs sat calmly in the shade that the building created, each attached to an iron railing. They all stared at Danny, eyes shining with doggy simplicity.

Inside, strip lighting illuminated a large room dotted with desks and noticeboards. There was a damp smell like over-boiled vegetables in the air. At several of the desks, heated conversations were taking place. "There's no way I could have done that job," implored a man, jabbing a crutch at a young woman who was avoiding eye contact. "I told you that last week," complained a large man who struggled to fit his bulk into the blue plastic chair. There were lots of people milling around too, mothers wheeling buggies, men dressed smartly in suits and other men, seemingly dressed in their pyjamas.

Danny spent a good twenty minutes not really being sure what to do, but he finally found his way to the one of the boards where cards listing jobs Danny had never heard of were pinned up with drawing pins. Every now and then, someone took a card down and carried it over to a desk. Danny felt unsure of himself - it felt presumptive to just grab a card and claim it and so he stood and gazed in bewilderment at the cards, hoping one would jump out at him. None of them said 'football reporter.'

Eventually, a woman with a badge announcing that she was called Claire approached him and asked if she could help. Danny's hesitancy answered for him, and she ushered him to a chair and said that she would go through a Careers Questionnaire with him and embarked on an endless run of quick-fire questions that Danny had to respond to with Strongly Agree, Agree, Neither Agree nor Disagree, Disagree or Strongly Disagree. Danny never ventured into strongly agreeing or disagreeing and his most common answer was 'Neither Agree nor Disagree,' but this response seemed to annoy Claire and so he found himself agreeing to having a growth-mindset and having the skill of ideation even though he had no real idea what these meant.

Finally, the questions ceased and Claire said that there was a job going at a Fencing shop in Hove. This seemed to bear no relation to the answers Danny had given, but suddenly, employment and money were within his grasp.

"Er, okay," Danny replied when asked whether he was interested, and Claire was instantly on the phone. The only information the Fencing shop wanted to know was how tall he was and Claire responded with "about six foot" - with Danny having met the desired height requirements, Claire cupped a hand over the phone and asked if Danny could get down to the shop that day and Danny briefly wondered how this would fit in with watching *Neighbours*, but didn't voice this concern, and said that he could, and thirty minutes later, he'd taken the walk in the late summer-sun along Hove seafront to the shop and agreed to commence employment the following day. It was only on arrival at the shop that Danny realised that fencing referred to garden fences and not sword-fighting. He was a little disappointed. He led with the fact that he couldn't work Saturdays and that hadn't gone down well, but it seemed that the shop would accept this - he was six foot after all.

"We pay under eighteens £2 an hour," said Derek, the owner of the shop, "and you'll get paid in cash at the end of each week."

By the time Danny had got home, *Neighbours* was over, but there was always the 5.35pm repeat.

"Mum, I've got a job. It's starting tomorrow."

"That's great, Danny. Now, listen. Now that you're working, I won't get Child Benefit for you anymore, so you're going to need to start paying rent."

"What? I have to pay to live here?"

"I can barely afford to feed us without your dad's money," replied his mum. "I wouldn't charge you if I didn't need to."

"How much will it be?"

"Child Benefit is £30, so I'll need you to match that."

Danny did some maths in his head as he walked to the newsagent to do his last paper-round. His sudden resignation didn't go down well, but Danny didn't feel like he had a choice. £2 an hour from the fencing shop would get him £80 a week, so he'd still have £50 after paying his mum which should open the door to some away days.

The next morning, Danny arrived at the shop. He had imagined standing behind a counter, listening to the radio and occasionally telling someone how much a fence cost, but Derek had other things in mind: namely, work. The first task of the morning was unloading fences from the back of a truck into the yard out the back. He understood the need for height now as he stretched his arms around the six-foot-by-six-foot panels, leaning them against his face as he bumped his way into the yard.

"Come on, you can take two at a time," chided Derek, who demonstrated with ease, but only once before returning to his copy of the *Daily Sport* and the tea with two sugars that Danny made him; "a cup on the hour every hour, please Danny," had been the request.

Every time a customer purchased a fence panel or a shed or a pole, it was Danny's job to load up their van and he regularly collected the wrong panel or pole, only to have to return it to the yard. In between lugging fence panels back and forth, he re-felted a shed roof, swept the yard, cleaned the windows at the front of the shop, swept the yard again, collected Derek's prescription from the chemist (a welcome relief to take a half-hour stroll away from the shop), loaded the van for the evening deliveries and swept the yard one last time. With every sweep of the broom, dust clouds billowed into the air, only to settle once again for Danny's next visit.

After a lengthy summer of lie-ins and idleness, a full working day exhausted Danny. The muscles in his arms ached and his hands were covered in nicks and splinters. A blood blister throbbed beneath the nail of the middle finger of his left hand, and the little finger of his right hand was swollen and wouldn't bend. He felt annoyed with Derek; he'd felt like a nag - at the end of every task, another one waited or there was a quibble with a task he'd already completed and as every new hour began, he wanted to know where his tea was.

The following morning, Danny arrived at the shop at 9.07am and Derek tapped his watch and said, "Time-keeping needs to be better young man. I'll let you off this time, but you'll lose an hour's pay if you aren't here by 9am each morning."

Danny had almost always been late for school, sometimes by ten minutes, but also by upwards of an hour and this went unremarked upon, the only recognition of his tardiness being the 8% punctuality mark he'd got in his annual report compared to his 96% attendance mark. He pretty much always made it into school, but very rarely before his name was read out in the register. Lateness had become habitual, his alarm clock belting out Radio One at a distorted high volume being a suggestion that he get up rather than a demand, and he often felt like he needed to summon the willingness to face the day and that usually took a while. There was no way that Derek would accept the early morning melancholy that overcame Danny as a reason for his lateness.

Day Two was much like Day One, Derek dreaming up jobs for Danny - an endless cycle of tasks. While Danny worked, Derek slurped tea and leered over naked women in the *Daily Sport*. When a greying gentlemen came into the shop mid-morning, his eye not so furtively glanced repeatedly at the flesh on display on Derek's desk.

"Can you believe the youth of the today, bringing this filth into this reputable business?" asked Derek with a knowing laugh.

The customer chuckled and Danny just stared awkwardly at the floor feeling like a peeping tom caught in the act. He was simply unprepared to brush off the banter or offer a witty reply and just seethed within. Derek wanted a boy who could make laddish jokes, make suggestive comments about shed erections and pergola poles at every opportunity and it was his awkwardness that was the reason why Derek found him endless jobs. His sullen presence in the shop was too much for him. He'd tried to engage Danny by telling him to check out page eight. Danny had opened the newspaper, thinking that perhaps there was some news about the Albion that Derek was kindly pointing out to him and when he just found soft porn, he responded with a noncommittal "Oh, right" and closed the paper, leaving Derek confused before telling Danny to go and sweep the yard for the third time that day.

Danny was on time on Friday and the workload continued to stretch his stamina and strength, but Derek was so fed up with

Danny's taciturn ways that he sent him out on repeated trips, to the bakery for an iced bun, to the off licence for a packet of *Benson and Hedges* and to the newsagent for, painfully, a copy of *The Daily Sport* which Danny found mortifying to buy, but the end of the day came around and three days' wages - £48 - were counted out into Danny's hand from the till. It was the most money Danny had ever had in his life. His mum had said that the paperwork hadn't gone through cancelling the Child Benefit yet, so he could keep the full wage packet for the first half-week.

The next day, Danny, Ethan and James were in the Albion Club Shop an hour before kick-off. It was a tiny Portakabin on the west side of the stadium and inside were programmes from previous games and an assortment of random sweatshirts each with the club's logo, a seagull in flight, emblazoned on them. It was a kit that was most desired though and Danny, who had never owned a coveted 'current' Brighton kit, only cheap outdated ones, was delighted to part with £35 for an XL away shirt, a fluorescent yellow top with a scattering of black squares on the right shoulder and the bottom of the right sleeve. The away shirt matched Danny's desire to be travelling up and down the country with his genuinely hard-earned wages. The XL was totally unnecessary on Danny's skinny frame - he was as tall as the fence panels he wrapped his arms around, but his arms were twigs and his ribcage overhung his stomach. It was an improvement on the XXXL third shirt though. Danny pulled the kit on over his t-shirt and it billowed in the breeze as the boys made their way towards the turnstiles.

"What's the job like?" asked Ethan.

"Pretty terrible," admitted Danny, "but seventeen and a half hours there gets me this," he said, clutching a chunk of his new shirt in his fist.

The world of work felt like a mystery to James and Ethan who, whilst claiming to hate school, got to hang out with their mates and kick a well-used football around a playground a couple of times a day.

"Have you heard about Dick Knight?" asked Ethan.

"Who's Dick Knight?" asked James.

"He's the guy who's going to save us," said Danny. "He wants to buy the club and make sure we stay in Brighton."

"What? We get to stay at The Goldstone?" asked James.

"No," said Ethan. "We've already sold it, but we might be able to play at the greyhound stadium."

"The greyhound track? How many can get in there?" asked James.

"I don't know, but it's better than going to Portsmouth."

It was better, far better. It gave the boys a chance to keep doing this. They wanted to do this for the rest of their lives, to grow old doing this and while the greyhound stadium wouldn't be the same as this place, that held almost a century of memories, it was still within walking distance of their homes, not forty-seven miles away in a different county.

The boys leaned against the rusting iron crush barriers. A man with a blue and white striped scarf that was so long that both ends dangled on the ground got an apple out of his pocket, carefully peeled the sticker off before affixing it to the barrier where it joined hundreds of others, a sticker to mark every match he'd attended: Royal Gala, Braeburn, Delbarestivale and Evelina stickers dotting the metal, a monument to the man's devotion.

Hope after the opening day victory had quickly evaporated with the team failing to find victory again. The attendance had noticeably dwindled, but the team were back in the mood against Scarborough. Stuart Storer had signed for the Albion from Exeter City for £15,000 the previous season. It had been exciting that Brighton had actually paid a fee for a player, but the moustachioed winger had disappointed and when he was missing from the line-up, a cruel rumour went round the North Stand that he'd been run over by a milk-float, but he'd shaved his energy-sapping moustache and a jab at his sluggishness was misplaced as he raced beyond the Scarborough defence in the first half and calmly slotted the ball into the far corner.

Cue bedlam in 'The Box' and then, "We've got Stu, Stu, Stu, Stu Storer on our wing, on our wing…"

Craig Maskell was the hero of the second half. He had joined in the previous summer and was part of the team that got relegated from Division 2. Maskell had been trying to make it as a Premiership striker at Southampton, but in two seasons, he'd only managed to score one goal, a neat header against Liverpool on a day that he was outshone by a Matt Le Tissier hat-trick.

Eventually, the Saints had lost faith in him and he'd dropped three divisions where goals were easier to come by. Against Scarborough, Storer rolled the ball across the face of goal for him to tap the ball into an open net in front of the North Stand - 2-0 - before he jigged and weaved in the box before scuffing a shot into the bottom corner. 3-0!

In the last ten minutes, Albion almost imploded, conceding twice, one coming from the bald head of ex-Brighton man Andy Ritchie, but the final whistle saved them. Hope was in the air. The team were winning again, and a Knight was preparing to slay the dragons who had been slumbering greedily for too long on the gold.

And Danny had even better news: "Boys, what do you say to a trip to Exeter next week? If I buy an adult ticket on the train, you boys can get a return ticket for a quid each 'cos I'll be, like, your guardian. We can stay with my nan. She lives up there."

Ethan and James leapt onto Danny, knocking him to the floor, delighted at the prospect of an away day following the Albion.

07/09/96: Brighton 3-2 Scarborough (Storer, Maskell 2)
10/09/96: Colchester United 2-0 Brighton

14th September 1996

Exeter City vs Brighton & Hove Albion

Another week of shifting fence panels was made bearable by the thought of the Friday night train trip to Exeter that the work was funding. At just over 3p a minute, Danny had to work for less than half an hour to pay for the entrance fee to the game thanks to Exeter's generous pricing policy, letting children in for just a pound. Ninety minutes' work would get all three boys through the turnstiles, but ninety minutes' work dragged by so much slower than a football match did.

Each morning, unloading the van exhausted Danny, his t-shirt soaked in sweat by the time he had put every fence panel in its place, and he was always surprised that it wasn't even ten o' clock when he had finished. Small, tiresome and physical tasks filled the day, but each task never took long and every look at the clock was a disappointment that so much of the day remained.

On Tuesday, Danny was seven minutes late and Derek told him that he would be docked an hour's wage. Danny tried to argue that if he was seven minutes late, then he should only be docked 21p, but Derek said that he was paid by the hour and if he didn't complete an hour's work, then he'd be docked an hour's pay. Danny was on time or at least close enough to 9am to stop Derek quibbling for the rest of the week, but each day, he wasted a minute here, a minute there, sitting on a wall outside the newsagent for a minute when sent on a cigarette errand, standing still in the yard gazing at the sky while he could hear Derek talking on the phone, waiting an extra minute in the kitchen before pressing the button on the kettle until he'd wasted all fifty-three minutes that Derek wasn't paying him for. Danny felt satisfied in his silent, petty protest.

Derek had stopped trying to make conversation with Danny, finding his awkward monosyllabic responses unfulfilling. The only communication between them were instructions delivered and complaints about the quality of Danny's work. Danny felt to blame for the silence that lingered in the shop when there were no customers. He saw Derek transform into an affable joker every time a customer arrived. He seemed to know a lot of the customers by name and the gloom that felt like a miasma within the shop walls instantly lifted whenever the bell on the door tinkled and a customer came in. Danny wanted the relationship the customers had with Derek, jolly chatting flowing back and forth, but he didn't know how to achieve this and as the days went by, he accepted his lot for the cash that it would bring.

As soon as the £78 was in his fist at the end of the day on Friday, Danny ran to Hove Station to meet Ethan and James. A hasty purchase of one adult and two child return tickets and they were sat around a table westwards-bound. The train tickets had cost more than half of Danny's wages and with £30 going to his mum, there wasn't much left, so the boys were grateful for Exeter's generous ticket prices. Danny's wages weren't going far, weren't going beyond the end of Saturday.

Tony Blair was campaigning for a minimum wage for ordinary working people, but there was an election to navigate first. The Tories had been in power for the entirety of Danny's life. Margaret Thatcher had felt like a monolith that would forever stand to Danny when he was at St Augustine's Primary School; as a young child watching the news, he had been scared by her gravelly proclamations. When he was ten, his mum had gone to London to protest against the introduction of the Poll tax and Danny had remembered his dad being racked with worry, watching the news later that day as the streets descended into chaos. Traffic cones were spearing through the air; police officers were swinging batons wildly and every now and then, there was the image of a protester or a police officer lying in a pool of their own blood. Danny was captivated by a man with an incredible Mohican leaping over the barrier into the Houses of Parliament, scattering paper everywhere before being wrestled to the floor.

Danny's mum arrived home later that evening and his parents embraced tearfully on the doorstep and Danny had never felt so loved, watching on. Thatcher hadn't lasted long after that. Danny remembered being in a reading group in the last year of Primary school and Mrs Abraham telling the group that Thatcher had resigned. No reading was done as the students asked question after question about what this meant. The Tories were still in charge explained Mrs Abraham, but there would be a new Prime Minister and ten-year-old Danny watched avidly to see who this new person would be. It turned out to be a man that would bore Danny, John Major droning political jargon in a way that was incomprehensible to him, and as he started secondary school, politics seemed an irrelevance. He heard his parents' grumbles about the Tories and associated them in his mind with privilege, a political party that made life more difficult for his family. Labour was the party for the poor, the party for people whose wages didn't stretch beyond the weekend and the fresh-faced Blair and his talks of minimum wage had piqued Danny's interest. Surely, Derek would be forced to pay him more than the paltry £2 an hour he was getting at the moment. An election was coming - there hadn't been one since 1992 and even then, the Conservative majority had shrunk considerably from the Thatcher years.

"Look what I've got," announced Ethan, withdrawing a battered Monopoly box from his bag, and for the first two hours of the journey, the boys bargained and argued over property.

James, in a needless expression of devotion to Brighton, was paying well over the odds for blue properties and chanted, "Seagulls, Seagulls" every time someone landed on them, much to the annoyance of other passengers.

His foolish tactics brought quick defeat and Danny and Ethan played out a more competitive game, Ethan's ownership of the orange set eventually proving to be decisive, bankrupting Danny. Ethan launched into, "I'm by far the greatest Monopoly player the world has ever seen." Again, annoyed glances sprang the boys' direction from other passengers.

"Have you spoken to your dad yet?" asked James, blunt and direct.

"No. If he was at home, I'd speak to him every morning, but I'm not sitting in on a Friday night waiting to talk to him." The reality was that Danny was sitting in most Friday nights, but that wasn't the point.

"What does your mum say about it?" asked Ethan.

"She thinks I should speak to him. She says, 'Even though he's done a terrible thing, he is your dad.'"

"It wouldn't hurt, would it, just to speak to him?" said Ethan.

That was the problem. It would hurt. It would be horrible and painful and awkward. He'd been rejected for this Sharon woman and talking to his dad was a reminder that he wasn't wanted. But, it was also painful not to talk to his dad, not to have him in his life. He knew that he wasn't going to delete him from his life forever. He'd let Brighton make the decision.

"I tell you what. If we beat Exeter tomorrow, I'll talk to him next Friday."

Casting the decision onto the fate of his football team felt like a way out that wasn't a decision, a way of the decision being made for him. If Brighton could bring him the jubilation of a victory, he would take that step into the muddy puddle of reconciliation, whatever that looked like, but if they didn't, he'd face the misery of defeat and let the misery of his estrangement from his dad continue.

For the rest of the journey, conversation became purely about football. Who was the superior winger, Stuart Storer or the new Scottish lad, Paul McDonald that they'd signed from Southampton? Danny and Ethan preferred Storer's all-action style, but James had thought McDonald was the more skilful. Isn't Jimmy Case still good enough to play for Brighton? He'd made two appearances the previous season, but he was forty-two now, surely too old to make an impact. Why had the board removed the non-profit clause? This seemed decidedly dodgy - the only reason to remove it was so that individuals could profit from the club, surely? Would we beat Exeter? Obviously and easily - they'd only won one game all season. Was it okay to have a second team? (James was considering Middlesbrough, lured by Juninho, Emerson and Ravenelli.) Under no circumstances could you show any support for another team - "It would be like wanting Sharon to be your mum. Do you want that?" chastised Danny, furious that James had even suggested such a betrayal.

After four and half hours of the train trundling through the evening, they arrived at Exeter Station and emerged to see Granny Danny as Ethan and James had named her, standing in her long brown coat waiting for them. Danny gave her a hug and introduced her to Ethan and James.

"You're so tall," was Granny Danny's first comment before adding, "This is much later than my normal bedtime."

Back at Granny Danny's house, they were shown their bedroom.

"You know where everything is, love," she said, "I need to get myself off to bed."

The boys had another game of Monopoly before going to bed with James repeating his tactic of only going for blues, but this time, he was mercilessly mocked every time he landed on the reds: "Go on, why don't you buy Trafalgar Square. It will match your Middlesbrough shirt."

The game went as it had done before with Ethan winning with the orange set and James going bankrupt first. They chatted away lying in their beds for a while, but soon, Danny found that he was explaining why he thought Jeff Minton would go on to play Premiership football to himself.

The following morning, Granny Danny had left a Kellogg's selection pack on the kitchen table and the boys argued over who would get the Frosties before playing Rock, Paper, Scissors for the packet. Granny Danny emerged from the front room and asked them how they'd slept before saying she'd got them a gift each.

"I've got you some scarves for the football. I went to the Club Shop yesterday. I know it's still warm, but you boys like to wave your scarves at the football, don't you?"

Three bright red Exeter scarves emerged from a paper bag.

"Thanks, Granny, James absolutely loves red," exclaimed Danny, wrapping the scarf forcibly around James' neck while he tried to wrestle it free, spilling his Coco Pops in the process.

Granny Danny was confused but pleased that her gift had gone down well.

"What are we going to do with these?" asked James once they'd left the house.

"You're going to wear all three aren't you," replied Ethan, "along with your Middlesbrough, Man United and Liverpool scarves."

"No," said James sulkily.

They eventually decided on hiding them in a hedge to collect on the way home to avoid hurting Granny Danny's feelings.

The boys followed other blue and white shirts they saw on their walk to find their way to the ground. It was nestled among some houses and suddenly sprang upon them when they rounded a corner, floodlights looming into the sky; the stadium was as dilapidated as the Goldstone Ground, paint peeling off the signs that hung over the narrow entrances. The away fans shuffled into a small, uncovered terrace and as kick-off approached, it was apparent that Brighton's away support was going to be pretty thin, barely more than a hundred dotted around the spacious terrace, but there was Barnet, leaning against a red barrier, cigarette in one hand, limp burger in the other. Danny wanted to be noticed by him and deliberately walked past him twice, but Barnet showed no recognition.

The away terrace, even at the highest point, barely got above pitch level while Exeter's vast Cowshed, holding their loudest fans, towered above the pitch and they had plenty to cheer about as Exeter dominated possession while Albion hacked it clear time and time again, only for the red and white shirts to surge back at them. By half-time, mercifully, it was only 1-0, the Exeter goal tucked away in front of the Brighton fans. Most of the fans in the away end were on their fourth away trip of the season and they'd yet to see Brighton pick up a point or even score a goal, so when the diminutive winger, Paul McDonald headed Brighton level two minutes into the second half, rare hope was kindled. To celebrate in such an open space was a strange experience for the boys. They were used to being crushed by a surge of bodies as soon as the ball hit the back of the net, but here, they were able to leap wildly about unencumbered. Half-time burgers that many fans were still finishing were creating a somewhat messy celebration with globules of relish and the odd half-eaten burger flying into the air. James got a mustard-covered onion on his cheek, but he didn't care.

It was Exeter, though, who were dominant once more and they were finally rewarded in the closing minutes. Danny, Ethan and James peered the length of the pitch as seemingly, Nicky Rust had made an excellent save, but his connection with the ball had just sent it looping up into the air; it seemed to soar in slow-motion before arcing into the back of net, bringing Exeter all three points.

The boys trudged dejectedly back to Granny Danny's, made worse by jeering Exeter fans driving past in cars, honking and yelling abuse. It felt like an insult to drag the Exeter scarves back out of the hedge when they reached their hiding place and James refused to even touch his, much to the annoyance of Danny who told him that he was going to offend his granny.

That evening, they played Scrabble with Granny Danny before watching *Match of the Day*. Middlesbrough had won 2-1 at Everton and for both Boro goals, James received several playful but significant punches as well having the Exeter scarves rammed into his face.

"I don't support them, I don't support them," he pleaded, but his inquiry over the legitimacy of following two teams would never be forgotten.

As they lay in bed that evening, Danny spoke into the darkness, "At least I can carry on ignoring my dad's phone calls."

"Next time we win, you should talk to him," said Ethan.

Danny paused before saying, "Okay."

He knew a time would come when we would talk to his dad once again and he hoped there would be a time when Brighton would win again.

14/09/1996: Exeter 2-1 Brighton (McDonald)

21st September 1996

Brighton & Hove Albion vs Torquay United

Danny was already planning how he was going to spend his money as he walked through the mizzle on Monday morning listening to Kula Shaker's 'Hey Dude,' recorded from the radio: annoyingly, Chris Evans had interrupted the end of the song. His wages would stretch as far as the entry fee to the Torquay match at the weekend, an XL home shirt and Kula Shaker's debut album, *K* that was out that week. The energy of 'Hey Dude' had helped quicken his pace, but not enough to make it to the shop by 9am.

On entering the fencing shop, four minutes late, Danny could see Derek's unshaven chin jiggling up and down, but Crispian Mills' guitar solo was drowning out his words. Popping a headphone out, he responded with unintentionally belligerent-sounding, "What?"

Derek stepped closer, saliva now flecking Danny's face as he spoke, "You need to be reliable, young man. You need to aim to be early so that you're ready to hit the ground running at nine. I'll give you one more chance this week, but it'll be another hour docked if you're late again."

Deep down, Danny knew that what Derek said made sense, that to be late when you were being paid to work wasn't okay and the fact that Derek wasn't docking his wages this time around was actually reasonably decent of him, but Danny was also annoyed, annoyed at his own ill-discipline. He was frustrated that his intentions of being on time weren't turning into a reality, that as his alarm clock screamed at him, he still lay there in a trance, wanting the peace that the half-awake state brings to last forever.

Why did people want fences anyway? What was the point in marking your territory off with ugly wooden rectangles?

Danny's mind was fleeing from self-criticism, rejecting the pain of recognising he was in the wrong. The world was in the wrong, his dad was in the wrong, the owners of Brighton were in the wrong and Derek was in the wrong. Why did he have to live in a world where dads walked out on their families, men in suits destroyed football clubs and fence-shop owners demanded punctuality from their employees? It all just hurt and it needed to be let out. Hollering abuse at the board on Saturday afternoons was cathartic, but Saturday was five days away.

"We need to get twenty pergola poles down from the top shelf for collection later today. My knee can't cope with the ladder, so you're going to need to get up there and pass them down to me," said Derek.

Still seething with the world, Danny climbed the ladder and went through the motions, roughly dragging each pole free before passing them down to Derek. They were getting into a rhythm, Danny pulling a pole free and then letting it drop into Derek's waiting hands. Fourteen poles in and it felt mechanical to Danny, pull, drop, pull, drop, pull, drop…

"Ow, for fuck's sake you clumsy little shit."

Danny looked down at Derek who was rubbing his head. Derek aimed a kick at the ladder which tottered an inch or two and Danny grabbed onto the shelf to steady himself.

"Watch where you're…"

The phone rang from inside the shop and Derek stormed inside, still rubbing his head. Danny got down from the ladder and walked straight out of the gate at the side of the yard, onto the open street. He needed to escape. He wasn't going to tolerate this treatment, wasn't going to be spoken to like that he told himself. In reality, it was an excuse, an excuse to flee a job he'd quickly come to hate. The march home didn't seem to exist; Danny just walked with head bowed, but with eyes raised, staring straight ahead, never looking to the right or the left for the entire journey home, fortunate that the roads he crossed were empty. When he got home, his mum tried to speak to him, but he walked straight past her to his bedroom and got into bed fully clothed and burst into tears. He gathered part of his sheet and bunched it up around his face to mop up the tears and just lay there, sobs making his body shudder until he felt like there was nothing left inside and he lay there numb until sleep overtook him.

The incident with Derek had been nothing, Derek's temper understandably flaring when he'd been whacked by a falling pole, but Danny could see no way back, no way to salvage the situation. He'd wouldn't be going back to the shop - no way.

Having slept most of the day away, at night, he tossed and turned until, overcome by a suffocating frustration, he jumped down from his top bunk, pulled on some clothes and walked out of the house, unsure of what he was doing or where he was going. He walked quickly under the orange glow of the streetlights, pacing quickly through the alleys of the Knoll Estate all the way up to Hangleton Road, through the cool night air all the way to Ethan's house. He didn't know what the time was, only knew it was the middle of the night. He couldn't just knock on the Browns' front door, so he opened their side gate, walked into their garden, and peered up at Ethan's bedroom window. There was a balcony at the back of the Brown house and if Danny could climb up to it, he could stick his head into Ethan's room and wake him up. He surveyed his options: the shed was close enough to the balcony to make a leap for it. To get onto the shed roof though, he would first need to climb the garden fence, so that's what he did. Getting in amongst the Browns' laurel, Danny clambered to the top of the fence, using the branches of the laurel to help. From there, he tentatively stepped onto the shed roof, keeping to the edges. Perched on top of the shed, it creaked under his weight, and he sidled his way around the shed roof to get within jumping distance of the balcony. He feared that a misplaced foot would plunge him through the felting, but he made it around two sides of the shed to the corner that was closest to the balcony. Once there, he made the leap. If he failed to make the distance, he would plunge down and collide with the patio doors, but he made it and was safely on the balcony.

Danny turned his head at an angle that would fit through the window and could make out Ethan lying in the dark. It took four times of slightly increasing the volume of calling his name to wake him up and strangely, he didn't seem surprised to see him.

"What do you want?"

"Let's go for a walk."

"What?!"

"I lost my job today. Let's go for a walk."

As if this were enough explanation, Ethan got out of bed, put some clothes on and the boys were out on the street.

"Where are we walking?" asked Ethan.

"Let's go to the Goldstone," said Danny. Somehow, it felt like the right place to go.

The route to the Goldstone went past James' house and with his bedroom on the ground floor, it was much easier to extract him from his house in the middle of the night. The harder task was shutting him up, so excited was he to be going on an adventure at night, but miraculously, he got out of his house without waking his parents.

The boys got to the Goldstone and circled it in an anti-clockwise direction, starting at the North Stand and arriving last at the largely unused East Stand. Entry to the ground was prevented here, only by revolving metal gates with thin metal bars too small for anyone to climb through. Above the gates were thick coils of impenetrable barbed wire, but not on every entrance. On the fifth one they approached, the barbed wire was missing and a gap opened up above the gate.

"Let's go in," said Danny.

Ethan and James paused. Traversing the ground at night was one thing that no one could complain about, but climbing into the ground was a different matter. To Ethan and James, it felt like a dangerous step, but Danny was off, using the bars of the gate as a ladder before climbing through the gap. It was a far easier task than getting onto the Browns' balcony. He was up and over in moments.

"Come on," he said and Ethan and James, unprepared to let Danny have all the fun, followed.

The East Stand was the place from where filming of the match took place and the ladder leading to the television gantry, a wooden box twenty feet up in the air, was what caught the boys' immediate attention as they walked through the weeds of the East Terrace. They climbed the ladder and sat looking out from the flimsy television gantry, the pitch dimly illumined by a nearly full moon.

It was a great view, far better than the one they had from the North Stand which made goals at the other end of the pitch difficult to decipher. Often, the boys had celebrated having known little about the goal other than that they had seen the sudden exciting shiver of the net.

Sitting with their backs leaned against the back wall of the gantry, Ethan asked, "What happened?"

Danny explained what had happened at work that day, exaggerating Derek's anger and the kick at the ladder. He did a dramatic enough job to create a shocking image of abuse in the workplace instead of a simple moment that could easily have been forgotten by lunchtime.

"What's next?" asked James.

"I don't know," admitted Danny.

Tossing and turning in his bed an hour earlier, he'd felt hopeless, alone. He still didn't know where to turn next, but he didn't feel alone as he sat there with his two friends in the early hours. They sat silently, drinking in the silence of the stadium. It seemed so peaceful, so beautiful.

The next day, Danny's mum told him he had to go to the Job Centre. He was reluctant and wanted to give it a day or two, but his mum told him that if he didn't have a job, then he needed to sign on and claim Jobseeker's Allowance and that she would still need £30 a week. At the Job Centre, he found himself sitting opposite Claire again. This time, she didn't have a ready-made job for him to start the next day, but did organise an interview for him at a clothes shop, Madhouse, on the main high street of central Brighton - Western Road. Then came endless and confusing form-filling to claim the Allowance which would give Danny £32.50 a week. Under the 'Reason for Leaving' his last job space on the form, Danny squeezed the phrase, 'Dropped a pole on my boss' head' which Claire asked him to clarify. Eventually, he was told that he could come back next Tuesday to collect his first JSA cheque and the Madhouse interview would be that afternoon as well, so, if he wanted, they could go through some interview techniques beforehand.

When Saturday came around, there was not enough money for the Brighton home shirt or the Kula Shaker album, but, with the sale of Reef's album, *Replenish* to Ethan, Danny was able to scrape enough to get through the turnstile and find his home back on the North Stand once more. Talk of Dick Knight saving the club had flooded the fans with hope. He'd looked like a kindly grandfather on the cover of *The Argus*, always smiling and genial, eyes hidden behind sunglasses and a grey goatee beard giving him a cool edge, but perhaps his cool was because the fans saw him as a saviour.

Barnet arrived minutes before kick-off and was ready once again to test and challenge the fans with his hand-clapping test of loyalty: "If you all went to Exeter, all went to Exeter, all went to Exeter, clap your hands."

Danny, Ethan and James launched into enthusiastic clapping. It was their turn to look around to see who else passed this test. Barnet glanced towards the boys doubtfully, but accepted that perhaps they had indeed been to Exeter. He then pulled his scarf from his neck, stretching it out in front of him so that the white letters of 'Brighton' were clear: "Why don't you give me a B…"

The crowd responded with a deep and lengthy 'B' and once Barnet had encouraged the crowd to spell out the whole name, perhaps leading his very own spelling test, he asked, "Who's gonna win?" to which the crowd responded, "BRIGHTON."

Back-to-back home victories would certainly be welcome. The boys glanced up at the television gantry where they had sat earlier that week. It didn't seem real that they'd sat up there as they looked at it in the bright light of day.

Torquay quickly established themselves as the better side when the match started, with reserve goalkeeper, Mark Ormerod, into the team in Nicky Rust's absence, under threat repeatedly. On a rare foray forward though, it was Brighton that took the lead, Ian Baird showing his class with a composed and classy finish. Then, a moment of madness from Ormerod, rushing off his line and getting nowhere near the ball, gifted Torquay an equaliser.

At half-time, one fan vented his frustration, leaping the advertising hoardings and charging for the centre circle. Once there, he took a seat. The possible three-point deduction was in the fans' minds, but this young man felt like a hero to Danny. When he'd been treated badly by his boss at work, he'd acted and when the owners had treated the club badly, this man was acting, showing the board that they couldn't treat the fans like this. Two stewards in long fluorescent coats walked slowly towards the man and he allowed them to walk him away so that the second half could commence.

Brighton continued to implode, this time, right-back, Peter Smith heading the ball straight to a Torquay striker who put the visitors ahead for the first time in the game. When Torquay were awarded a penalty deep into the second half, it looked like it was game over, but Ormerod made up for his earlier error, leaping to his left to palm the ball away and finally, the momentum of the match swung as Torquay attempted to cling onto their victory. Jeff Minton, who had been quiet for most of the match, was suddenly inspired in central midfield, running at the Torquay defence repeatedly, jinking through gaps and finally, he found an opening, rescuing a point with a well-taken goal.

As the crowd departed, huge numbers seemed to be heading around to the West Stand, walking down the narrow Newtown Road, rather than the big dual carriageway of Old Shoreham Road that was most people's route home. Newtown Road had the entrances to the stands on the west of the ground, but this was also where the club's offices were, and this was where the fans were headed. They desperately wanted Dick Knight and his consortium to wrestle control from the current owners, but every day, the newspapers had depressing headlines of delays and disagreements. The fans were on their way to make it clear who they wanted in charge of their club. Danny, Ethan and James followed the crowd and found a brick wall to stand on.

"Sack the board, sack the board, sack the board!" rang around the streets.

The West Stand loomed over them, offices and windows encased in teak. Danny imagined the Chief Executive, David Bellotti sat in one of those darkened offices listening to the crowd outside. Bellotti was the only member of the board that ever attended matches. He sat peering through huge glasses at the game, alone in one half of the Directors' Box. The other half was always full of members of the opposing board and their entourage, but no one wanted anything to do with the Brighton board, didn't want their name dragged into the dirt. Sometimes, David Bellotti's wife would be with him, but the more the anger of the crowd grew, the scarcer her attendance became and who could blame her?

One fan attempted to build a bonfire in the street, mildly

successful in that he managed to light a small pile of newspapers, but it was quickly extinguished and gradually, the crowd dispersed feeling angry and impotent.

The boys walked back up the hill towards Ethan's house. Mr Brown had said that they would order a curry in the evening and on remembering this, the boys quickened their walk.

"Our home form's good," Mr Brown said an hour later as the boys munched their way through the poppadoms. "We haven't lost yet. If we can just start picking up points away from home."

Mr Brown rarely went to games anymore, but he still followed Brighton, reading the local paper every day and enjoying it vicariously through his son. Danny looked at Mr Brown as he continued to ply the boys with questions, asking how Mark Ormerod compared to Nicky Rust, whether the club should have offered Ian Chapman another contract or was Stuart Tuck proving to be a good replacement, whether Kevin McGarrigle deserved to start at the back. Danny saw the presence of this generous caring man who invited him into his home and fed him takeaway curry and he thought about his own dad, who he hadn't spoken to for eight months. Brighton hadn't won today. The silence would continue.

21/09/96: Brighton 2-2 Torquay United (Baird, Minton)
28/09/96: Northampton Town 3-0 Brighton

1st October 1996

Brighton & Hove Albion vs Lincoln City

On Tuesday morning, Danny meandered down to the Job Centre at midday. He'd hoped that he would manage to avoid Claire and be able to just pick up his cheque and go, but she spotted him before he could escape and beckoned him over.

"How are you feeling about your interview today?" she asked.

"Okay," responded Danny.

"What are you going to wear?" Claire asked.

"Just this," said Danny, indicating the clothes he had on: baggy blue jeans and a navy-blue Adidas jumper with three stripes running down each sleeve.

"It's important that you make a good impression," said Claire. "Have you got a shirt and some smart trousers?"

Danny still had his school trousers and there was probably the grey shirt that he'd been forced to wear for his auntie's wedding a year ago crumpled somewhere in his room. He told Claire that he thought he had something smart and she said he should wear it.

"You only get one chance to make a first impression," she said.

Danny did want the job at Madhouse. He'd appreciated having the money that the job at the fencing shop had given him and it had allowed him to go to the Exeter away game. If he could get another job, he'd be able to keep following Brighton away. Working in a clothes shop sounded easier as well - t-shirts hung on hangers were not going to cover his hands in calluses the way the fence panels had.

Claire kept the advice coming, telling him to think about skills he'd got and evidence to back them up. Danny didn't really know if he had any skills. At school, he'd liked writing, but that wasn't going to be relevant to working in a shop and he was alright at Maths which might be a little bit helpful, but the tills did all the adding up for you.

He'd been intending to go straight from the Job Centre to the

Post Office (to cash the Job Seeker's Allowance cheque) and then onto Madhouse, but Claire's suggestion of an outfit change meant that he had to take a detour back to his house. His old school trousers were still scrunched up in a ball in the corner of his bedroom. It had been over four months since he'd left school and there they had lain, discarded on the floor on that final day and untouched ever since. He couldn't find the grey shirt, but found a black polo shirt that loosely resembled smartness. He felt self-conscious, not himself somehow in this vaguely smart outfit, used to jeans, football shirts and sweat-shirts without deviation. He sat down on his bed for a moment, daunted by the idea of trying to impress someone with answers to questions. He felt like this was something totally beyond him and for a moment, he was tempted back into his bed where he could just lie and feel nothing and let the day drift by, but he didn't succumb and at two o' clock, he walked into Madhouse and told the woman at the till that he was here for an interview.

He was shown into a small room at the back of the shop. Clothes were piled on the shelves around the room and two plastic chairs were in the middle. A woman in her forties indicated the red chair and Danny sat down.

"Hello, my name's Donna. I'm just going to ask you some questions, nothing to worry about; it's just a chance to for us to get to know you and decide whether you'll fit in with our team here. So, firstly, do you have any experience of working in retail?"

"Er, sorry, what's retail?" asked Danny. This wasn't a good start.

Donna explained what retail was and Danny told her about working in the fencing shop, but then she asked why he'd stopped working in the fencing shop and Danny didn't want to be dishonest, so he explained how there had been an accident where he'd dropped a pole on his boss' head and that his boss had got angry and Danny hadn't liked being talked to like that, so he had decided to leave. Danny did his best to make it sound reasonable, not mentioning the fact that he'd just disappeared out the back door, but however you told the story, it didn't sound great.

The questions kept coming and Danny was aware that a lot

of the questions, he was answering very briefly, sometimes with just one word and every time he finished a short answer, Donna would sit there, allowing an awkward silence to linger before writing something down on the piece of paper on her clipboard. The biro scratching across the surface of the paper sounded uncomfortably loud as Danny sat and waited for the next question.

"What would you say is your worst quality?" asked Donna.

Danny paused. This was a strange question, one that seemed impossible to answer in an impressive way. Danny didn't like the way he looked but that was irrelevant. He felt frustrated by his inability to articulate himself. He got angry, most often with himself. After a moment's indecision, he decided on, "Laziness." Yes, that seemed right. He stayed in bed until the afternoon when he had the chance and was often overcome with a feeling of lethargy and fatigue.

Donna put her notebook down in her lap. "Do you want this job?" she asked.

This wasn't an interview question.

"Yes," replied Danny. Like every answer he'd given, it was the truth.

Donna looked doubtfully at Danny, confused by this boy who would have got the job had he just gone through the motions of giving insincere obvious responses to each question, but he hadn't played the game, hadn't given her what she wanted.

"I'm afraid, we're not going to offer you a position," she said.

"Oh, okay," said Danny.

With the fencing job, he'd just had to turn up and be six foot tall, but this seemed more complicated. There were things he had said that had closed the door for him and so he walked out of Madhouse, not sure how to feel. It seemed like such a blunt rejection. Donna had given no reason for not giving him the job. He didn't especially want to work in Madhouse any more than he wanted to work anywhere else, but he didn't like this. He wasn't distraught, just numb.

He noticed a Post Office on the other side of the road and finally completed the last of the day's tasks, cashing his £32.50 cheque of which he would see a whole £2.50. Fortunately, there was no Brighton home game until the following Tuesday and by then, he would have received another cheque and would have just enough money to get into the game.

The week went by, back to the routine that he'd kept all summer. Not working gave him ample time to indulge in lengthy sessions of *Sensible World of Soccer*. He'd taken Brighton all the way to the Premiership and lifted the European Cup with them, Robbie Fowler scoring 116 goals in one season. He'd visited the Browns a lot, sitting around their circular dining table and Mr Brown had asked about Danny's work and Danny felt like he was letting him down, telling him that at the moment, he wasn't working.

"I still think your thing is writing, Danny," Mr Brown said. "Ethan showed me the match report you wrote of the Hull game last season. It was really good."

As a piece of homework last year, Danny's class had written newspaper articles and Danny had opted to describe a rare victory for Brighton. His teacher wasn't a football fan and had given it some faint praise, but Mr Brown had loved it. When he read it, he told Danny that he was really gifted and that he should think about writing in the future. To be told this had buoyed Danny hugely and despite not doing anything to pursue a career in journalism, he still carried the dream that he would, one day, stumble into a career in writing.

On the Friday, the boys disappeared to the Rec for a couple of hours of football when Ethan and James had finished school. When they arrived back at the Browns' house, muddy and sticky, Mr Brown showed them the back cover of *The Argus*. It revealed that talks between Bill Archer, the current Brighton chairman and the Knight in shining armour, riding in to save the day, had broken down. There had been a meeting in a London hotel, but despite Archer's claims that he would sell the club for the £56.25 fee that he bought it for, he was, in reality, unprepared to relinquish the club to Knight.

"What does he want?" asked Danny.

"Money? Power?" suggested Mr Brown. "What does any man want?"

The next day, Ivor Caplin was on the back of *The Argus*. He was the leader of Hove Borough Council and was getting ready to try and claim Hove for Labour in the General Election the following year. Hove had been in the Conservative's grip for all time, a seat that they could be complacent over, but Caplin was a Brighton fan, a man who wanted the club to be the heartbeat of the town and he also knew that standing against Bill Archer publicly would bring in thousands of votes from Brighton fans who saw an alignment between the fans defeating the board and Labour defeating the Tories.

On Tuesday, Danny tried and failed to avoid Claire and found himself having to explain to her that he hadn't got the job at Madhouse. Yes, he'd got changed into smarter clothing. Yes, he'd arrived on time. Yes, he'd answered all the questions. Danny didn't tell her exactly what he had said, and Claire was slightly bemused at why Danny had failed to get the job, but she also sensed that he probably wasn't the best interview candidate. She showed him some more jobs and Danny went away with three different phone numbers that he could call to arrange interviews. Once home, he put them on top of his meagre book collection and decided that phoning them was a job that could wait until tomorrow. A task a day seemed like a reasonable approach, and he'd already visited the Job Centre and cashed the cheque for his Job Seeker's Allowance, £1.50 saved from the previous week to be topped up to £4 with this week's money to grant him access to the game against Lincoln City that evening.

The Argus that day had reminded fans that the potential three-point penalty was still hanging over the club. The newspaper was very clear in its criticism of the Brighton board, but it was also cautionary of supporter conduct, knowing that the breakdown in talks was likely to catapult the fans into reckless and desperate acts.

On the North Stand that evening, the boys could sense the increased anger in the air. The Directors' Box was empty, David Bellotti not risking an appearance in this fevered atmosphere. The match seemed almost an irrelevance as every chant angrily railed against the board instead of supporting the team. No one wanted to clap their hands because they'd been to Northampton on the Saturday. In fact, Barnet was conspicuous by his absence. He'd been a surly ever-present member of 'The Box,' leading chants whilst superciliously looking down on the lesser supporters around him.

Peter Smith rose in the box to head Brighton into the lead and the crowd went through the motions of letting their limbs spasm in uncontrollable joy. But then it was Lincoln's turn and in front of the North Stand, they levelled. As the net shivered, the first legs were over the hoardings and the Lincoln players, instead of celebrating, were fleeing, heading for the tunnel, as bodies swarmed onto the pitch. Danny watched, halfway up the stand, not close enough to clamber the barriers. If he'd been closer, he would have been on the pitch, but the moment was over before he'd decided to wrestle through the crowds to the front of the terrace.

Most fans applauded the pitch-invaders, but in amongst the applause, shouts of anger: "Get off the pitch" broke through, but those shouts were sparse. For most people, and certainly for Danny, Ethan and James, the existence of the club was at stake. The FA could take their petty points away for this pitch invasion if they wanted to, but if it cared about keeping this club going, they needed to step in and make these talks work and there was only one way of them working for the Brighton fans.

Chants hung in the air, sung angrily to the vacant seats in the Directors' Box and then eventually, the fans on the pitch plodded proudly back to the North Stand, warmly applauded, and responding themselves with arms raised aloft, returning the applause.

The players emerged back into the strange atmosphere and Brighton's composure, had it ever existed, was lost. They just about saw out the first half with the scores still level.

In the second half, Lincoln were by far the better side and everyone knew that there was going to be a goal and then, the fans would be back on the pitch and of course, it happened and once again, the players sprinted for the tunnel as fans spilled onto the pitch once more. They lingered for less time on the second occasion. They'd already made their point, already disrupted the game, so the second time felt a bit strange, slightly unnecessary.

The routine was set. Out came the teams: Brighton, poor, Lincoln, excellent and once again, Lincoln scored and this time, it felt silly and only around forty people spilled onto the pitch and they didn't get far, realising that they'd misjudged it and that a third invasion was excessive. The players paused at the entrance to the tunnel, realising that perhaps, they might actually be able to play out the rest of this game. Lincoln kept the ball and at 3-1 up, they seemed to just want to get the job done and get the game finished before midnight.

The whistle to end the match finally went and the boys, along with thousands of other fans, made their way round to Newtown Road to continue their protests, their anger not dissipating, only growing. This game had felt like a veering back into the chaos that dominated the end of the previous season. Just three months in, hope had been stamped upon and the team had nosedived to second bottom in the league. There was no win to celebrate, no future to look forward to, no chance of Danny responding to his dad's phone-call and no reason for him to get out of bed the next morning.

01/10/96: Brighton 1-3 Lincoln (Smith)
05/10/96: Wigan 1-0 Brighton

12th October 1996

Brighton & Hove Albion vs Cambridge United

Danny finally got around to phoning the numbers Claire had given him the following Monday, fearing that turning up to collect his Job Seeker's Allowance having not made an effort would make her doubt that he was actively seeking a job. She had explained that it was an expectation of people claiming the benefit that they "actively seek employment." All of the positions had already been filled, having been given out to all the other 'seekers,' people demonstrating a little more proactivity than Danny.

Danny had spent almost two hours of Saturday staring at the Ceefax pages scrolling through the Division 3 latest scores. Once Brighton had gone 1-0 down to Wigan, nothing had changed and for the first time that season, Brighton had sunk to rock bottom. Danny had been desperate to attend the Wigan game once he'd heard that there was a planned protest march direct to the front door of Bill Archer's house in the nearby village of Mellor, but no job meant no funds for away days. The march had been featured on the local news and Danny, Ethan and James, after enjoying Mrs Browns' shepherds' pie, watched on the evening news as a crowd of around a hundred had stood outside Bill Archer's house. Instead of bricks being lobbed through windows and an eruption of violence, punk-poet and Brighton fan, Attila the Stockbroker had recited a poem narrating the mismanagement and demise of the club. The news showed a fragment and the footage was at odds with images of angry men running onto football pitches and pulling down crossbars. Danny had felt inspired and had tried to write a poem himself when he got home: "Stuart Storer, super scorer, explorer of the right-wing border; if he had a wife, he'd never bore her." Danny's intense rhyme scheme meant it quickly petered out and he couldn't think of many rhymes for McDonald, Maskell or Baird.

On Wednesday, Danny, Ethan and James were back at the Rec with James' recently acquired birthday present, a Mitre

Ultimax. Ethan was by far the best player out of the three and the three-and-in competitions they played on repeat were predictable: Ethan would beat Danny who would outmuscle the four-years-younger James before Ethan destroyed James and so it would repeat, the game slowing down as they neared the second hour of play, but becoming no less predictable.

Lying exhausted on the weed-strewn grass, they peered to the other end of the Rec where two men were swinging golf clubs, sending their balls hurtling up and into a goalmouth a hundred yards away. The men followed their golf balls, getting closer to the boys and it was James that realised who they were first.

"That's Mark Ormerod… and Kevin McGarrigle," he squealed excitedly.

Danny and Ethan sat bolt upright, watching the men approach. Their identical haircuts, carefully gelled centre-partings only differentiated by colour: Ormerod's, a dark brown, McGarrigle's, approaching ginger, immediately identified them as the Brighton reserve goalkeeper, who had made a couple of appearances in Nicky Rust's absence, and the centre-back who had largely warmed the bench so far.

Danny jumped up: "Do you fancy a game?" he shouted, sending the Ultimax sailing through the air towards them.

McGarrigle trapped the ball and looked at Ormerod, momentarily indecisive, but then incredibly to the boys, McGarrigle responded with, "Go on then."

Energy immediately restored, the boys were on their feet, chucking sweaty jumpers down for goalposts, eager that this opportunity not slip away.

The game started and Ormerod and McGarrigle sprayed passes between each other, playing over-elaborately to demonstrate their far-superior ability before knocking the ball between the jumpers with a casual back-heel or playing keepy-up while crossing the line, but they were also playing lazily, not bothering to track runners and if the boys managed to launch the ball the length of the pitch to a goal-hanging player beyond Ormerod and McGarrigle's high-line, there were chances for the boys to roll the ball into an open goal, and it felt glorious to score against these professional footballers, a thrill of exhilaration coursing through Danny as he finished the simplest of chances. The boys were still well behind and the last goal of the game came from the foot of Ormerod, spotting James off his line, and launching the ball over his head from the halfway line as James flailed backwards, tripping over his own feet as the ball landed perfectly in the centre of the goal.

McGarrigle and Ormerod stuck around for a penalty shoot-out, and the boys found that beating a professional goalkeeper was a much harder task than the open goal they'd been allowed during the match. When McGarrigle went in goal for James' penalty, he turned around and let out a rasping fart before back-heeling James' tame effort away from goal.

"What do you think of Bellotti?" asked Ethan as James scurried away to collect the ball.

"He's an alright bloke," responded McGarrigle.

It was a disappointing response. The boys wanted them to share their righteous anger, but the players were talking about men who had given them a chance to fulfil their dream, to play football for a living. That had been their hope, a dream that had been realised, but still hung in the balance as to how long it would last, so they weren't going to let loose words slip to a bunch of kids at the Rec.

"Lads, thanks for the game," said Ormerod. "We'll see you at the Goldstone, yeah?"

"See you Saturday," replied Danny.

Ormerod and McGarrigle walked away and the boys looked at each other.

"Can you believe that?" said Ethan.

"I wish it had been Nicky Rust," said James.

Footballers felt otherworldly to the boys, figures that emerged from the tunnel on a Saturday afternoon and then disappeared back to Planet Football until the next game. Other than the very occasional glimpses of Denny Mundee, once in his underwear, in his front room when Danny delivered him his paper, the boys had never seen a footballer in the flesh outside of a football match and they had just had this magical experience, playing football with their heroes.

That Saturday, it felt different seeing the Brighton players warming up before the game. Playing football with Ormerod and McGarrigle had humanised the players to the boys. They were blokes, immature blokes who still found farting funny. McGarrigle, at nineteen, was only three years older than Danny and Ormerod was only one year older than that and here they were, carrying the hopes of men and women who allowed the irrelevance of a result in a football match to define their mood, and for Brighton fans, the mood was getting bleaker, bottom of the league and the future looking dire. Barnet was absent yet again - perhaps the self-proclaimed loyal supporter's commitment had been stretched to breaking point and this thought satisfied Danny as he joined in with, "Brighton 'til I die, I'm Brighton 'til I die, I know I am, I'm sure I am, I'm Brighton 'til I die." Life seemed like a vast expanse in front of him. He couldn't imagine himself an adult doing adult things. It felt like he'd stay at this stage for the rest of his life. The older he'd got, the worse life had got. As a young child, life had been so carefree, but now life had bashed him about: a cruel school, the departure of his dad and the crumbling of his football club. Things that seemed so certain had turned out to be fragile and temporary.

On the pitch, the defending against Cambridge in the first half was sloppy and chaotic; the running of the club was being mirrored on the pitch with terrible, calamitous, rash decisions repeatedly made by the back four. In front of the North Stand, Cambridge strolled to a 2-0 lead at the break and it should have been more. Stuart Storer restored some hope at the beginning of the second half and the game became more of a contest with Cambridge retreating and desperately trying to cling onto their lead the closer it got to the final whistle. Brighton had lots of possession, but chances were scarce with hopeful balls whacked into the box from deep positions to be headed clear time and time again. As Danny watched the balls fly into the box, it felt like they were his dad's phone calls, rebuffed by the Cambridge United defence and rebuffed by Danny. It had been four weeks since he'd told Ethan and James that he'd talk to his dad when he next saw Brighton win and deep down, he wanted both things to happen: to reconnect with his dad and to see the Albion climb off the bottom of the table, but his words bound him and he would stick by them even with the news that Simon was to bring that evening.

Back at home, watching *Gladiators* with his younger brother, Simon announced, "Dad's coming home on Monday and he's bringing Ryan."

Lightning clambering up The Wall to wrestle an opponent seemed of little importance suddenly.

"What? Who's Ryan? What do you mean he's coming home?"

"He's coming here on Monday with Ryan."

"You're saying the same thing again. I've no idea who Ryan is and what do you mean, he's coming home? He's not coming to live with us again, is he?"

"No. He's just coming to stay Monday night and then go to the football match. Ryan is Sharon's son."

Danny had no idea that Sharon had a son and the news was physically painful. His breath caught; it felt like he'd forgotten how to breathe. He felt winded. *Gladiators* had gone to an advert break before Danny spoke again.

"So, Ryan's his new son?"

"He told me that he's his stepson and that it's not the same as a real son."

"Why are they going to the football? Dad doesn't go to the football."

Danny's dad had only been to the Goldstone Ground once, taking Danny to his first ever football match in 1991. They'd gone to watch Brighton against Liverpool in the FA Cup and Brighton had been glorious that day, drawing 2-2 with Kenny Dalglish's Liverpool, a team featuring John Barnes and Ian Rush and a team that would go on to win the league that season. Brighton would have their last good season that year, making the Play-off Final, only to lose 3-1 to Notts County. If they'd triumphed at Wembley, they would have made it the top flight one year before the dawn of the Premier League, the moment when big money started to roll into football, a sliding doors moment with the door firmly slamming shut on Brighton. They were relegated the following season and then finished 9th, 14th, 16th, then 23rd in their four consecutive seasons in the third tier, getting gradually worse year on year and now, here they were, the worst league team in England.

"Ryan supports Hartford," said Simon.

"You mean, Hereford," replied Danny.

Every bit of information was a further wound. On Tuesday, his dad would be erasing that beautiful first memory of going to a football match by taking this Hereford boy to the Goldstone and sitting in the away end. Could there be anything more traitorous than that?

12/10/96: Brighton 1-2 Cambridge (Storer)

15th October 1996

Brighton & Hove Albion vs Hereford United

Danny couldn't bear to be at home. He'd said that he wasn't going to speak to his dad until he'd seen Brighton win. Perhaps, he might have relented for a personal visit from his dad, but there was no chance he was going to be at home, welcoming this Ryan. Danny couldn't believe that his mum was letting this happen. She'd spoken to Danny about Ryan sleeping in his room. Simon had agreed that he could have his bed and that he would sleep on the floor. Danny was sure his dad would be sleeping in the front room on the sofa - surely, he wouldn't get back into the double-bed with his mum. It was all so weird and painful, and Danny was going to be nowhere near any of it, and he didn't want to be found either. His mum and his dad would know that he'd be at Ethan's or James' house if he wasn't at home and he didn't want them attempting to collect him, so he needed another plan.

It came to him as he woke up on Monday afternoon. He stuffed three thick jumpers into his old school rucksack, an extra pair of socks and *To Kill a Mockingbird,* grabbed from the bottom of the bookshelf, and made his way to Ethan's house, aiming to arrive at the same time as he would be returning from school. His anxiety had quickened his pace and he was sitting on Ethan's doorstep when he arrived home.

"We're going to sleep at the Goldstone tonight," he said.

"What?"

"I can't be at home. My dad's there with his new son."

Ethan wasn't sure. He wanted to say the right thing, give advice that was good, give advice that was kind.

"Do you think…" he started.

"No - there's no way that I'm going to be at home tonight."

Ethan could see that there was going to be no negotiation. No compromise. The pain of going home was too much for Danny and tonight, Ethan needed to be there for his friend.

"Just let your mum know so she doesn't worry," he said.

Danny hadn't even thought about his mum and how she'd worry if he didn't turn up, but he agreed that it would be cruel to just disappear, so he phoned his home number from Ethan's phone and told his mum not to worry, but that he wasn't going to be home until after his dad had gone. She pleaded, got angry, started crying, but Danny just stood resolute, letting her emotions burn themselves out before finally saying, "Bye, mum" when she paused, and he put the phone down before she had a chance to respond.

Danny filled his rucksack with crisps, a couple of apples and a pack of sausage rolls from the Browns' house and then walked down to the Goldstone Ground as the light faded.

He'd arranged to meet Ethan at eleven o' clock in front of the Club Shop, but there were a few hours to fill and the first task was figuring out where he was going to sleep. Around the back of the East terrace was the best place to explore with most of it no longer in use. The most concealed area was a Portakabin that had been used in the past to sell programmes from. It had since had the windows smashed and the wooden door was just about clinging to its frame by one rusty hinge. The door swung open without resistance and inside, the floor was covered with broken glass. There were two tables and Danny flipped them over, thinking that the underside of the tables could create a makeshift bed.

He sat with his back to the wall of the hut and pulled the sausage rolls and *To Kill a Mockingbird* from his bag. He'd studied the book for his English Literature GCSE, but sitting in his lessons at school, he'd just stared out of the window watching the Year 8s play football - their PE lesson always coincided with his English lesson - and as his teacher had read the book aloud in a monotone, he'd let the words wash over him, none of them connecting into coherent sentences in his mind. He only had the loosest sense of what the story was about, but as it had been drawing to an end while Atticus Finch's speeches, imploring the jury not to judge Tom Robinson guilty just because he was black were read, Danny had stopped looking out of the window and been momentarily captivated by the words, despite the fact that they were delivered in an unemotional drawl.

As he opened the book in the Portakabin, the first time he'd opened a book since leaving school, he felt excited to read it properly, but after twenty minutes, the light had faded and even with the book brought as close to his face as possible, he could no longer make out the words.

He realised that he had no way of being able to tell the time and the only way he could think of to find it out was to walk down to Hove Station and look at the clock. He'd tried to estimate the time, not wanting to spend longer at the station than he needed to, but when he finally decided to make the walk, he'd massively underestimated how much time had gone past, those lonely moments sat on the underside of a table dragging by.

He arrived at the station at 8.44pm and found a seat on a cold, red iron bench, the bars feeling like ice against his thighs. The light of the train station allowed him to resume reading and he followed Scout's childhood, getting into scrapes and fights in school and trying to get a glimpse of her reclusive neighbour, Boo Radley. Despite the cold biting at his fingers with each page turned, he kept reading. With every chapter read, a chunk of minutes passed and at a quarter to eleven, he started walking back to the Goldstone Ground, attempting to continue reading as he walked with the illumination of the street lights, but this was a frustrating experience with the lampposts spread out in a way which meant that the book was plunged into darkness for a good few strides between each post.

When Danny got to the Club Shop, Ethan wasn't there, but within a couple of minutes, two figures turned onto Newtown Road.

"Look who I've got with me," said Ethan pointing to James, who had been collected with a rap on his window on the way to the ground. Ethan knew that sleeping at the ground was something that James would not want to miss.

Danny walked the boys round the ground to the Portakabin: "Gentlemen, welcome to the Goldstone Hotel," said Danny as he stood in the doorway.

The boys settled themselves onto the upturned undersides of the tables. Ethan had brought three sleeping bags with him and the boys got themselves as comfortable as they could. Ethan pulled a flask of hot chocolate out of his bag and they took turns using the only cup. Inside the Portakabin, there wasn't enough room for them all to lie down, so they got themselves into an awkward, reclined sitting position.

"Who's this new son that your dad's bringing?" Ethan asked.

Danny told the boys about Ryan: "I feel like he's stolen my dad," he said. "I was going to talk to my dad the next time Brighton won. I was going to give him a chance, but having this Hereford-kid on the scene is just horrible."

"Don't worry. We'll smash Hereford tomorrow," said James, missing the point entirely.

"This Ryan doesn't change how your dad feels about you," said Ethan.

Danny didn't respond. He wanted this to be true but didn't know if it was. The existence of this surrogate son might help his dad assuage his guilt, knowing that he was still fulfilling the role of a father.

The boys continued to talk and began to shiver despite the sleeping bags. Talk quickly turned to football. Brighton desperately needed a win and tomorrow was the perfect time to get it. Hereford were only just above Brighton and if Brighton could win, they would drag Hereford towards the relegation zone with them. To send Ryan's Hereford crashing down the table would feel like some kind of justice. But there was a more important battle to fight, against the board and that day's *Argus* had announced that there was going to be a walk-out protest fifteen minutes before the end of the match, that en masse, the crowd would up and leave to show their contempt for the board.

"I've got an idea," said Danny.

"What?" chorused Ethan and James.

"Let's take those fifteen minutes back that we're going to miss tomorrow. Let's go into the ground now."

Shivering inside their sleeping bags was beginning to feel a little unbearable, so, no sooner was the suggestion made, the boys were up and out of the Portakabin. As they walked down Goldstone Lane, James spotted a football on the front lawn of one of the houses. He tiptoed up the steps to the garden and grabbed the ball before the boys started scrambling into the ground once more, through the same gap above one of the East Terrace ticket stalls that should have been blocked with barbed wire.

Into the ground, they stood on the top step of the East

Terrace looking out onto the pitch. There were lights on in the South Stand and the pitch was partially lit, the light dimming as it approached the North Stand.

"We've got to go and score a goal in front of the North Stand," said Danny.

With a football in their hands, it felt like an irresistible temptation and so they scampered down the steps and climbed over the advertising hoardings. The light coming from the other end of the pitch was just enough so they could see what they were doing, but was also, not so bright as to make it likely that they would be spotted by anyone looking out of their windows in Goldstone Lane.

The boys passed the ball around before taking it in turns to take penalties against each other. They were all careful to keep their shots on target, fearful that a wild shot sailing into the North Stand would create a loud echoing noise. Each time the ball hit the net, it made a delightful rippling sound. They were used to the nets at the Rec which were put up every Friday by the council. These hung loose and swayed in the wind, nothing like the taut beauty of these nets. Each boy had scored a few goals and every one of them was then celebrated in front of the empty North Stand. The idea of doing this in front of a heaving mass of fervent bodies was an incredible thought and this was the closest the boys could ever get to that experience.

A siren pierced the silence of the night and the boys ran and leapt into the North Stand, lying flat to the floor, but it wailed past and the noise disappeared into the distance. However, it felt like a warning and the boys decided that they'd had their moment and it was time to get back to the Portakabin.

They returned the football on the way - they weren't thieves. Little would the owners know that it had been nestled in the goal in front of the North Stand during the night. The adrenaline and energy of feeling like footballers had warmed the boys up and after excitedly talking through their glorious finishes, they were warm enough to finally fall asleep in the early hours of the morning.

They awoke with the morning light a few hours later and as they emerged, a hedgehog was curled in a ball in front of the Portakabin. Ethan and James had to get home before their parents awoke and Danny needed to fill his day without going home. It was a Tuesday, and, in a few hours, he was expected at the Job Centre. Danny filled the rest of his day in search of warmth, walking the aisles of Co-op, returning to Hove Station, and sitting on a train that wasn't going to depart for half an hour and getting off just before it did and crawling under a bush in a cemetery, hoping that the branches might provide warmth. They didn't.

That evening, instead of getting into the North Stand early and watching the players warm up, Danny said he'd meet Ethan and James in a bit, and he headed around to the entrance for away fans. He pulled his Brighton scarf up and over his mouth and nose and pulled his hood up so that just his eyes were visible and stood at a distance and watched as the Hereford fans made their way into the ground.

He'd been there ten minutes, wondering what he was trying to achieve, when he saw his dad walking with a teenager who looked a similar age to Danny. This must be Ryan, he thought. His dad looked no different. He hadn't changed his hair in years: it was still just a boring middle-aged man's haircut, short grey hair. He still had the moustache that made him look like he was stuck in the '80s. Ryan was wearing his Hereford shirt over a black jumper. He wasn't as tall as Danny, but not by much He had short spiky hair and slightly chubby cheeks. Danny was pleased that he didn't look like the cool kids at school. He just looked normal, a kid who loved football and looked excited for a Tuesday night out in Brighton.

Danny walked away. The last time he'd seen his dad had been when he watched from his bedroom window as his dad drove away and here he was, back at the Goldstone for his second ever match, watching the same game as Danny, their eyes following the same ball, the same men. Danny felt a connection to his dad that he tried to fight. He's in the Hereford end, he thought. We're not on the same side.

The Brighton team were in a rut, lacking confidence and making mistakes, but Hereford weren't much better. It was certainly the visitors though who were on top, due to Brighton repeatedly trying to play a passing game without having the ability to actually string three passes together, so possession was turned over repeatedly. The fans were frustrated, to a degree, but they had other things on their mind and their chants were directed predominantly at the board.

In the second half, Hereford took the lead and Brighton did not look like even creating a chance, let alone, actually scoring so as the second half ticked by, it was clear that the fans were twitchy, looking for the signal that would lead to their mass exodus. It would be a fascinating moment. With the Lincoln pitch invasion and the march in Mellor, there had been no more than a hundred people taking part. Breaking the law and the risk of a points deduction had stopped many at home to Lincoln and the fans who travelled to the away game at Wigan were a small gathering, but anybody could walk out of a game, but how many would?

In the 75th minute, fireworks erupted from one of the gardens on Goldstone Lane. As they exploded across the sky, the crowd turned as one, walking from the game with reluctance and determination. Paul McDonald had been in front of the North Stand, preparing to deliver a cross, but as Danny glanced back, he saw that he'd lost the ball and was looking round in bewilderment as the fans surged for the exits. Once outside, it was round to Newtown Road where songs of "Sack the board" and "Build a bonfire…" filled the air.

The crowd wasn't dispersing quickly, after a few songs, as it had done before, but were here to make its voice heard. Danny, Ethan and James hadn't seen how many people had remained in the ground, but it seemed like everyone was here, not just the loud-mouthed lads who loved the jostling of the North Stand, but all around, there were elderly people and families all standing together, all desperately pleading with Bill Archer to let the club go, to give it up and let Dick Knight lead them towards a future.

As the full-time whistle went, Danny slipped away, back to the away end where he saw jubilant Hereford fans departing, "1-0 to the Hereford…" In the fans' absence, no goals had been scored. Those fifteen minutes felt like they hadn't existed. If only Brighton had Danny, Ethan and James as a front three banging in the goals like they had done the previous night. Danny saw his dad and Ryan emerge, Ryan looking ecstatic, singing with the other fans, but his dad's was a sad face amongst a sea of happiness. He was looking around as if he might see Danny, but there was no chance of that. Danny was hidden in the darkness, watching as his dad boarded the coach for the long journey back to Hereford. It dawned on Danny that this must be where his dad now lived. He hadn't even known where he'd gone. He watched as the coach pulled away. If Brighton had won, would he have stepped out the gloom and approached his dad? He doubted it, but perhaps the words that he'd uttered on the journey to Exeter would have compelled him, but no, Brighton had lost and Danny felt like loss was what defined him.

15/10/96: Brighton 0-1 Hereford
19/10/96: Doncaster Rovers 3-0 Brighton

26th October 1996

Brighton & Hove Albion vs Fulham

When Danny arrived home after the Hereford game, his mum opened the door before he could get his key in the lock. She reached out and hugged him. Danny couldn't remember the last time his mum had hugged him. When he was young, she'd come to the side of his bed after he'd had a bad dream and she'd hugged him until he wasn't scared any more, but that was years ago.

He sat on the sofa awkwardly, knowing that it wouldn't be right just to disappear to his room.

"I know having your dad coming here was hard for you, Danny. It was hard for me too."

Danny hadn't given much thought to how his mum might feel. He was so absorbed in his own feelings of frustration and rejection that his mind didn't have space for anyone else.

"It was stupid of him to bring Ryan," she said. "He's a nice boy, Ryan is. All that's happened isn't his fault."

"I saw him."

"What?"

"I saw him at the Brighton match with Dad. He didn't see me. I hid in the shadows."

Danny's mum wiped away a tear.

"I love you, Danny," she said.

He wanted to say it back, but it felt like the words weren't there to say. He loved his mum, but he didn't know how to say it, couldn't cope with allowing the emotion of the phrase to slip out. Ethan was always saying a casual, "Love you too," to his mum as if it was just another way of saying goodbye, but Danny just didn't know how, the monosyllabic words not in his vocabulary.

That night, he got into his bed. By the smell of it, he could tell that Ryan had slept there, a strange staleness that wasn't his own. Yesterday, he would have been furious, would have shouted at his mum if she'd suggested that he give up his bed for his replacement, but seeing his mum tonight made him feel like it didn't matter. He didn't regret not seeing his dad or Ryan, or at least, not letting them see him, but he felt different. He hoped once again that Brighton would win and then he would answer the Friday phone call and hear his dad's voice again.

As he put his head on his pillow, he heard a rustle and reached under it to pull out a piece of paper: *It's crap when your dad leaves. My dad left five years ago. I don't want to take your place. I hope I get to meet you one day. UP THE BULLS. Ryan.*

Danny read the note over and over again and then folded it in half and put it into *To Kill a Mockingbird* on the page he'd got to.

The next day, Danny was sat playing *Sensible World of Soccer* when Simon got home from school.

"Where were you?" asked Simon.

There was pain in his brother's voice. Danny realised he'd not only left his mum to cope with his dad's visit, but also his brother.

"I didn't want to see him," he replied, and after a pause, "What was he like?"

"He took me to McDonald's," said Simon as if this was all the answer that was required. "He told me to say that he misses you."

Danny didn't pause in his gameplay or respond, but just let the words hover in the air before disappearing.

"Ryan was nice," Simon said. "He played *Mariokart* with me, but he wasn't very good. Do you want to play?"

"Alright - just let me finish this match first," he responded, sending a curling effort beyond the reach of Peter Schmeichel to give Brighton a 5-0 lead.

The brothers switched the game to *Mariokart* and selected their drivers. During the third race, Danny mumbled, "I'm sorry I wasn't here."

"It's okay," replied Simon in a singsong voice.

The following Tuesday, it was raining heavily, but Danny knew that he had to get to the Job Centre to collect his JSA. Paying his mum and topping up the tiny amount of money he had to go to the Fulham game on the Saturday was essential. Danny had put the walk off until after *Neighbours* and watched in shock as Harold Bishop walked back onto Ramsey Street. Five years earlier, Danny had thought he'd watched him drown, but here he was as, an amnesiac wandering the street he once lived on and pausing in half-remembrance at every familiar name. It was as if the script-writers couldn't handle the death of the show's icon, that they knew no one wanted permanent endings - that's not why they watched soaps - but wanted life to be perpetual, eternal. It's what Danny wanted for Brighton too.

Madge and Harold had visited Danny's primary school shortly before Harold's apparent drowning. They were performing in a pantomime of *Dick Whittington* at the Brighton Dome and Danny's friend, Sam had won an art competition and the whole class were given free tickets to the first night. Madge and Harold had come to the school for an assembly and Danny had been chosen to press play on the tape player, so that they could enter to the *Neighbours* theme tune. It seemed almost impossible that they had flown around the world and there they were, standing in front of excitable school children.

The rain hammered down on Danny's window throughout Harold's reappearance, contrasting the constant sunniness of Ramsey Street and Danny was forced to face the downpour to collect his cheque. There was no delaying - if you failed to turn up on the right day, you lost the allowance.

At the Job Centre, there was a lengthy queue at the collection point, the person at the front of it undoubtedly the cause of the backlog. Everyone in the queue looked awkwardly at their feet while the man at the front repeated the same phrase over and over again with increasing volume.

"I'm not going anywhere until I get my money."

"As I've explained…" began the toothy man behind the counter, but he did not get the chance to explain before he was interrupted and the conversation circled back round.

Claire spotted Danny in the queue and told him to come and see her when he'd collected his cheque. It was another thirty minutes before Danny got his cheque. It had taken a burly security guard to remove the now-livid man at the front of the queue and after that, people were swiftly served.

"This is the fifth Tuesday running that you've collected your allowance, Danny. On the sixth week, if you're under eighteen, we start the process of placing you on a scheme for the long-term unemployed," explained Claire. "Now, there are a few options for placements. But what is it that you want to do?" Claire asked.

Danny wondered. What he wanted to do was to have enough money for away games, but then he remembered Mr Brown's words and he said, "Journalism."

Claire looked at him as if he'd said "Terrorism," but she only let the look linger for a moment before typing into her keyboard and then, looking pleased with the results she'd found.

"I wasn't sure that we'd have anything so specific, but there is a project in Brighton for young people that are interested in journalism, graphic design and photography. That sounds perfect for you. Now, I can't make an application until you've been technically, long-term unemployed which will be next week, so let's wait a week and then, we'll make the application next Tuesday. Does that sound good?"

It did sound good - too good. Surely, sixteen-year-olds couldn't go from unemployment to becoming journalists out of nothing, but that seemed to be what Claire was suggesting, that next week, she'd try and make it happen. On the way to the Job Centre, the rain that penetrated through Danny's clothes to his skin made him feel utterly miserable, but on the way back, it didn't bother him.

That evening, at the Browns' house, lasagne was on the menu and Danny didn't dread the question that he knew would come at some point from Mr Brown.

"How's the hunt for jobs going, Danny?" he asked before he'd even touched his lasagne.

"It's good," he replied. "Next week, there's an opportunity to apply to be a journalist."

"Really?" said Mr Brown, looking a little surprised, "Well, that's really good news, Danny. I said that you're good with words, didn't I? Good on you. I really hope it happens for you. Did you see today's *Argus*? Maybe, this could be your first article," he said, reaching over to the work surface where *The Argus* lay and then holding up the back page for Danny and Ethan to see.

Emblazoned across the back page were the words

'PROTEST MARCH' and below the title, the details. That Saturday, before the match, fans were going to march through the town to make it clear, yet again, that there was no place for Archer and Bellotti at the club.

"I might even join you for this one, boys," said Mr Brown.

There was no way the boys were going to miss the march and on Saturday, they were milling around under the arch leading into Brighton Station, eager to walk the streets proudly for their club. The previous evening, Danny had listened angrily to Bill Archer on the radio and as soon as he had finished talking, he had flicked to Radio One where not even Reef's new single, 'Place Your Hands' could cheer him up. It was rare that the Brighton chairman talked to the media, but he had been tempted out by news of the march: "The players are traumatised when they play at home," he claimed, ignoring the fact that the away form was even worse than the home form. Danny, Ethan and James were quick to volunteer to carry a banner and each grabbed a chunk of an eighteen-foot plastic banner that read, "Homeless - broke. The board's a joke" and waited for it to start. There was a constant flow of fans, getting off trains to join the masses or walking from every by-street to join the crowd.

Eventually, the march started and the boys' banner was chosen to be the one that would lead the march. They headed directly south to start with, down Queens Road towards the Clock Tower. Shoppers stopped to gawp in confusion while above the shops, people crowded onto balconies and stood at their windows, many applauding as the crowd broke into song. In front of the marching crowd, a group of a dozen police officers were accompanied by a film crew scuttling backwards to document the action.

At the Clock Tower, the seething snake of supporters turned right along Western Road, the main high street of the town. The plastic flapped against the boys' ankles and while Danny and Ethan were able to hold the banner at chest height, James had to hoist the banner above his head and walk blind with the plastic sheeting in his face, unable to see the shoppers distracted momentarily from looking for new outfits.

Danny felt like he owned the street, marching at the head of the crowd, walking through the middle of the road, singing songs of defiance, feeling like there was no way that their voices could be ignored. Inside the stadium, their chants against the board sometimes felt hollow and a hopeless claustrophobia sometimes enveloped him, like the angry voices of the North Stand were just screaming into a vacuum, but here, out on the streets, there was a freedom - their voices like the call of the seagulls in the grey sky overhead, wild and untamed.

When they reached the turning for George Street (a narrow pedestrianised street teeming with charity shops) the police motorbikes continued on, but the crowd didn't want their route defined for them, so they veered right and the one policeman on foot was unable to stop the snake from turning. Other than a bit of futile finger-pointing, he had to concede to the masses and on the crowd surged, choosing an unwise narrow route that would lead them up some steps and over the even narrower bridge that led across the train tracks at Hove Station. For a brief time, their banners and flags had to be tucked away until they emerged back onto the wider Old Shoreham Road, leading them down to The Goldstone Ground.

Once there, a man clambered onto a brick wall and bellowed to the crowd: "Let's get into the West Stand where the Directors' Box is. Let's get up close to them and tell them to get out," and for a moment, it felt like the crowd surged in that direction, but then everyone was mixed together, with people battling through to get to their own area of the ground. Danny, Ethan and James had followed this man's voice and found themselves standing outside the West Stand where tickets were double the price and people sat on polished wooden seats in a far more civilised fashion than the rowdy frenzy of the North Stand.

Danny looked up at the prices above the West Stand. It was an extra four pounds, four pounds more than Danny had, but Ethan said, "I'll pay the extra. We've got to go in the West today," and through they went.

It felt strange to see the North Stand heave and sway as an observer and as the boys looked over, they felt a longing to be there, but it was too late. They walked to the row directly behind the Directors' Box and sat down. In front of them was a small wall separating their seats from those of the owners of the club.

Square cushions were laid out on each seat of the Directors' Box, not one person in position with still twenty minutes until kick-off.

A few minutes later, the boys looked up to see a group of men in their fifties and sixties standing over them, each of them wearing sophisticated and expensive coats, only one of them wearing an item of clothing defining himself as a Brighton supporter, a blue and white striped scarf, double-knotted carefully and then tucked beneath the lapels of his coat.

"You're in our seats," said the man with the scarf.

"Oh, er, sorry," said Danny and the boys shuffled off, slightly embarrassed.

There was no indication that any seat was reserved or that there were places they couldn't sit. They'd just walked through the turnstile and handed over the money. Danny was glad to be away from the Directors' Box though. It felt strange sitting so close to it. He had no idea what he would do when David Bellotti emerged. He knew he wouldn't go leaping in and doing anything stupid, but what would he say and do? It was alright singing, "Bellotti out" from the North Stand, but to shout it at a man who sat a row in front of you would feel intimate and uncomfortable. Bellotti would suddenly be a real man in front of him, not a cartoonish villain.

As the boys walked the aisles of the West Stand, from the top row, a group of men launched into a rendition of, "We love you Brighton, we do" and the boys knew immediately that this was where they needed to be and joined in with the ending phrase, "Oh, Brighton, we love you."

Before the game kicked off, there was an eruption of noise in the North Stand and the boys could see a commotion at the front. Moments later, a small group of Fulham fans were led through the emergency gate at the front of the stand to loud boos and escorted around the edge of the pitch to the away terrace.

The Fulham directors had made their way to their seats, but the Brighton half of the Directors' Box was still empty at kick-off, but not for long. Two minutes into the game, David Bellotti emerged. Presumably, he'd hoped that appearing while the game was going on would mean that people would be distracted and not notice his presence, but there was no chance of that.

Protesting was more important than the football to the majority of the crowd and a chorus of boos greeted his arrival.

The North Stand swivelled their attention away from the pitch, directly towards the Directors' Box and the small North-west terrace just below the Directors' Box turned their back on the game to direct a cacophony of insults towards the sole member of the Brighton board who had braved it out into the open.

Why was he there? It was obvious that this would happen. It surely couldn't be enjoyable to sit there and be screamed at, to be one man against thousands. Next to Danny, a lad with a pockmarked face and a tattoo that looked like it had been done by a toddler pulled a red tube from his pocket. Danny wasn't sure what it was, but realised quickly when he pulled a lighter out and lit the end which started sizzling instantly. The banger was launched through the air, landing in the empty space behind where Bellotti was sitting and erupting with an unmistakable and loud bang and Bellotti leapt up and scuttled away.

The crowd turned. It was obvious where the banger had come from, the loud boys on the back row.

"There's kids down here."

"What the hell are you doing?"

The men Danny, Ethan and James were with shouted back at the crowd of angry voices, swearing, gesticulating, doing everything they could to show they didn't care for these objectors and Danny, Ethan and James just stood there, paralysed by the situation, not feeling able to walk away and distance themselves while angry faces stared at them as if they had just shoved a lit firework down their children's trousers.

The clamour eventually died down and the crowd turned back to the game. At half-time, the boys used the bustle to get half-time drinks to find themselves other seats. They watched the rest of the match, frustrated that they'd spent their money on putting themselves into this uncomfortable situation.

Fulham were the better side, controlling possession and creating chances. They were fighting at the other end of the table to Brighton, but it was Brighton who were doing the battling that day. Gone was the hapless defending of the previous matches. Crunching slide tackles, heroic last-ditch blocks and towering headers kept Fulham at bay and whilst there was rarely a foray forward, Brighton deserved the 0-0 draw they eventually ground out.

The march through town before the match had carried with it frustration at the situation, but also hope, that the supporters were grasping their own destiny, not letting it fritter away. The hope seemed to infect the players who played with a belief and passion that had rarely been seen that season. The fact that the march had caused the crowd to swell and double in number had helped too. There were no gaps in the terraces and once Bellotti had made his early departure, the crowd had switched at least some of their attention to roaring the team on. After a run of six successive defeats, although not a win, a point was precious. Not precious enough to accept the Friday phone-call though.

26/10/96: Brighton 0-0 Fulham
29/10/96: Rochdale 3-0 Brighton
02/11/96: Hartlepool United 2-3 Brighton (Mundee (pen), Minton, Morris)

9th November 1996

Brighton & Hove Albion vs Mansfield Town

On Tuesday, Danny returned to the Job Centre to collect his JSA, but there was no need to avoid Claire - in reality, there had never been any need, but on most Tuesdays, the gaping nothingness that filled each day was something that he'd wanted to cling to; the blank void of purposelessness had felt miserably comforting and he hadn't wanted to be cajoled out of it.

There were other days though when a longing pierced the gloomy surface of the lake, a fish coming up for air having lain half-dazed in the grimy depths for days and this was one of those days. The possibility of doing something he enjoyed for a living quickened his pulse. Doing something meaningful with his life had felt out of reach, inaccessible, and now suddenly, a door had been opened.

As he sat opposite Claire, she could see the difference: a smile and a certainty instead of a weary shyness that had been his default setting.

"Let me see," said Claire as she tapped away on her keyboard. "This project says that they employ people between the age of sixteen and twenty-one who are long-term unemployed - and today, that's you - and young offenders. They're based in Kemptown on Rock Place. Shall I give them a call and see if they've got a space for you?"

"Yes, please," replied Danny, eager that this might work.

Claire picked up the phone, dialled the number and explained that she'd got a keen and eager young man who was interested in journalism and then, there were lots of "Uh-huhs" and "Yeses," and Danny had no idea what was being said on the other end of the line. After a couple of minutes, Claire covered the receiver with her hand and asked Danny whether he was able to go in on Friday for an interview. Danny's calendar only included Brighton games and Friday was totally clear.

"Okay," said Claire, once she was off the phone. "The interview is just an informal thing, a chance for them to get to know you. There's a space for you with them if you accept. This is a project set up to support and train you, so it doesn't pay like a normal job would, but they will top up your Job Seekers' Allowance to £48 a week. I know it's not much, but this opportunity will give you some really valuable skills. I really hope it works for you."

As Danny left the Job Centre, he was happy although the £48 a week was disappointing and certainly wouldn't be funding any away days after he'd paid his mum.

Danny made the most of staying in bed until the afternoon, playing *Sensible World of Soccer* and meeting Ethan and James at the Rec for football for the next couple of days, knowing that he wasn't going to be able to have such a leisurely schedule soon.

On Friday morning, he caught the bus to Brighton Pavilion. He'd never really been into Kemptown, an area beyond the bustling town centre stretching into the east of Brighton. He had to look at a map to find Rock Place, a small road just off the eclectic St James' Street - a busy thoroughfare crammed with colourful shops, pubs emblazoned with rainbow flags, and takeaway venues. Walking up St James' Street, Danny peered into the shops - so many of them seemed to sell such a random collection of things: sprawling unidentifiable sculptures, weaponised underwear and heavyweight copper jewellery. There were lots of second-hand record shops as well and because Danny was early for the interview, he went into one and flicked through the CDs, wishing that he had enough money to extend his collection. Kurt Cobain was growling through his headphones as he clacked the CDs forward; he made a mental list of what he'd like to buy.

Set above some garages was the building for his interview, and after pressing the buzzer to be admitted, he was led up a narrow staircase covered in a shag-pile carpet that squelched under his feet and smelt like damp dog.

"Hello, come in," said a man in a broad Scottish accent when Danny arrived at the top of the stairs.

He followed the man into an office with four computers with a black, leather swivel chair at each one. The man spun a chair and wheeled it to Danny who caught it as it rolled towards him.

"Grab a seat, young man," said the man.

He was dressed in a baggy long-sleeved black t-shirt and cargo trousers. His head looked like it had been shaved a couple of months ago and was now wispy and grown out and although he was probably only in his late twenties, his face sagged like a bloodhound, his cheeks covered in thin red veins crisscrossing chaotically.

"My name's Bram," said the man, "and this project is an amazing thing. Every month we create a magazine. We've got a deal with WHSmith and they stock it in lots of their branches which is great. We also take it round to local newsagents and give them copies for free just to build the exposure. The magazine is made totally by us, all the articles, all the photos, all the design. If you want in, I can give you a place here for six months. You'll get to learn a load of skills and then after that, see where they'll take you. Are you interested?"

Danny wanted to show his keenness with more than just one word, but he could think of nothing more to say than, "Yes."

"Excellent," said Bram. "Now, I've got to warn you. We let all sorts work for us. There are some pretty crazy characters, so you're going to need to be able to handle yourself. Some of the guys have been unemployed for a while. I understand that's true for you."

"Yes," said Danny.

"Some of these guys have just got out of juvie. Do you know what that is?"

"Er, no, sorry."

"It's prison for people who are too young to go to prison. Some of these kids have made some pretty bad mistakes and we want to help everyone, to give them something good in their lives. But people here still make mistakes."

A crash was heard from the adjoining room and then some raised voices as if to make Bram's point.

"Excuse me one moment," said Bram.

He returned a few minutes later: "Just some of the lads getting a little bit excitable," he said. "So, are you in?"

Just the word "Yes" sufficed again and then the details were worked through. There was some paperwork to sort out and one of the boys had one more week to go, and so it was decided that

Danny would start a week, Monday.

Making his way back over the damp carpet, he felt excited and nervous. It was what he wanted, what Mr Brown had told him he was good at, but this also seemed like an unpredictable environment.

During the following week, *The Argus* reported another protest. Some of the national newspapers had reported on the march through the city streets and pressure seemed to be mounting on the Brighton board. This time, they wanted to hit them in their pockets by boycotting the next match. From by far the biggest attendance of the season, it looked like Brighton were going to plummet to their lowest attendance of the season. Danny was grateful that he would save the £4 entry fee.

David Bellotti had reacted to the hostility at the last game by creating an exclusion zone around the Directors' Box. Now, only season ticket holders were allowed in the North-west terrace, the closest area of terracing to him.

It had also emerged that a new ground-share for the following season was being organised, this time with Gillingham. It didn't really matter where it was if it wasn't in Brighton, but this was an extra twenty-eight miles further than Portsmouth. Carlisle's chairman, Michael Knighton had joked that Brighton could share with them.

On the Saturday, the boys wondered what they would do and decided to head down to the ground to just mill around outside, hundreds of fans deciding to do exactly the same. Standing on the Old Shoreham Road, they watched the North Stand turnstiles. Very few fans were making their way in, but there was a trickle.

"Don't give Archer your money," Danny shouted as two men walked towards the turnstile.

They looked at Danny like they had no idea what he was talking about, like they didn't know that their club was on the brink of extinction.

Once the game had started, there was no one entering the ground and therefore, no one to persuade not to enter and although the few hundred chanted a little, it felt odd to Danny, Ethan and James to just be loitering outside the ground while inside, Brighton were playing. They decided to walk round to the

East Terrace to see if they could get any view of what was happening inside. As long as they weren't paying to get in, it was fine to watch the game they reasoned. The best view they could find was if they lay on their stomachs and looked underneath a gate. It gave them a reasonable view of some of the pitch and one of the goals and they saw Mansfield take the lead this way.

Other fans meandered round to join them, some climbing onto garden walls, some climbing up lampposts. Between them, they could have created a collage of the whole pitch. From where Danny, Ethan and James were, they could see the South-east terrace. There were so few people there, spread out sparsely. Danny had stood in that stand to watch a reserve game once against Arsenal and there had been a similar number of fans present on that day.

As half-time approached, a group of men started shaking one of the gates, wobbling it back and forth. It creaked on its ancient hinges and then more people piled in, running and then launching themselves against the gate. One man in a home shirt caught his head on an overhanging rusty pole as he leapt and blood started to pour down his face. He swiped at with his hand, but made no real attempt to stem the flow and it dripped down onto the white stripes of his shirt.

The attack on the gate was becoming more frenzied with repeated charges, each one causing the gate to heave inwards, each time threatening to burst open and then, finally, it happened, and the gate was open and the fans poured in. The gate led them directly into the Mansfield Town away supporters and they turned to face the Brighton fans, a moment of uncertainty on both sets of fans' faces, but as soon as the Mansfield fans lifted their hands above their heads and applauded the invaders, there was embracing and shirt-swapping.

The boys had followed the crowd in. It had seemed like the thing to do, but they felt less sure of themselves as they walked past a policeman with a large camera on his shoulder filming them. It was half-time and after the initial welcome from the Mansfield fans, what next? The recklessness of breaking in made them feel invincible, like they were an army that had conquered the enemy and where was the enemy territory? The Directors' Box.

Hundreds swarmed across the pitch and Danny, Ethan and James, caught up in the moment, followed, wondering where this would end, not even sure where they were going. Reaching the North-west terrace, they clambered over the advertising hoardings and into the newly-created exclusion zone, but even this wasn't enough.

"Come on," shouted a man from the West Stand reaching down his hand and Danny ran to it and was pulled up and into the seated area above the terraces. In front of Danny was the empty Directors' Box, vacated at half-time. It was the fans that should be in control of this club, thought Danny and he clambered over one more wall, into the Box and sat down on a soft cushion, the exact one that David Bellotti's backside had been warming during the first half. The crowd behind him cheered and more came, dads with their children, men and women, Ethan and James, until the Directors' Box was full of fans. There was no way that Bellotti was going to be able to come out for the second half. It felt like a symbol - this is our club, but in reality, it meant nothing. Until the club was signed over to the fans' man, Dick Knight, the future remained uncertain.

The teams emerged for the second half to a roar of welcome and players who had spent the first half playing in front of a handful of spectators in a muted atmosphere looked around in surprise at the crowd that had bulged at the break.

Brighton were dominant in the second half - the electric atmosphere created by the invading fans, who were now scattered across the ground, filling them with an energy they had been lacking in the first half, but Mansfield were resolute, thwarting attempts repeatedly until finally, Albion got a break. Young striker, Phil Andrews, making a rare appearance in the team due to injuries, tumbled in the box and Denny Mundee picked up the ball. Danny clasped his hands together and whispered a prayer. Could he will this in with his prayers? Denny stepped up and sent the ball crashing into the net.

Brighton poured forward but couldn't find the goal to turn this into a precious victory. A point was important, and they'd picked up their first away win of the season the previous weekend at Hartlepool, but that win had come after eleven failed attempts at picking up three points and they were getting cut adrift at the bottom of the table. A winning goal against Mansfield was not to be found and Danny's silence would continue. He was ready for it to end, ready to talk to his dad, but Brighton needed to make that happen.

09/11/96: Brighton 1-1 Mansfield (Mundee (pen))
19/11/96: Swansea City 1-0 Brighton

23rd November 1996

Brighton & Hove Albion vs Carlisle United

When Danny arrived at Rock Place on Monday morning, the office was empty other than Bram who asked him about his weekend. Danny said he'd gone to watch Brighton play, but didn't want to go into the detail of entering the ground through a forced-open gate and climbing into the Directors' Box. It didn't seem like the ideal first impression to make. The second person to arrive was a nervous girl with sandy-coloured hair. She was wearing a black jacket that was far too big for her. It was her first day too. Danny made faltering conversation, asking her name: Tracey, and where she lived: a couple of roads away in a safe house. Danny didn't know what she meant by a safe house. She said she lived with seven other girls and had moved in two weeks earlier.

Bram showed Danny and Tracey how to get logged onto the computers and said that as a starter task, he wanted them to design a front cover for the magazine. He told them it was called *Sorted*. He told them to open a programme called QuarkXPress and showed them the menu bar where they could choose to insert text boxes and images. He said that for the next edition, they were going to feature an article with Brighton-resident and middleweight boxer, Chris Eubank, so he should be the main image on the front cover. A pile of old magazines was next to the computers and they flicked through them for ideas of what to make the front cover look like.

Close to ten o' clock, a more experienced member of the team arrived. He introduced himself as Mickey McMashup. He was a lanky boy with hollow cheeks and hair gelled flat against his head. He had 'LOVE' tattooed on the knuckles of one hand and 'HATE' on the other, both words looking like they'd been applied by a someone writing with their wrong hand. He was friendly with a manic energy, beat-boxing between comments. He logged onto a computer and said he was working on an article about drugs. He described it as a guide.

Next to arrive was Garth the Goth, a teenager with jet-black hair hanging below his waist. He wore tight black leather trousers and a black and red checked shirt. He didn't acknowledge Danny or Tracey; his headphones were blasting out heavy metal at a volume that made it audible to the whole office. Mickey jumped up behind him, playing air guitar, getting closer and closer to Garth who only reacted when Mickey hoisted his leg up onto the arm of his chair and started thrusting his groin into his face. Garth pushed him gently away and Mickey went from playful thrusting to strutting aggression instantly, plucking a headphone from his ear, and saying, "Come on, Goth-boy," arms outspread, fingers beckoning.

Bram got slowly to his feet and walked over to Mickey, putting his hand on his shoulder and growling, "Sit down, Mickey."

Mickey shrugged him off with a surly glance towards Garth, but he did what he was told and walked back to his seat.

The rest of the morning passed without incident, Mickey's beat-boxing the soundtrack of the office, filling the room whenever he wasn't leaning over and telling Danny how amazing the drug was that he was currently writing about: "This one is proper-good… Have you ever had…? I was off my head on this…"

Danny found a photo of Chris Eubank gazing with characteristic arrogance into the middle-distance before a fight. The picture was taken from below and had a black background; it made a perfect cover image. He filled the page with the image and then started scattering text boxes in front of it before scrolling through the fonts, selecting a different one for each box.

Bram sat at a large table in the centre of the room, strolling intermittently between Danny, Mickey, Garth and Tracey, commenting on their work and guiding them. For Danny and Tracey, he talked about choosing colour schemes and splitting the page into thirds. He showed them how to crop images and remove backgrounds. With Mickey, he was futilely attempting to persuade him to include the dangers of each drug in his erratic compendium. Garth wasn't much more receptive of Bram's guidance, removing his earphones reluctantly, nodding noncommittally to Bram's suggestions, seemingly in an attempt to rid himself of the interruption to his metal session.

At lunchtime, Mickey asked Danny if he wanted to go the pier and with no other invitation, Danny accepted. They stopped off at a fish 'n' chip shop, unimaginatively called 'Fish 'n' Chips' and Danny realised that he'd need to fit lunch purchases into his weekly budget. He only had £2.90 in his wallet and nothing more was coming until Friday, so he went with a small bag of chips for £1.10 and wondered how he was going to last the week. Mickey seemed to be more flush and bought chips and a chicken and mushroom pie. They ate as they walked down Rock Place to the seafront before turning right and walking along the promenade towards the pier.

Mickey monologued all the way, telling Danny about his weekend which had involved witnessing, encouraging and occasionally getting involved in fights. Mickey spoke about violence as if it were a hobby or a way of relaxing. Each moment had seemed so needless, the strangest being a story where Mickey had exchanged punches with his landlord over the paying of rent. According to Mickey, the landlord had burst into his bedroom on Saturday morning and woken him up by punching him straight in the face repeatedly until Mickey, stark naked, had squirmed out of bed, kicked his landlord to the floor and pinned him by putting his knee on his neck. The incident had somehow ended with Mickey paying his rent.

Brighton Pier stretched five-hundred metres into the English Channel, two large arcades punctuating the journey to the end where it expanded to include a small collection of fairground rides and a karaoke bar. Danny had always been excited by the pier, but his most common experience had been watching people enjoy rides he couldn't afford, eat doughnuts he couldn't afford, play on arcade games he couldn't afford. Once, he'd seen a girl vomit all over herself and her friends on The Waltzer. Even though the girls had stumbled off with regurgitated candy floss and chips all over them, he had still felt a little jealous.

As they walked onto the pier, Danny looked through the gaps between the boards, at the grey sea foaming below them. Seagulls floated overhead before landing elegantly on the railings, casting their beady eyes around for tourists inattentive to their chips, but Danny and Mickey had both finished their lunch and were heading for the arcades. Mickey changed a twenty-pound note into pound coins and headed straight for the fruit machines. He walked up and down, eyeing each one before declaring, "This one's about to pay out."

He spoke with such authority that Danny felt sure that he was about to win as he fed the first pound coin in. Danny had no idea how the machines worked, how you earned an extra nudge, why parts of the machine were lighting up, but he started to feel doubtful of Mickey's expertise as he fed coin after coin in, swearing and shaking the machine so that it wobbled on its base between each failure. It took less than ten minutes for Mickey to feed all twenty pound coins in, at which point, he asked, "Have you got any money?"

Wanting to be honest, Danny told him the exact amount he had.

"Give me a quid and I'll give you two quid in a second," said Mickey confidently.

Danny's lunch budget for the week was already tight, but he didn't want to say no. Mickey had been the friendliest of the 'journalists' at *Sorted* and giving him a quid felt like a demonstration of gratitude and trust. The potential to double his money felt exciting but unlikely, and he was also a little intimidated by the stories of violence although there didn't really seem like there was any threat of that.

He handed over the pound and Mickey said, "I guarantee you; it's going to pay out this time," and then thirty seconds later, he was thumping the machine in frustration.

They walked back to the *Sorted* offices, Mickey explaining how the machines must have been rigged to fail, that he'd never failed like that before and that he was going to go down there with his pay cheque on Friday and if they didn't work then, he was going to smash the machines up.

The next day, Bram told them that there was going to be a planning meeting that afternoon and that all the contributors to the magazine would be arriving. He gave each of them a responsibility for the meeting and Danny was given some money to go to Safeway and buy snacks. Thinking that this could double as lunch, he bought sausages rolls, mini scotch eggs, Monster

Munch and packs of Maryland cookies. The food would need to be shared around, but he would take advantage of this bonus food by not buying lunch and keeping his 80p for another day.

That afternoon, twenty-three people crammed around the rectangular table in the middle of the main office and Bram led the meeting, first getting everyone to introduce themselves before asking people what articles they thought would be good to go in next month's magazine. The most vocal amongst the group was a twelve-year-old girl, still in her school uniform and bright pink trainers. She was full of ideas about which pop stars she wanted to see feature in the magazine, the Spice Girls being top of her list.

Bram created a mind-map on a flip-chart and the page filled up quickly with ideas: a fashion page, a new music page, a review of the best music of 1996, a makeup tutorial, film reviews, a crossword, a Christmas quiz, star signs, TV shows to watch over Christmas, an interview with Michael Jackson, how to be fashionable on a budget, photos of hot celebrities, lyrics to songs that aren't in the CD booklets, do UFOs exist?, predictions for who's going to win the Premiership and a guide to drugs.

Once the ideas filled the page, Bram said that he had some opportunities for possible articles. The magazine had been given two tickets to see Alisha's Attic at the Brighton Centre; there was a new radio station that was being created, Surf FM, and he had organised an interview with the founder of the station, and a computer game based on *The Rocky Horror Show* was coming out and he had tickets for the launch party.

Then, the articles to be written were divvied out amongst everyone present. Danny felt like he was the new boy. He didn't feel like he could demand any of the opportunities on offer and they all went to people who had come in for the day to scoff his mini scotch eggs - they were, annoyingly, at the other end of the table - but he did come away with an article that excited him, a list of the top ten albums of 1996. His own personal collection of CDs were all released narrowly earlier than the current year, but he'd enjoy the research.

The next day, he spent the whole morning in HMV and Virgin Records, putting on the oversized headphones at the listening booths and staying put until the album had played out for the entire length, scrawling comments in a notebook he'd taken from the office and giving each album a mark out of ten to help him order them when it came to the final article. When he made his way back to the office, *1977* by Ash was top of his list, the building beauty and euphoria of 'Girl from Mars' sending it above *Moseley Shoals* by Ocean Colour Scene, *Everything Must Go* by the Manic Street Preachers and *C'mon Kids* by the Boo Radleys.

On his way back, he'd returned to Safeway once again, finding himself a flatbread covered in cheese, tomato and onion costing just 39p for lunch.

Danny spent the rest of the week carefully creating his list and writing up descriptions of the albums. He found it hard to find different ways of describing the albums which were all by male-fronted guitar bands and all featured distorted guitar riffs and growled vocals. On Thursday, he'd gone into WHSmith and looked through *NME* and copied down phrases they'd used: "incandescent pop song," "punk irreverence," "brawny musicality" - he didn't know what they all meant, but he'd look up the words he didn't understand in the dictionary and decide which albums they fitted.

On Friday, Danny was to receive his first pay cheque, but the fact that it was a cheque was problematic. He'd been planning to buy lunch with it and more importantly, to use it to gain entry into the Brighton game. He didn't have time to wait for the cheque to clear, but Mickey came up with a solution, showing him what he did with his pay.

At lunchtime, they walked to Cash Converters, a shop full of second-hand games consoles, vacuum cleaners, cuddly toys, anything that someone in dire need of cash could easily part with. At the back of the store was a desk where you could bring your goods, but they also offered a service where they would cash a cheque instantly, deducting 10% for the service. £4.80 of his wages were instantly extinguished, but after paying his mum, he still had enough for lunch and admission to the Goldstone Ground the following day. Money would still be tight, but not as tight as it had been - he was able to return to a portion of chips for his lunch and at the end of the day, he treated himself to caramel bun from the bakery opposite the *Sorted* office, reduced to 10p with only ten minutes of opening time remaining.

That evening, Danny went to the Browns' house - they ordered an Indian takeaway and Danny was glad to be able to tell Mr Brown about his first week in the *Sorted* office, pride in his voice as he described the article he was constructing. Mr Brown showed him his record collection, telling him that Lynyrd Skynyrd was his favourite band.

The following day, Danny, Ethan and James were back on the North Stand. After sitting in the Directors' Box for some of the Mansfield game and having made the bad decision to go into the West Stand for the Fulham game, it had felt good to be watching the game from behind the goal once more, staring over the crossbar at the action. They'd created a home for themselves in this exact spot with the same familiar faces around them.

Danny absentmindedly picked an apple sticker affixed to the crash barriers before pushing it back into place once he'd pried it loose. For the past few matches, there had been a specific protest, but today, there was nothing but a vague sense of unrest, an unsettling anger in the air that only seemed to dissipate slightly when the crowd launched into their songs that recognised the bleakness of their situation and demanded a change: "We've sold the ground and now we're going down; sack the board, sack the board."

There really didn't seem to be much hope in either the boardroom or on the football pitch and answering the phone to his dad seemed to Danny like something that might never take place, but despite the pessimism of the fans, Danny's week had filled him with a sense of purpose. He hadn't found it difficult to get out of bed when his alarm clock had summoned him even though he had to get up even earlier for the *Sorted* offices than he had for the job at the fencing shop. A renewed positivity had sown a seed of hope and when the fans greeted the players with, "Seagulls, seagulls, seagulls," Danny believed today was a day for victory.

During the opening exchanges, the crowd were distracted by the appearance of David Bellotti in the Directors' Box. Despite the fact that the terrace just below had just a handful of people in, because of the creation of the exclusion zone, that handful started clambering up towards him and shouting up to the Directors' Box, roared on by the North Stand, and Bellotti went scampering back down the corridor and out of sight before he'd had time to settle in his seat.

With the crowd's attention back on the game, Brighton took the lead, Ian Baird scrambling an effort into the goal and the glorious sound of "1-0 to the Albion" rang around the stadium, but by half-time, the briefly inflated balloon had been popped by two Carlisle goals, celebrated wildly by the few away fans who had made the long journey.

At half-time, the boys sat down on the steps of the terracing, the ice-cold concrete sending shivers through their body. It was the only time they were ever cold at games. They never wore coats - it was either just the replica shirt on the top half or the shirt worn over a sweatshirt. In amongst the mass of swaying bodies, it always felt warm. In the summer, it was stifling. When bees defend their hive against a wasp, they surround the wasp and vibrate, their slightly higher body heat slowly cooking the wasp to death and that's what fixtures in August felt like, but in December, the warmth of the masses was a happy respite against the cold.

The stadium announcer started reading through the half-time scores at other grounds. There was a customary cheer when it was announced that Crystal Palace were losing at home to Wolves. As the announcer started on Division 3, Danny listened for the teams near Brighton at the bottom, thinking momentarily of his dad when he heard that Hereford were losing at Cardiff.

After the half-time scores, it was usually birthdays and engagements and most of the crowd switched off, arguing about which player should come on at half-time to rescue the match, but the sombre tone of the announcer felt jarringly different to the normal bouncy tone. Danny hadn't caught the beginning of the announcement, but as it progressed, he tuned in, nudging Ethan and James to listen.

"… his passing is a huge loss to his family and to the football club. He loved Brighton and Hove Albion and watched home games from the North Stand. He regularly followed the Seagulls to away games and always supported the team. Despite being only nineteen, he was a mature and kind man who will be greatly missed."

After a pause, Ethan asked, "Was that about Barnet?"

The boys looked around and the familiar scowl of Barnet was nowhere to be seen. When had they last seen him? No one could remember the game, but it seemed like he hadn't been there for weeks. Had he been ill and unable to attend? The boys didn't even know his name.

"I think it must have been," Danny said.

"It was definitely him," said James with certainty.

The boys didn't know what to say. They hadn't really known this boy, this man, but he'd felt like one of them and it seemed weird that he was just gone. Danny had never known anyone to die. He'd sat and listened to Ethan when he'd told him that his gran had died, and he'd not really known what to do other than to say "Sorry" as if he was responsible somehow.

"I can't believe he's dead," said Danny.

It didn't seem real that Barnet didn't exist anymore.

It was only the emergence of the players for the second half that managed to distract the boys away from thoughts about Barnet, but the players played in a discordant way, passing the ball straight off the pitch when under no pressure and dallying on the ball, allowing the Carlisle players to dispossess them repeatedly. The hope of the early Baird goal was truly gone, and it was Carlisle who looked likely to score with every attack. Mercifully, their shooting was wild and careless and they only once found the net again.

Outside the ground at the end of the game, fans milled around, half-heartedly gathering on Newtown Road to shout up at the closed windows of the offices, but they'd shouted the same words before and the futility and misery of it was too much and they quickly drifted away.

23/11/96: Brighton 1-3 Carlisle United (Baird)

3rd December 1996

Brighton & Hove Albion vs Darlington

The next week, Danny put the finishing touches to his top ten albums of 1996 article. Everything had to be submitted by the end of the month if it was going to be featured in the magazine. In an office upstairs, Bebop - nicknamed after the mutant warthog in *Teenage Mutant Hero Turtles* - put the magazine together. Occasionally, he came down to Bram's office to ask about articles, always complaining that the downstairs office stank of meat.

No one else in the office completed an article in time for the deadline, but articles from the mysterious contributors who arrived for the monthly meetings to scoff mini scotch eggs were plentiful. Despite lots of talk, Mickey had written very few words of his drugs guide. Garth the Goth had become a little more communicative, insisting that Danny include Depressive Age and Carcass into his album list. Danny had been struggling for a tenth album to complete the list, so included Depressive Age after Garth had lent him his headphones so that Danny's eardrums could be battered by a deluge of noise.

Tracey gave the impression of productivity without actually producing anything. Mickey had started going around to her house after work and he showed Danny the CDs that he'd managed to steal from Tracey's housemates when Tracey had gone to the toilet. Danny didn't know what to do with the information that Mickey had stolen from Tracey's house - telling Tracey would create huge issues and Mickey would know that it had been Danny that had said something. He liked Mickey and didn't feel threatened by him, but he was wary of getting on the wrong side of him. He knew that he was never going to invite Mickey back to his house.

On Thursday, Bram had set them a photography challenge, sending them out in pairs to take photos of the best graffiti Brighton had to offer. Danny paired up with Mickey, but Mickey was intent on pointing the camera at himself, announcing, "I'm Mickey McMashup" and then clicking the button. They hadn't even found any graffiti and Danny hadn't even touched the camera when the film was used up with twenty-four photos of Mickey's face. When they got back to the office, Mickey claimed to have taken loads of amazing photos, his lie lasting only until the following day when the photos were collected from Boots.

"I really liked your albums article," Bram said, on Friday morning, "Bebop has said that it's going in the December issue."

It felt amazing that what he'd written would be in print on a shelf in WHSmith.

"I'd like there to be a feature on politics in the next issue," Bram continued. "It feels like next year is going to be a big year, maybe a change in government. What do you think? Would you like to write it?"

Danny wasn't sure. He'd paid no real attention to politics, distrustful of the droning dullness of men in suits who seemed to be irrelevant to his existence.

Bram sensed his reluctance: "Everything's political, Danny. Last month when you were picking up your JSA, how much you got was decided by the government; what you studied at school is decided by the government; this project is funded by the government; kids ending up in prison is political; your football team getting a new stadium: that's political and who people vote for makes a difference. Did you see that *Rock the Vote* thing with Radiohead earlier this year?"

Danny hadn't.

"They're an organisation that are trying to get young people engaged in politics. They want young people to have a say in the future, so they're making sure that everyone is registered to vote."

"I'm not old enough to vote."

"I know. I wish you could vote, but if we do an exciting article with the bands and comedians that have supported *Rock the Vote*, we could try and get our readers to vote in the election next year. You can't vote, but you could get other people to."

"Okay, I'll do it."

Bram's words had inspired Danny. He remembered years ago, his mum going to London to protest against the Poll tax. He didn't know exactly what had happened as a result of those protests, but he knew that the Poll tax didn't exist anymore, that his mum's voice, joined by others, had created a clamour that had forced change. Could Danny write an article that would get young people going to the voting booths next year? Danny imagined the seat at Brighton coming down to a single vote and someone who had read his article deciding that it was worth voting after all. Ten minutes earlier, Danny had cared nothing for politics, but hearing Bram say that even football was political, that Thom Yorke wanted people to vote, had transformed him into someone that wanted to use his words to get people politically engaged. Bram said he'd bring a copy of the *Rock the Vote* CD in after the weekend and Danny could use that as a basis for his article.

Danny paid another visit to Cash Converters before going home and Mickey joined him to sell the stolen CDs. With another Brighton game on Tuesday evening, he didn't want to risk the cheque not clearing in time, so another 10% of his wages was immediately swallowed up.

Danny had been desperate to attend another away day. this time to Fulham. It wasn't just another away game: the fans were on the march again, this time through London right up to the FA Headquarters where they would deliver a petition demanding the removal of the Brighton board. It was only sixty miles to Fulham and on Friday evening, Danny tried to persuade Ethan and James to walk the distance. It was the travel that was financially prohibitive - he could stretch his money to entry for the game.

"If we start now," said Danny at eight o' clock in the evening, "we'd get there in the morning and be able to join the march. It would be our own protest march all the way from here."

"How would we even know the way?" asked Ethan.

It was a good point. They couldn't walk along the motorway, so they'd have to just meander north, hoping that they were heading in the right direction.

Instead of attending, they'd had to wait for *Football League*

Extra on ITV on Monday night to watch the Brighton fans taking over the capital. The boys were sat in the Browns' front room watching the fans walk past London landmarks. The camera captured bemused taxi drivers wondering what was going on. Three fans skipped through the streets, dressed as clowns as a parody of the board. The programme revealed that even ground-sharing with Gillingham was something that was not a certain thing, the FA saying that it would only ratify the move if there was a clear timescale for the club returning to Brighton and with the board still sticking to their plan to build in a location that wasn't going to receive planning permission, it seemed like an utter mess. Bill Archer appeared to tell the fans to "Stop pressing the self-destruct button."

Mr Brown, normally so calm and measured, swore loudly, "It's not the fans that are destroying this club," he said, jabbing his finger at the television. "Sorry, boys," he said, regaining his composure, but there was no need to apologise. The boys had loved his outburst.

On Tuesday, Danny walked straight from the *Sorted* offices to Ethan's house to prepare for the home game against Darlington - a significantly shorter journey by foot than the aborted trip to Fulham. Bram had let him copy his *Rock the Vote* CD onto a tape and he listened to every track as he walked, a mixture of rock bands, and short comedy pieces from Eddie Izzard, Steve Coogan and Jo Brand. There was no political content in the tracks, but instructions on how to register to vote were in the CD sleeve. It seemed unlikely to Danny that anyone who had bought this compilation would end up keeping the status quo and voting for the Tories. The encouragement for the young to vote was only going to be good for Labour. Damon Albarn had recently announced that he would definitely be voting Labour and his words were far more persuasive than any politicians'.

Danny arrived at the Browns' as dinner was being served up, a creamy chicken dish with mashed potato. Danny and Ethan ate quickly, eager to get to the ground as early as possible, so, once the dinner was wolfed down, they were out the door and on their way to pick up James.

Although they were later than they usually were to games, the ground had not yet filled and wouldn't. Normally, bodies were packed together, but on a cold December night and with victories rare, people had just not bothered to come and only those that would never miss a game were there.

With 'The Box' virtually empty, the boys made their way down to the front of the North Stand, leaning against the advertising hoardings bordering the pitch.

The game kicked off and, like the previous few games, the Chief Executive, David Bellotti emerged a few minutes in, hoping and obviously failing to slip in unnoticed. With every appearance he made, the fury seemed to increase and despite the lack of numbers, a roar of anger burst from the crowd and then suddenly, fans in the North Stand were vaulting the barriers and running towards the North-west terrace, just below the Directors' Box.

The first over the barrier was Barnet and at the sight of this resurrected redhead, Danny exclaimed, "He's alive!" and leapt the barrier, the sight of Barnet propelling him into an impulsive act, and as soon as he was on the pitch, Ethan was clambering the barriers followed by James.

Once in the North-west terrace, the boys showed no interest in directing any ire towards Bellotti. They were exhilarated by the act of running across the corner of the pitch while the game continued at the other end and they were shocked by Barnet's sudden appearance, seemingly, leaping out of the grave and onto the pitch and now, here he was, shouting abuse at the empty seat where Bellotti had been.

"He's like Harold Bishop," said Danny.

"Barnet Bishop!" laughed Ethan.

James launched into a chant, "We thought you were dead, we thought you were dead, Barnet Bishop, we thought you were dead."

The noise of the crowd drowned out James' high-pitched singing. As the fans turned away from the Directors' Box and back to the game, the boys couldn't help stealing glances towards Barnet just to reassure themselves that he was actually alive and well and back.

On the pitch, Brighton took the lead against their closest

relegation-rivals, Darlington, a long-throw causing the ball to bounce around the penalty box, eluding everyone until Craig Maskell headed the bouncing ball into the back of the net. Darlington quickly equalised, but Brighton were back in front with more chaos in the box, Maskell sending a shot straight into the backside of Ian Baird who was no more than two yards from the goal. Five players lunged for the loose ball, but it was Baird who managed to nudge the ball goalwards, the ball trickling in.

Brighton retreated and tried to defend their lead. Danny wondered if the phone call in three days' time would be one he would answer. He wanted to tell his dad about working at *Sorted*. He had things in his life that he thought his dad would be proud of and he wanted to hear him tell him that he was proud of him, wanted to hear those words, but he wasn't going to break his word, was only going to answer that phone call if Brighton could hold on.

The final quarter of the game was painful to watch - Brighton seemed to be inviting Darlington to score, gifting them the ball time and time again. They scored an inevitable equaliser and as time ticked away, in the final moments of the game, they grabbed a winner. There were so few away supporters that the celebration for the goal was drowned out by shouts of anger from the Brighton fans.

"CASE OUT!" roared Barnet and his call for the manager's head was joined by others.

There Jimmy Case stood, thumb and forefinger stroking his moustache on the edge of the pitch, just watching as the last few seconds of the game ebbed away. When the final whistle went, he turned quickly as boos resounded and walked straight down the tunnel.

Danny looked around at his fellow fans, amazed that they were calling for Jimmy to be sacked. He was a hero, a legend. He was working in an impossible situation. He couldn't be expected to win games in these circumstances, but while not everyone shouted for his sacking, there were no voices defending him, no voices singing his name defiantly. Results had been poor. This was the fourth consecutive defeat and they'd only won one of their last seventeen games. They were nine points adrift at the bottom of the football league. He was in charge of the football and the football was undeniably terrible.

"I can't believe they want Case out," said Danny as they walked through the darkness of Hove Park.

"It's not his fault that we're losing. It's the board's," agreed Ethan.

But James was not so sure, his disappointment at results wearing his patience thin: "Case has got to go. We're losing every game."

"Who would we get? No one's going to want to come here," said Danny.

"Kenny Dalglish," said James. "Get King Kenny in. He'll sort us out."

Danny and Ethan erupted in laughter at James' suggestion.

"What? What?" he protested. "He hasn't got a club at the moment."

The next day, Danny walked into Cherries newsagent on his way to *Sorted* and turned over the back cover of *The Argus*. He saw that the scattered voices calling for Case to be dismissed had been heard: 'CASE SACKED' read the simple headline. It had only taken a few shouts of dissent and he'd gone, but it wasn't him that Danny wanted gone from the club. It was the board who were telling the fans to get behind whoever was appointed. Danny resolved in his mind that he wouldn't support the new manager. He'd be a puppet of the board, a yes-man who'd say the right things and praise the board in the press. Danny put the paper back on the pile and walked out of the shop.

30/11/96: Fulham 2-0 Brighton
03/12/96: Brighton 2-3 Darlington (Maskell, Baird)

14th December 1996

Brighton & Hove Albion vs Hull City

"Mum, why did you do go to the Poll tax protest?" Danny asked.

He'd caught his mum off guard. They'd just watched Supergrass perform 'Going Out' on *TFI Friday*, cameras swirling, guitars roaring, although his mum hadn't really been paying attention, chipping the remains of long-ago applied nail polish from her fingernails. Danny had been absorbed by the song, eager for the next Supergrass album, but now *TFI Friday* had gone to an advert break and the four-minute gap until Chris Evans reappeared gave Danny a window to understand his mum's former political passion that had faded as life's pressures piled up.

Danny's mum didn't reply immediately, letting Gary Lineker steal a cheque from a nun as part of a Walker's Crisps advert before saying wearily, "It just seemed so unfair. The rich would stay rich and the poor would only get poorer… I just felt so frustrated and angry and I wanted to make a stand."

"How did it make the poor poorer?"

"It's to do with how people are taxed. Poor families suddenly had to pay much higher amounts, as much as people that were much richer. I just hated it."

"Were you scared at the protests?"

"No, I was never in any danger. Sometimes, I sensed there might be violence and I just moved away from it. I wanted to make a point, but peacefully."

"Did it work?"

"We got rid of the Poll tax, but I don't know if things are really much better."

"Why not?"

"The poor are still poor. We're still poor. I don't want to charge you rent. It hurts to ask you for thirty quid each week. You know that, don't know?"

Danny had never really thought about it, hadn't really considered that his mum hated the position she was in, trapped into asking her son for rent so that she could afford to pay the bills and feed the family.

"I know, Mum."

He did now.

"I love you, son."

"I know, Mum."

Chris Evans was back on the television, Samuel L. Jackson strolling through the bar, high-fiving beer-drinking members of the audience and Danny and his mum's conversation petered out.

On the Monday morning, as he sat down to start his political article, he wrote about his mum and the battle she had fought. He thought that making it personal would make it interesting. He knew that readers of the magazine would flick quickly past his article, hoping to find something about Peter Andre instead, but perhaps if he told a story of injustice and struggle, some readers might linger and capture a little bit of the fire that he had found. "Nothing's changed," he wrote, echoing his mum, "but that doesn't mean that nothing can ever change." He was proud of that line.

It was tough to write. He didn't really feel like he knew enough and when Bram wasn't distracted by Mickey, who was amusing himself by sticking as many post-it notes as he could to Garth the Goth's back, he talked to Danny, telling him how a Conservative MP, John Gorst, had resigned and this now meant that the Tories no longer had a majority. Danny didn't really know what that meant and Bram drew a diagram of the House of Commons, explaining how a government was formed by getting more than half of the seats in the house and how the country was split into areas that were each represented by an MP. John Gorst's resignation was significant, Bram explained. The Conservative Party had held a majority in the House of Commons since 1979, but in recent years it had shrunk, the public longing for change and filled with disillusionment after sleazy tabloid stories about politicians that seemed to hit the headlines every other week.

"Is Ivor Caplin an MP?" Danny asked.

"No, but he'll be trying to become one next year in the election," Bram replied.

Danny was surprised at how interested he was becoming and decided that Ivor Caplin would feature in his article. Caplin's recent criticism of the Brighton board had made him something of a hero on the North Stand, his name being sung at home matches. He was someone who was standing up to Bill Archer and David Bellotti, and had some power to actually achieve something.

That evening, it was toad in the hole at the Browns' house. On arrival, Danny was greeted by Ethan holding up the back page of *The Argus*. The FA had decided on a punishment for the pitch invasion against Lincoln City and Brighton were being docked two points. That stretched the gap at the bottom of the football league to eleven. In their opening twenty-two matches, they'd only amassed thirteen points and two of those had now been taken away. Teams above them would continue to pick up points and the idea that they might actually stay in the football league seemed utterly impossible: a team devoid of confidence, a board at war with the fans and no manager.

"It only seems like yesterday that we were in the FA Cup final," said Mr Brown. "Has there ever been a club that has crumbled as quickly as we have?"

Danny and Ethan hadn't really known anything different. Brighton had always been a team that lost games to them, every season, a decline from the previous one.

Two days later, there was more news for Brighton, the appointment of a new manager, but this was greeted with as much enthusiasm as the points deduction by Danny and Ethan. Steve Gritt was the man given the unenviable task of rescuing something from the disaster of a season, like a chef asked to make a gourmet meal out of a compost heap. Where to start, the rotten carrot of ownership, the eggshells of the first team or the discarded teabags that were the fans? Gritt would need to be a miracle worker to make anything out of this decaying mess.

"I'll support the team, but Gritt is just a puppet of the board," said Danny, perched on the garden wall of James' house.

"Who is he, anyway?" asked Ethan.

Gritt had spent most of his playing career at Charlton

Athletic before becoming joint manager in 1991 with Alan Curbishley, while still making occasional playing appearances. After four years sharing the reins, Gritt was cut loose after a disappointing fifteenth place finish in the First Division. Charlton had ambitions to become a Premiership club and the change they decided on was to cut half of the duo - Gritt had been without a club for a year and a half.

"He used to manage Charlton," said James. "I reckon he's going to be good. He'll be better than Case, anyway."

At that, James was shoved backwards off the wall and into a holly bush, his feet still dangling at the top of the wall while he writhed to avoid being stabbed.

At the Goldstone Ground on the Saturday, feelings were mixed. "GRIT IS SHIT" graffiti had been daubed across the back of the West Stand, but many fans wanted to give the man a chance. The mess wasn't his fault. He was coming in to do a job.

Outside the ground, whistles were being handed out from fans with carrier bags full of them. With their voices ignored, a new higher-pitched form of protest was being employed. As the start of the game came closer, the whistles joined to create an ear-numbing scream. Flecks of spit shot out of sound holes as peas rattled ferociously.

Before the game started, Gritt was escorted out into the centre circle of the pitch accompanied by a photographer. He turned to each side of the ground, waving a friendly greeting towards a not so friendly crowd. The whistles abated for a moment and then the chant went up, "GRITT OUT," and Danny and Ethan joined their voices to those that just felt any form of football was futile if the club was on the verge of extinction; other voices rose, shouting down the harshness of instantaneous rejection of Gritt, and as the crowd fragmented and whistles drowned out arguments and accusations, the players quickly distracted everyone from their squabbles once the game had started. Craig Maskell sent a looping cross into the box and there was Paul McDonald, rising to nod the ball downwards, sending it skidding towards the bottom corner and everything was forgotten because the pure pleasure of a goal going in sent bodies colliding in ecstatic abandon. Barnet Bishop tumbled to the floor and Danny ended up sitting on his chest. Barely five minutes had been played and the Albion were in front.

In front and the arguments were forgotten. Brighton were playing effective, attacking football, Stuart Storer surging down the right-wing, Paul McDonald jinking down the left, Maskell and Ian Baird throwing their bodies at crosses while the maroon shirts of Hull chased the ball down fruitlessly. Albion's players were stroking the ball around with freedom and confidence, as if they'd forgotten that they were the worst team in the football league.

At half-time, the score was still only 1-0, but it had been hugely encouraging. Without the distraction of football during the half-time interval though, the crowd grew restless, a reckless anger again in the air. Danny, Ethan and James looked out onto the pitch wondering what would happen and then, a man leapt the advertising hoardings and sprinted towards the goal before handcuffing himself to the post in front of the North Stand, his free arm held aloft. Men surged forward and a few burst through the small group of stewards and were out and onto the pitch, heading for the centre circle. Again, the crowd didn't know how they felt, didn't want to lose more points, but wanted to fight the board and cheers and boos for the pitch invaders mingled in the air as the dozen fans on the pitch scattered, scrambling back onto the terraces while the handcuffed man in the goalmouth was cut free and led away.

The second half began and Brighton continued to dominate and more goals came, Maskell crossing for Storer who swept home and then Maskell, emerging from the fog of mediocrity that had been his recent performances, battled in the box, shooting first, straight at a defender, then, straight at the goalkeeper before steering a bobbling ball beyond the keeper as he fell to the ground. He was simply hungrier for the ball, the static Hull defenders watching on as he pounced upon the ball again and again before finding his target.

The game was won. Hull couldn't get a touch and the fans celebrated, but in the midst of the happiness that victory brings, they didn't forget to protest. "Archer Out," went up the cry and then from the Hull end, the cry was echoed, "Archer Out, Fish Out." Brighton weren't the only ones longing for change and as

Hull joined the Brighton chants, adding their own Chairman to the demand, the Brighton fans applauded. Here were a set of fans, being humiliated by the team bottom of the football league, having travelled hundreds of miles, and they knew that victories and petty rivalries were nothing in comparison to fighting for your club's survival.

"I told you Gritt would be good," James said as they walked out onto the Old Shoreham Road.

"It's one game," said Danny, unwilling to concede, unwilling to let himself believe that something good might actually be happening.

"It's one game, Danny, but it was only one win that was needed for you to talk to your dad," said Ethan.

In the excitement of the victory, Danny had forgotten about his dad. With every failure to win, he had walked away feeling the frustrating anger of longing for a win and not getting it, but at a deeper level, he had felt a hollowness at the thought that he wouldn't be speaking to his dad and now, it had happened: the elusive victory had been achieved. This man he hadn't wanted, hadn't welcomed, Steve Gritt, had brought the man he so desperately wanted back into his life. The goals had pried open a door that had been slammed angrily shut almost a year ago, but Danny was ready, told himself he was ready to speak to his dad and let him back in.

On Friday, Danny sat by the phone, drumming his fingers on the arm of the chair. For the first time since he'd started at *Sorted*, he had not taken his pay cheque to Cash Converters, but had instead walked briskly to Churchill Square and deposited the money into his account at Alliance and Leicester. His bank card had been unused for over a year, his 76p sitting there gaining interest.

Simon was playing *Smash Tennis* on the SNES and had tried to get Danny to join in, but Danny couldn't handle anything other than the impending phone-call. Finally, it came. Danny let Simon answer it first and sat listening to one side of the conversation, irritated as Simon told a long-winded story about how he had won a hundred Pogs from one of his classmates and as Danny paced the room, he heard his brother say, "Yes, he's here" and

"He's going to speak to you today," and the warm handset was pressed against his ear and he heard his dad's voice, crackly and distant, and here and now.

"Danny, thank you so much for speaking to me. I've missed you so much."

Danny couldn't communicate emotion, couldn't tell his dad that it had been unbearable to be separated from him, that his soul had been fractured the day his dad had left and that although time had made things gradually less immediately painful, it was like the fracture had never healed properly, and still, when he least expected it, he'd wince in pain as he was stabbed by a shard of bone.

All he said to his dad was, "Yes" and Danny's dad steered the conversation towards practical, easier things to discuss.

"Your mum said you're working for a magazine. That sounds amazing. What is it like?"

Danny told his dad about his article about the best albums of 1996 and how he had been working on an article about politics. He didn't mention the sometimes chaotic working environment. He wanted his dad to be impressed with what he was doing and the mayhem of Mickey McMashup wasn't the picture he wanted to create in his dad's mind.

They moved on to talk about football which Danny's dad feigned an interest in. When he was nine, Danny remembered his dad phoning up one of his friend's dads to ask about how football worked and his dad had scribbled down notes: three points for a win, one point for a draw, three teams relegated, three teams promoted. Afterwards, they'd looked at a league table together. Liverpool had been top of the First Division and Newcastle United bottom. They figured out most of the columns, but some of them were still a mystery to them.

As Danny finished explaining that Brighton had a new manager, but they were still certain to be relegated, his dad said, "Listen, Danny. I'd really love to come and see you at Christmas, but, I know last time I came down, you weren't ready to see me and I understand that. I can drive down on Boxing Day, but only if that's okay with you. I don't want the same thing to happen as last time. I don't think your mum could take that."

Danny paused. He didn't feel quite ready to actually see his dad and Brighton were at home to Colchester United on that day. He'd opened the door though, let his dad back into his world and it felt good to hear his dad's voice, but it still hurt.

"Brighton are playing that day," he replied, not sure where this piece of information would lead the conversation. He didn't want to turn down or accept his dad's suggestion.

"Oh, okay," his dad said and then coughed. "That's okay - when you're ready…" He left the sentence hanging. "It's good to hear your voice, Danny."

Danny clumsily said goodbye and put the phone down and sat silently, his mind empty, his emotions indecipherable. He hadn't meant to turn his dad down, but his reluctance had been implied and his dad had backed away.

14/12/96: Brighton 3-0 Hull (McDonald, Storer, Maskell)
22/12/96: Leyton Orient 2-0 Brighton

26th December 1996

Brighton & Hove Albion vs Colchester United

On Monday morning, thousands of copies of the December *Sorted* magazine had been delivered to the offices. For the first hour of the day, Danny looked through the magazine, lingering proudly on his article. He kept smoothing the page, looking at his name at the foot of the article. He wondered whether he should have put Ocean Colour Scene higher. Garth and Tracey arrived at varying degrees of lateness and when Mickey finally walked in, he was covered in vomit and oblivious to the sour stench that he was carrying. Bram ripped some holes in a bin-bag and made him wear it as a vest and then drove him home.

Garth and Tracey flicked through the magazine disinterestedly, not having any articles in it.

"How can you put these soft-rock whiners above Depressive Age?" was Garth's only real engagement.

When Bram returned, they were tasked with taking the magazines to every newsagent within walking distance of the offices. Other than the deal with WHSmith to stock the magazine, there was nowhere else that it could be bought so their job was to give the magazine away to shops for free in the hope that this would get the magazines into people's hands.

Bram had got some paper-round bags and they each put two-hundred copies of the thin magazine into their bags and set off in different directions.

In the first shop, Danny felt awkward, but once he'd stutteringly explained that the magazine was free and all they had to do was to put it on their shelf, the man behind the counter said, "Yeah, okay. Stick a few on the rack," and Danny slotted ten magazines between *Smash Hits* and *Just 17*, making them as prominent as he could.

Most shops accepted the free offer of magazines once they'd got over their suspicion, but a few said they'd need to check with the owners or just refused, sometimes in a rude manner: "That rubbish won't sell," one woman told Danny.

Each time, Danny put the magazines on a rack, he stood for a moment, looking at how easily it slotted in alongside its more famous competitors. He was doing something significant and people would pay to read his words, read his thoughts. He didn't imagine that he'd be boosting Depressive Age's album sales, but just his words in a stranger's hands felt amazing.

At lunch-time, they came back to the office before heading out again with a further two-hundred magazines. On Tuesday, they were back out and this time, Danny was joined by Mickey who complained all the way round that he wasn't Bram's slave, but when he got to the shops, he transformed into an energetic salesman and convinced a couple of shop-owners to let him help himself to a can of coke or a Mars bar in exchange for the magazines.

It was the last week of the year that the offices would be open and Danny was excited by the idea that he was going to be paid for being on holiday the following week.

On Wednesday, it was time for another meeting, with Danny being sent once more down to Safeway to stock up on snacks for the arrival of the mysterious contributors who arrived at Rock Place once a month. The mind-map drawn up by Bram was almost identical to the one drawn up the previous month, but no one made this observation, everyone presenting their fanciful ideas as fresh and new. When it came to Danny though, he felt more confident, willing to say what he really wanted to write about.

"I think it would be good to have an article about Brighton and how the club is being destroyed."

"We're meant to be a national magazine," said a heavily tattooed woman at the other end of the table. "Brighton aren't any good, are they?"

"It's not about how good they are at football," said Danny. "It's about the owners destroying the club. What's happening at Brighton could happen to any club. We were on *Match of the Day* last year when we got the game abandoned. I reckon the country will be interested."

"Let's stick it in the mix," said Bram, scrawling, 'Brighton Football' at the end of a line sprouting out from the mind-map. "There's a good chance we could get an interview with someone from the club, so let's see what we can do."

An interview! Danny imagined sitting down and chatting with Stuart Storer, his mind wandering as the conversation turned to The Fugees.

On the final Friday of the working year, Bram announced that it was time for Christmas dinner so Danny, Mickey, Tracey and Garth followed Bram down St James' Street to Grubbs Burgers and he told them that they could order what they liked. Danny and Mickey both chose triple Malaysian burgers, three patties topped with lettuce, chilli and peanut butter. Back at the office, Danny declared it to be the best burger he had ever eaten and proved Bram wrong who had claimed that Danny and Mickey's eyes were bigger than their bellies. At the end of the day, they each got a double pay-packet to cover the Christmas week.

Danny and Mickey walked out of the door together, out onto the frosty street at the end of the day. Their breath billowed before them and they both pulled their tracksuit tops close, neither of them wearing a coat.

"What are you doing for Christmas?" Danny asked.

Mickey coughed, rubbed his cold hands together before blowing on them.

"I don't know," he said.

"Aren't you going to see your family?"

"No," said Mickey, offering no further explanation.

"Why not?"

"I got kicked out of home on my sixteenth birthday," Mickey said. "I haven't seen my family since."

"Oh," said Danny. He didn't know how to respond. He'd looked at his own family and thought it couldn't get much worse, but here was Mickey, abandoned and alone at Christmas.

"Do you want a game of snooker?" Mickey asked.

"Er, okay," said Danny. "Where?"

Mickey led Danny to the Castle Snooker Bar. Having lunch bought for him by Bram meant that he had enough money in his pocket to pay for an hour's rental of a table. There was a hushed atmosphere inside with only two other tables being used by grey-haired men nursing pints of bitter. Mickey bought a Coke, having been turned down when he'd asked for JD and Coke. The boys played out an hour of abysmal snooker, Mickey slightly better than Danny, but foul shots outscored the points scored by balls potted and Mickey's eventual tally of more than two-hundred points were largely provided by Danny missing the ball he was aiming for completely or potting the white ball.

"Thanks for the game," Mickey said as they parted an hour later.

"No worries," Danny replied. "Have a nice Christmas," he added, knowing that it was unlikely.

With only one Brighton game to pay for, Danny, for once, had some spare money and once the pay cheque had cleared, Danny walked into town to buy a present for his mum, his granny and Simon. For his mum, he went to The Body Shop and bought a small selection of mint shower gels and soap - he had no ideas whether she'd like it - and for his brother, he found a second-hand copy of *Paperboy 2* for the SNES. For his granny, he spent ages staring at the biscuit selection in Woolworths, deciding on which box looked expensive but wasn't, finally deciding on the smallest Fox's selection box. Just as he was about to leave, he decided to get the Browns a box of Quality Street.

On Christmas Day, Danny couldn't help thinking back to one year ago. That was the last day that he had lived in ignorance of his parents' disintegrating relationship. He'd been self-absorbed and ignored the signs of unhappiness that they both showed, thinking it was normal, but normal is just what you get used to, what you accept because there is no alternative. It was just a few weeks later that his dad left and until last week, he had not spoken to him. The only time he'd seen him had been at the Hereford game where he'd watched from a distance as he walked into the away end, a symbol of his betrayal, with Ryan.

Christmas was stirring up those memories, the pain and the anger, but he squashed those feelings, for his mum, for his brother. Danny's granny had come to visit, paying £200 for a taxi to take her door-to-door, arriving on Christmas Eve with a suitcase full of gifts. She'd knitted Simon and Danny identical jumpers that Danny wore on Christmas Day, certain that this was going to be the only time he ever put it on, other than perhaps on cold nights when he needed to layer up before getting into bed. She'd also got him a voucher that could be used in a long list of shops.

Danny's mum had got him *K* by Kula Shaker - he knew what a stretch it would have been for her to buy him this album and he tried to say thank you in a way which sounded heartfelt, but it came out wooden and cold and Danny was inwardly frustrated that he couldn't communicate emotion. Danny's mum was far better at gratitude and she wiped a tear from her eye when she opened the gift from Danny and came over to him and kissed the top of his head.

They had roast chicken for Christmas dinner and then sat down for a game of Scrabble before settling down to see out the day with what the BBC had to offer: *Jurassic Park* - a film Danny had been so excited to see three years earlier at the cinema; an *Eastenders* Christmas special in which the Mitchells screamed at each other over dinner and Phil got raucously drunk and the *Only Fools and Horses* Christmas special, Del Boy and Rodney foiling a mugging, running through the foggy streets dressed as Batman and Robin.

Danny's granny fell asleep first, shortly followed by his mum. Simon nestled into his mum and when the closing lyrics to *Only Fools and Horses* were singing about Trevor Francis tracksuits, Danny looked around, realising that he was the only one who was still awake. He went up to his room and put *K* into his CD player and lay on his bed and let the album roll through.

On Boxing Day, Danny arrived at the Browns', having wrapped the box of Quality Streets in the same wrapping paper that his jumper had been wrapped in. It was a little torn, but it did the job. Mr Brown opened the door and Danny just held out the gift without saying anything.

"Oh, thank you, Danny, that's really kind," said Mr Brown. "I hope you've had a good Christmas."

Mr Brown unwrapped the gift immediately and offered the box to Danny and he took a Toffee Penny. The Browns had a huge, real Christmas tree in their lounge. It looked like the ones in shop windows, perfectly decorated. Fairy lights trailed across the mantelpiece and around pictures and mirror frames.

Hundreds of Christmas cards rested on every surface with more Blu-tacked to the door. Danny was mesmerised by what he saw, immediately aware of how different this was to his home where a two-foot, bedraggled, white Christmas tree, that had been dragged down from the loft two days before Christmas, had been the only decoration.

In the kitchen, there was food everywhere and Danny tucked into cold turkey, leftover pigs in blankets, mince pies and a chocolate orange. Tupperware containers filled with food seemed to be everywhere, an abundance of food that would keep the Browns going until New Year.

Well-fed, the boys set out for the Goldstone Ground, calling in on James along the way. James was wearing his new Brighton home shirt, training top, scarf and woolly hat with pride, his Christmas presents entirely purchased from the club shop.

At the ground, the Christmas atmosphere felt a little muted. A couple of fans wore blue Santa outfits, but the energy of the previous match wasn't there. An away defeat at Leyton Orient had burst the irrational optimism that a few fans had and a funereal march towards relegation or oblivion seemed once again the path the team were on.

This was further cemented when Colchester took the lead, a low free-kick squirming past Nicky Rust. The North Stand groaned in frustration and James monologued about how the shot was unstoppable, that Rust was unsighted, that even the greatest goalkeepers make mistakes.

"Go and ask him for his gloves," said Danny and James shut up and leaned his chin against the barrier.

Colchester, having scored their goal, retreated, hoping that the one goal might be enough to win the game, but the invitation of pressure did not work and as Brighton delivered hopeful ball after hopeful ball, eventually, one landed at the feet of Ian Baird and as he tried to turn the defender, like a bin lorry in a cul-de-sac, his legs were swept from under him and the referee blew his whistle and pointed to the spot. Denny Mundee stepped up, slamming the ball into the top corner to equalise.

As soon as Brighton scored, Colchester abandoned their defensive strategy and tried to find their gangly target-man, but their balls were overhit or mis-controlled while Brighton's attempts to release Stuart Storer or Paul McDonald down the wings were thwarted, usually by an aggressive tackle. On the rare occasions that one of the wingers got beyond their man, their crosses sailed out of play or straight into the keeper's arms. Neither team seemed good enough to actually score another goal, their set pieces in the first half gifting them easier chances than they could create in open play.

A point was no disaster, but Brighton were losing touch with the rest of the league, cast adrift at the bottom of the table, an island soon to be claimed by the Vauxhall Conference if the FA would even allow Brighton's presence in non-league football without a ground to call their own.

"I talked to my dad on Friday," said Danny as they walked back through Hove Park after the game.

"Because of the Hull match?" asked Ethan.

"Yes."

"You were so weird about that," said James, waving a sausage roll that had been flattened in his pocket during the match and was only now emerging from its plastic wrapping.

"I know. I'd started to feel ready, but I wanted to stick to my word and wait until Brighton won."

"What was it like?" asked Ethan.

"It was weird and, kind of, normal. It was a bit awkward. I don't know," said Danny, struggling to describe the enormity of the very ordinary conversation he'd had with his dad.

"I think it was a good thing to do," said Ethan.

"Yeah," said Danny, the simple word carrying a weight that he couldn't properly explain.

A seagull swooped down and plucked the sausage roll clean out of James' hand and the moment was gone. The seagull landed a few feet in front of the boys and mockingly, arched its neck backwards and swallowed the sausage roll in one greedy gulp before taking flight again. Danny and Ethan were rolling on the floor, unable to control their laughter while James chased the seagull waving a fist.

"Seagulls, seagulls," Danny managed to get out, while regaining momentary composure of himself.

26/12/96: Brighton 1-1 Colchester (Mundee (pen))
28/12/96: Scarborough 1-1 Brighton (Storer)
01/01/97: Torquay United 2-1 Brighton (Andrews)
18/01/97: Lincoln City 2-1 Brighton (Storer)

25th January 1997

Brighton & Hove Albion vs Rochdale

Each Friday, the phone calls came. It was difficult for Danny and his dad to find things to talk about. When they had lived together, they had co-existed around the practicalities of the day: Do you want a bacon sandwich? What time are you going to be in? Have you done your homework? When are you going to tidy your room? Days used to be punctuated by questions and demands that were now rendered irrelevant by his dad's departure. Now, their conversations demanded to be meaningful, yet neither Danny nor his dad could meet this challenge and once Danny had delivered the factual details: "I've written an article about politics;" "Dennis, next door, has been arrested;" "Brighton lost to Torquay," neither of them could manage to conjure anything to prolong the phone call and it ended after just a few minutes.

Simon was much better, tedious stories of playground squabbles and teacher tantrums. He started every story with, "Can you believe..." before launching into something utterly believable and Danny knew that Simon's unfettered enthusiasm meant that he connected with his dad in a way that Danny found it impossible to do, awkward long pauses creating an accidental barrier between them.

Danny felt tied to the ritual of the phone call now that he'd conceded. To avoid it would feel like a huge statement that he didn't want to make, but each time, after the conversation, he walked up the stairs and sat on his bed with his head in his hands, blaming himself for his lack of effusiveness, for this horrible hollow feeling. Sometimes, Nirvana purged away the pain and sometimes he'd wallow with The Verve before emerging to face the world once more.

A cloud of tension hung over the *Sorted* office when Danny returned. Mickey had gone to Tracey's on New Year's Eve. He'd used the opportunity, again, to nab a few CDs, but had been caught in the act by one of Tracey's housemate's boyfriends and an inevitable fight had ensued. Tracey described it to Danny one morning before Mickey arrived. Lamps and plates had been used as weapons and Mickey had been eventually thrown out onto the street and been attempting to kick the front door in when the sound of sirens sent him scurrying. When Mickey arrived, neither of them said a word to each other and the silence infected the whole room. All that could be heard was the tapping of fingers on keyboards and the distorted echo of Garth's music coming from his headphones.

Bram didn't know what had happened, but it was clear that things weren't right and he tried to gather everyone together so they could "air their grievances." Danny and Garth said they didn't have a problem with anyone. Tracey would only say, "Ask Mickey" while Mickey refused to say anything and was taken away for further interrogation in the office next door.

Three days later, as Tracey walked out of the door at the end of the day, she announced that she was leaving and despite Bram following her and speaking to her in the street, she was true to her word. The next day, she wasn't there and Mickey was instantly back to his ebullient self, talking up his still unfinished drugs article, gyrating his groin at Garth on repeat and suggesting another visit to Grubbs every single day.

Danny joined him for another game of snooker on the second Friday of the year. With three away games in a row, he'd not had to pay to get into a match for a while. He even managed to afford a Coke on this visit. Neither Mickey's nor Danny's snooker was any better and they left after an hour, Danny to his weekly phone-call and Mickey to whatever chaos the weekend would bring.

The following week, Danny walked into the offices on Monday. He'd finished *To Kill a Mockingbird* on the bus journey into work, gripped as Scout's ham costume saved her life.

Normally, Bram would gently inquire about the weekend, but instead, he animatedly accosted Danny with an energetic question: "Guess what?"

"What?"

"Brighton have been in touch. They've agreed to an interview."

The bleariness of a Monday morning was gone as a thrill of

excitement shot through Danny.

"Who?"

"Steve Gritt."

"When?"

"Next Tuesday. Are you up for it?"

Danny's right leg wobbled. It felt too big to be true. He'd chanted 'GRITT OUT!' weeks before, but that Gritt had been a stranger in the distance, an imposter in Jimmy Case's shoes, but time had dulled his absurd righteous anger and although Brighton hadn't won since Gritt's opening game: two draws and two defeats, the win that opened the door to his dad being back in his life still felt important. Sitting and having a conversation with the Brighton manager made Danny feel giddy and sick, exhilarated and jittery.

"Yes," he responded. There was no other answer.

All Danny could do for the rest of the week was write and edit, draft and craft a list of questions. He discussed the interview in microscopic detail with Bram. "Is it okay to ask this?" "Do you think I should wear my Brighton shirt?" "How many questions should I ask?"

When he told Ethan and James about the interview, they were equally incredulous, excited and jealous.

"Are you going to tell him you don't want him as the Brighton manager?" James asked.

"I've changed my mind about that," responded Danny.

A defeat away at Lincoln at the weekend meant that Brighton were back on a bleak winless streak, the euphoria of the Hull game fading back into the inevitability that the jaws of relegation were open wide for the Albion.

Danny had hoped that a victory on the road would have made for a more positive interview, but his excitement hadn't been quelled by the result.

Danny had been given money from a red tin in one of the upstairs offices to pay for the bus journey up to Sussex University where Brighton trained and where he would meet Steve Gritt. He got on the number twenty-five bus in front of Brighton Pavilion. He looked over at the Georgian palace from the top deck of the bus; he'd always thought that the domes looked like giant onions. He'd been inside once, years ago, on a school trip and he'd been most interested in the servants' quarters, a sudden shift in tone from the luxury of the rooms that had once been frequented by King George IV.

The bus rumbled up Lewes Road and Danny checked in panic when he thought for a moment that he'd forgotten his list of questions. He read them through again, wondering if there were enough and wondering how he was meant to start the interview.

The bus turned into the university campus and Danny followed the signs to the Sports Centre only to find that there were two separate Sports Centres and that he'd gone to the wrong one. He worried that he would be late, but there were still forty-five minutes to go and after a quick march back through the university grounds, he found himself climbing the path up to the training pitches where the team prepared for matches.

He hung around in the car park, watching people come and go for half an hour, not wanting to be too early, but five minutes before the interview was due, he walked up to the main building, a big grey block, and told a woman sitting behind a desk that he had arrived to interview Steve Gritt. She pointed up the stairs and told him that Steve's office would be the second door he came to.

Standing outside the office, he could feel his heart hammering and he took a moment to swallow what felt like excess saliva in his mouth and then he knocked.

Steve Gritt opened the door and smiled broadly and held out a hand. He gripped Danny's hand firmly and gave one solid shake before releasing his hand and saying, "Come in, it's Danny, isn't it?"

"Yes," said Danny, following Steve into his office.

There were two desks in an L-shape, each with a computer on and papers in neat piles. The walls were grey and bare, broken up by one large window that overlooked a few football pitches that were currently full of players. Jeff Minton was juggling a football on the edge of the closest pitch, but Danny only had time to glance before taking his seat.

"Would you like a drink?" asked Steve.

"No, thank you," replied Danny.

He feared spilling a drink or choking on his words. He clumsily got his Dictaphone out of his pocket and asked if it was okay to record their interview and Steve confirmed that it was fine.

"I've got some questions," said Danny. He wished he'd thought of a better start to the interview.

Danny started by asking him about why he decided to join Brighton and Steve spoke honestly about how he'd being doing "bits and pieces" since leaving Charlton eighteen months earlier and that he wanted to get back involved with football and when the opportunity came up to manage Brighton, he went for it and here he was. He spoke about having played against Brighton back when they were in the top flight in the early '80s, how he'd once lost 7-0 at the Goldstone and he wanted to bring those good times back to the club and he was glad that he'd started by bringing a much-needed win.

"How did you feel about the reception the fans gave you at the Hull game?"

Danny couldn't bring himself to tell Steve that he had chanted for his dismissal before the whistle had even been kicked, but it was obvious what the question was asking.

"It was a surprising reception," Steve said. "I know the fans care deeply for the club and they feel frustrated and I understand that and I guess, I received some of that frustration. I'm here to be a football manager and to try and win as many games of football as I can, and if I can get Brighton winning, then I'm sure I'll win the fans round."

There was an edge of empathy to Steve's response. It was immediately clear that he wasn't a big ego using Brighton as a stepping stone. Would he stray into criticising Bill Archer and David Bellotti? That's what Danny really wanted to ask about. The football was important, but not as important as the future of the club.

He falteringly read his question aloud: "Do you agree with the fans' criticisms of Bill Archer and David Bellotti?"

Steve paused. "When I was at Charlton, we couldn't play at our ground and that was a tough time. I'm not here to get involved in the boardroom matters. I'm here to figure out how to get this team winning football matches, but I do understand what the fans are going through."

He'd not criticised the board, but to do so would have been suicidal. There was a sense, though, that he understood what it was to be a football fan, understood what matters. He could have been angry with the reception he'd got from the fans, but he'd accepted it and recognised that it wasn't a rejection of him.

"What is your plan to get us winning football matches?"

"When I arrived, I quickly realised that we've got good players here, that this set of lads shouldn't be bottom of the football league. You've seen that I've set the team up in a 4-4-2 formation. Storer and McDonald are fantastic wingers and we've got two great strikers in Bairdy and Maskell. If we get it out wide and get balls into the box, we'll score goals. Then, we just need to be solid at the back, have a hard-working midfield that protects the back four. I want the whole of the midfield to be tracking back and supporting the defence when we haven't got the ball. If we all do our jobs properly, we'll get results."

"Do we need any new players?"

"We could do with some reinforcements and I've got a couple of deals that I'm hoping to get over the line. I feel like we need an extra option up front. Bairdy and Maskell are great, but if they get injured, we haven't got back up in that position. There's a lad I'd love to get. I've seen him score goals off the bench and that could be important for us, to have an option late in the game. We'll see."

"Who is it?"

Danny couldn't believe that Steve was going to let slip a bit of transfer gossip to him that no one else knew.

"I can't say his name yet. I tell you what, you can't put this in the article, but I'll give you the initials: R.R."

R.R.? Danny's mind buzzed between the next question he was going to ask and who this player might be. The only name that came to mind was the Hereford legend, Ronnie Radford, but he would have retired years ago.

"If you could sign any player to help Brighton stay up, who would it be?"

Steve chuckled. "Imagine Alan Shearer getting on the end of Storer and McDonald's crosses. That would be good, wouldn't it? But if I had that kind of money, I'd spread it across a few players. This lad I'm hoping to bring in, he'll do a good job for us."

"Who do you think is the best player for Brighton?"

"There's a lot of good players here. Let me talk about one player, though, who I think is going to be really important for us between now and the end of the season: Kerry Mayo. He's a young lad, figuring himself out, but I love his energy and passion. He's exactly what I need in centre-midfield. There are players with great natural ability, but I want a fighter in there and even though he's young, I think I can trust him."

Danny came to the end of his questions and thanked Steve. He'd been unhurried and genuine, not rushing through perfunctory answers, but really thinking through Danny's questions.

"Come, have a look at the lads training," Steve said, beckoning Danny to the window.

Out on the pitches, the players were running through a drill where a player in the centre circle sent a drilled pass into the path of one of the wingers who then delivered the ball into the box. Steve explained what the players were doing and talked Danny through how he was hoping this might translate to a match-day scenario. Danny stood and watched with Steve for another half-hour, Steve explaining each training drill and asking Danny's opinion on how players had performed before his arrival.

When the players started wandering back up towards the building, Steve said, "Good luck with the article, Danny. You did a great job asking questions. There were some in there that I've never been asked before, and thanks for your support from the terraces. We need the fans."

Danny returned to the office and enthusiastically took Bram through the interview, question by question.

"He was such a good bloke," said Danny. "He thanked me for my support. What a legend."

Danny logged onto a computer and spent the rest of the day transcribing every word Steve had said into a document so that he knew what material he had to work with. The task took him into the next day and when he'd finally finished, he went through and changed every quote he wanted to include in the article to red before finally settling down to write the article. It seemed impossible to find words to match what had been an incredible meeting and he didn't want his article to just be one that heaped praise on Gritt. It was important that the article properly discuss the wrongs that been done to the club by the board.

"What was he like?" Ethan asked as they walked to the Goldstone Ground on Saturday.

"He was amazing. He's really got a plan to get us winning games and we're signing Ronny Rosenthal," Danny said.

Danny had trawled through the *Sensible World of Soccer* database, trying to find who the mysterious R.R. might be and had convinced himself that it must be the low-scoring Tottenham Hotspurs striker.

"Ronny Rosenthal!" exclaimed James. "Isn't he that player that hit the bar when he had an open goal?"

"Yeah, but he's a Premiership striker. He'd be amazing down at this level. He looked great when he first started playing for Liverpool. I remember seeing him score a hat-trick on *Saint and Greavsie*," said Danny.

"It's too late, though," said Ethan. "We've got no chance of staying up."

The gradual point-gathering since Gritt's arrival had coincided with nearest rivals Hereford losing six consecutive games, so whilst the form hadn't been brilliant, the gap between the sides had narrowed to a still-substantial seven points.

"If we win today, we could be four points off Hereford," said James.

Danny spent large chunks of the game looking over at Steve Gritt, stood with his arms crossed on the touchline looking on, his plan put in place, now hoping that the players might execute it. Occasionally, Gritt would become suddenly animated, cupping a hand around his mouth and shouting while waving his free arm backwards, forwards, up and down, directing his players, trying to get his orchestra to find its rhythm.

Brighton were unusually kicking towards the North Stand in the first half, having been turned around by Rochdale, a ploy that seemed to be done to unsettle Brighton. However, it was to no avail, Brighton dominating possession and creating all the chances. Craig Maskell gave Brighton the lead, glancing a header in off the post from Paul McDonald's cross. It looked almost identical to the training ground move that Danny had stood watching from Steve's office window. In the second half, Rochdale had a player sent off and Danny, Ethan and James enjoyed the glorious gloating "Cheerio" chants as he trudged from the field. A long throw launched into the box was flicked on and into the path of Maskell who swept the ball home to double the lead and then Stuart Storer raced down the right-wing and drilled a low cross into the path of Ian Baird who tucked the ball neatly beyond the keeper.

At the end of the game, the players lingered to applaud the crowd. The clamour to oust the board was there, chanted about, demanded as fervently as ever, but there was a shift in the atmosphere that a win brought, a coming together of the players and the fans.

As the boys exited the stadium, a man clutching a radio to his ear announced loudly, "Hereford won," and swear words collided in the air.

25/01/97: Brighton 3-0 Rochdale (Maskell 2, Baird)
01/02/97: Mansfield Town 1-1 Brighton (Mundee)

Brighton & Hove Albion vs Hartlepool United

"Danny, there's something I want to ask you and it's totally fine if you say no."

Danny expected that his dad was going to suggest another visit. He'd grown accustomed to the awkwardness of the weekly phone-calls and he wouldn't reject his dad if that was what he was going to suggest.

"Ryan wants to come down to Brighton for the game next weekend. He says it's some Fans United thing. I know it might be weird, but could he come to the game with you?"

Danny pictured the spiky-haired, chubby-cheeked boy entering the away end at the Goldstone a few months ago. He'd been angry that this boy had taken his place, but the note he'd left under his pillow had destroyed that anger. He was a boy, like him, who loved a terrible football team and had been through the agony of his dad walking out on him.

"It's fine; he can come," said Danny.

"Thank you, son. That's really good of you."

The next Friday night, Danny, Ethan and James were standing on the concourse at Brighton Station trying to figure out which train Ryan would be arriving on. Ryan had said that he would be wearing a Hereford shirt - there couldn't have been many teenagers wandering around Brighton Station in a Hereford shirt on a Friday night. Danny hadn't let on that he'd seen him before, as he stood in the shadows, looking on with a heavy heart.

The following day, it wasn't just going to be Ryan's Hereford shirt as an anomaly at the Goldstone Ground. A few months earlier, a teenage Plymouth fan had posted on a message board: "I'm a Plymouth fan and I think that one week when we're away, I'm going to come down and support your protest. I think it would be a good idea if LOADS of fans from different clubs turned up at Brighton (with their shirts on) and joined in. It would show that we're behind you, 100%."

Brighton fans had latched onto the idea and the Hartlepool game had been chosen as it coincided with an international break, meaning that fans of Premiership teams might be tempted down.

"Do you think they'll be many fans from other clubs at the game tomorrow?" asked James.

"I don't think so," said Ethan. "I don't reckon other clubs will care about us."

But Ryan clearly cared. Despite the fact that Hereford and Brighton were toiling away at the foot of the table together, he'd chosen to come to Brighton rather than follow his own team on an away day to Barnet.

Danny, Ethan and James were still staring at the board searching for Hereford, not realising that Ryan had changed train twice and had just arrived on the final leg of his journey from St Pancras.

"Is that him?" said James, pointing at a boy in a Hereford shirt with a backpack who was scanning the station.

Danny, Ethan and James approached Ryan.

"Ryan, I'm Danny."

Danny introduced Ethan and James and the boys quickly settled into the comfortable common ground of football. Ryan narrated Hereford's season, explaining how they'd turned a corner recently with back-to-back wins against Cambridge and Wigan. He explained his frustrations, how they'd made the play-offs the previous season, but that this time round, they'd nosedived.

"I do hope you boys stay up," said Ryan. "I hope we both stay up. Exeter, Torquay, Hartlepool - they could all get dragged in."

That night, Danny let Ryan have his bed. He took the cushions from the sofa and laid them on the floor of his bedroom and made himself as comfortable as he could, a tricky task as the cushions shifted and separated every time he changed position.

"Why did you want to come to this game?" Danny asked.

"I saw it on our fans' forum and I just thought that this could happen to any football club. It's not right and I decided that I wanted to join the protest, stop these people from ruining a football club and warn other people at other clubs that they won't be allowed to destroy clubs."

"It's cool that you're here."

Danny wanted to thank him for the note he had left under his pillow. The darkness of the room allowed an intimacy that light would not allow.

"What happened with your dad?" Danny asked.

There were a few beats of silence as Ryan searched for how to explain.

"I was just about to start secondary school and in the last week of the summer holidays, my dad came and told me that he was leaving us. I remember asking why and he didn't explain, just said that it was something he needed to do. There wasn't another woman or anything. There didn't seem to be a reason, but he must have had his reasons. He's never explained it to me."

"Do you still see him?"

"Yeah. He lives in Hereford. I usually go and see him on Sundays. He doesn't really know how to be a dad though."

"What do you mean?"

"I don't know. I mean, there are things you want from a dad, I think. Like, you want advice even though you'd never ask for it and you want encouragement, you know, someone to say what you've done is great even when it isn't. But that's not my dad's personality. He's doesn't mean to be crap. He just doesn't know how to be anything else. Your dad's much better."

Danny rolled over, facing the bookshelf, the spines just distinguishable in the darkness.

"I'm sorry," said Ryan. "That was a stupid thing to say."

"It's okay," said Danny. "It's not your fault. It's hard to accept that there are good things about him because I was angry at him for so long. I sort of still am, but it's draining and miserable to be angry all the time."

"I know what you mean. I was angry for ages and then, it started drifting away and I tried to hold onto it. The anger was, sort of, comforting, but I remember talking to this guy at my church and he talked about forgiveness and how it wasn't about the other person and letting them off, but it was about freeing us from the negative emotions and it, kind of, made sense."

Danny hadn't expected Ryan to start talking about religious

stuff, but what he'd said about forgiveness did make sense. He'd always thought that accepting an apology was weak, that there were things that were unforgivable, but he realised that accepting his dad's phone-calls was a way of forgiving him for what he'd done, even though he didn't deserve it. He'd felt better, lighter somehow, since he'd done that.

The next day, Danny and Ryan walked the two miles to Ethan's house. A thick fog swirled around them, meaning they could barely see twenty metres in front of them.

"If it's like this, we're not going to be able to see the South Stand goal," said Danny.

They played a game of naming footballers beginning with S, neither of them faltering the entire journey. Hereford seemed to have an unlikely number of sibilant stars: Smith, Stoker, Sandeman, Sutton and Danny had no way to query them.

When they arrived at the Browns' house, Ethan had fast-forwarded through his *101 Great Goals* video and paused it just before Ronnie Radford's famous thunderbolt, when Hereford had shocked Newcastle United in the FA Cup before any of the boys were even born. As Danny and Ryan entered, he pressed play. The sound was down and he launched into the commentary himself.

"Tremendous spirit in this Hereford side. They're not giving this up by any means. Radford…"

Ryan joined in. He'd watched this goal thousands of times, loved this goal. "Tudor's gone down for Newcastle."

Danny and James, who had seen it enough times, sat on Ethan's sofa to join in as Radford shaped to shoot: "Radford again. Oh, what a goal! What a goal!"

As hundreds of children in snorkel parkas charged onto the Edgar Street pitch, the boys in the Browns' living room acted as if they were watching the match live and piled into an exhilarated mess in the middle of the floor.

"You've got your knee in my balls. You've got your knee in my balls," squealed James as the video moved on to show Ted Macdougall scoring for Bournemouth against Arsenal.

The boys disentangled themselves and James lay, clutching himself and groaning as goal after goal played out on the screen.

Mr Brown came in with some bacon sandwiches and the boys tucked in, eating quickly in their eagerness to get down to the ground.

The fog gave Hove Park an eerie atmosphere as they walked through, shapes shifting in the trees, noises coming from the gloom. There were still over two hours until kick-off, but the ground was already bustling. A coach pulled up in front of the North Stand and out poured men, women and children, all wearing Charlton Athletic shirts. Standing beneath a lamppost was a huge man wearing a black and white checkered top hat. Back and forth, he waved an Eintracht Frankfurt flag, chanting something in German.

From everywhere, shirts from different clubs were emerging: Norwich City, Bournemouth, Torquay United, Wimbledon, Lincoln City, York City. Some shirts, the boys recognised instantly; others, they approached surreptitiously, checking out the badge to know the team. Two Crystal Palace fans stood smoking, leaning against a brick wall. Even Brighton's rivals didn't want their demise. The pantomime of a rivalry was something you wanted and even though they hadn't been in the same division for a number of years, they hoped that one day, they could reignite those tetchy days when Alan Mullery and Terry Venables quarrelled.

The boys' conversation was simply pointing out shirts that they'd spotted. When they spotted a Middlesbrough fan, Danny and Ethan asked James why he wasn't wearing his Boro shirt. Between them, they counted up forty-three different clubs represented by shirts. Club identity was so important, following your team to the exclusion of any other club, but this moment was transcending the tribalism of football, fans stepping away from their insular focus and seeing football as something bigger, a world where they were all interconnected and a world that needed protecting and here they were, signing up for the battle, wearing their colours, but for a cause that was not their own.

As the boys glanced up and down the road, forty-four, forty-five, forty-six stepped out of the fog like they were on a film-set. It felt like a war movie where a small group of soldiers know that all is lost, that they are about to lose their lives, when suddenly, seemingly from nowhere, a crowd of reinforcements arrive and sweep them to victory. Surely, this moment couldn't be ignored. They'd run on the pitch, pulled down the goal-posts, marched through the city, refused to attend, left early, blown whistles, but none of that compared to this moment. This was a statement from the entire football community. This club matters. This club must be saved.

This club mattered, not because there was anything unique about it. It mattered because all football clubs matter. All football clubs exist within communities and each club are their very own communities. The Eintracht Frankfurt fan waving his flag; the Palace fans leaning against the wall having their pre-match fags; the Charlton fans descending from their coach: they all knew that what was happening to Brighton could happen to them and that standing with Brighton was sending a message to all owners everywhere that the fans are the club.

From the North Stand, the goal in front of the South Stand was just about visible shrouded in fog, and the ball was regularly, but only momentarily, lost by the fans when it got caught in a melee of players. Danny, Ethan and James took Ryan into 'The Box'. Barnet Bishop was there and incredibly, stood next to him, was a man in a Barnet shirt. Fans of other clubs were dotted everywhere. In the West Stand, a large banner read, 'Real Madrid Want Archer Out.' Had someone really been watching Davor Šuker and Raúl the previous week and now, here they were, demanding that Bill Archer relinquish the reins of Brighton and Hove Albion?

On the pitch, the doubled crowd inspired the players. In the distance, the boys watched as Ian Baird stooped to head home Paul McDonald's corner and the place went wild. Danny could see Ryan punching the air and letting himself be swept along by the celebrations while Danny found himself pinned to a Liverpool fan who he suspected of living locally. Craig Maskell made it 2-0 and then 3-0 before half-time, heading in a cross and then finishing from close range when it looked like Baird had been fouled in the box.

At half-time, scores from around the country were announced and fans from opposing teams mocked one another if they were beating them. Ryan let out a triumphant, "Yes" and gave a self-satisfied smile and nod towards the Barnet fan when it was revealed that they were leading at half-time.

As the second-half started, a tubby Chelsea fan at the bottom of the North Stand clambered up onto the crash barriers, demanding in a slurred voice that others hold his legs steady. For ten minutes, he serenaded the crowd with a gruff, call-and-response army song: "Go left, go left; go left, right, left; go left, go right, go pick up the step, go left, go right, go left."

He was only toppled from his perch when Gary Hobson headed Brighton into a 4-0 lead.

"It's just like watching Brazil," sung the fans and then Craig Maskell finished from a tight angle to complete his hat-trick and give Brighton an incredible five-goal lead.

Teams are often buoyed on by their fans, the home advantage giving them a psychological edge and with what seemed like the world behind them, the players had turned into world-conquering superstars, scoring at will, Hartlepool blown away like a crisp packet in a hurricane.

The Charlton fans gathered at the front of the stand launched into song for their ex-manager: "Stevie Gritt, Stevie Gritt, Stevie, Stevie Gritt; he's got no hair, but we don't care, Stevie, Stevie Gritt."

Gritt's name had never been sung before. The process of accepting him had been slow, but he'd transformed the team, particularly at home where they were unbeaten since his appointment, and so, the fans were willing to make the statement that his male pattern baldness did not bother them, that they would accept him for the joy he brought them, for the football he inspired the team to play.

When the final whistle blew, the crowd erupted in cheers and Maskell collected the match ball from the referee. He knew that the normally treasured possession of a match ball for a hat-trick scorer did not belong to him. This day was for the fans and he jogged to the North Stand where the fans warmly applauded and launched the ball, looping up and into a melee of bodies who dived over each other, clamouring to grab the souvenir.

"I don't even support Brighton, but that was the greatest game I've ever been to," said Ryan as they walked down to the station at the end of the match.

"That was special," said James.

"And Hereford won," said Ryan. "We're both staying up. I'm sure of it."

The boys launched into a rendition of, "We are staying up, say, we are staying up."

"You're a legend for coming down to support," said Ethan as they arrived at the station.

"Yeah, thanks… for everything," said Danny, trying to capture how much he valued Ryan's empathy and hoping that his simple words would translate what he felt.

"No worries," said Ryan, patting Danny of the shoulder.

Ryan leaned out of the open window of the train as it pulled away and Ethan shouted, "RADFORD AGAIN…"

"OH, WHAT A GOAL!" screamed Ryan as the train trundled away and then, Danny, Ethan and James charged around the platform, arms aloft in celebration while a rainbow of fans in shirts of every colour laughed and cheered at these three Brighton fans who they had joined for the day.

08/02/97: Brighton 5-0 Hartlepool United (Baird, Maskell 3, Hobson)

11th February 1997

Brighton & Hove Albion vs Exeter City

"I've got tickets for three films that are coming out soon," explained Bram to Danny, Mickey and Garth. "The Odeon put on midnight showings for journalists, so we can go along and review the films before they come out."

"What are the films. I bet they're crap," said Mickey.

"So, we've got *A Portrait of a Lady.*"

"Bor-ing," chimed Mickey.

"*Trainspotting.*"

"A film about spotting trains!" Mickey was incredulous that such a film would even be made.

"And *Mars Attacks!*"

"I'm going to that one," declared Mickey.

"Hold on. Let's do this fairly. Which film does everyone want to see?"

Everyone chose *Mars Attacks!* and Bram said that he was going to write everyone's names down on a piece of paper and that the first to get chosen would get first choice. Bram tore three small squares of paper from an A4 sheet and wrote down the boys' names, screwed each piece of paper up and shuffled them around in his cupped hands before laying them on the table.

"Who wants to choose first?" he asked.

"Me," said Mickey, grabbing for one of the scrunched up balls.

Bram held out his hand and Mickey dropped the ball into it. Slowly, the ball was unravelled to reveal Garth's name.

"What film do you want to see, Garth?" Bram asked.

"*Mars Attacks!*" said Garth.

Instantly, Mickey was over the table, knocking Garth backwards and off his chair. Chair, Garth and Mickey were in a pile on the floor and Mickey's forearm was pressed against Garth's neck. There was indistinguishable shouting from Mickey; then Bram had a hold of Mickey's shoulders and was dragging him backwards while Mickey writhed, screamed and then burst into tears, freeing himself from Bram's grip and running out the door.

Garth lay motionless on the floor, unharmed, but stationary.

Danny just sat there, the sudden explosion of anger and violence making his heart thump audibly in his chest.

"Are you okay, Garth?" Bram asked as if he was checking in on him after a mild case of hiccups. "No harm done?"

"Er, no," said Garth, inelegantly getting to his feet and righting his chair.

"I was about to tell him that there are two tickets for each film, but I think, after that little outburst, that it wouldn't be a good idea for you two to have a little date at the cinema. Mickey will have to choose one of the other films."

It seemed a pretty mild punishment for leaping the desk and attacking a colleague.

"Danny, do you want to choose the next name?"

Danny picked the pieces of paper off the floor and then, picked his own name.

"What film do you want to watch?" Bram asked.

He'd wanted to watch *Mars Attacks!*, not so desperately that he was going to attack someone for the privilege though. He could still choose that film, but he wanted to write his own review, not share one with Garth and he was also nervous about what Mickey's reaction would be when he returned to the office to find that he was the only one missing out on the favoured film.

Neither *Trainspotting* nor *The Portrait of a Lady* sounded remotely interesting, but Danny chose *Trainspotting*, hoping that there might be a little more to it than its title suggested.

The films were showing over the next three evenings and *Trainspotting* was first up. With the film not starting until midnight, he was told that he didn't need to come in until lunchtime the following day.

When he went to get lunch - with two Brighton games in four days, it was going to have to be the 39p Safeway flatbread for the entire week - he found Mickey, sat with his back against the brick wall of the building. His eyes were red and blotchy and he was only wearing his tight pale blue t-shirt despite the temperature hovering around zero.

"Do you want to come and see that film, *Trainspotting*, with me tonight?" Danny asked.

"No."

That evening, Danny walked down West Street just before midnight, a few Monday night-clubbers staggering through the streets, the girls with arms interlinked and looking like they were going to drag each other to the floor any moment, the boys, jostling and laughing at one another. As he reached the door of The Odeon, there was Mickey, still in just a t-shirt, smoking a roll-up, sucking in each breath until his cheeks hollowed.

Danny said nothing about the rejection of his invitation earlier in the day and just accepted that he was here, ready to spend the early hours of Tuesday morning in front of a screen. On the door, a man in a baggy suit seemed dubious that Danny and Mickey were journalists, but when they told him they were from *Sorted* magazine, he checked his list and was surprised to find that there were two spaces reserved.

They were shown into a small room where three men sat reading newspapers. There was a raised counter with a man behind it and behind him, a fridge stocked with beer.

"What would you like to drink?" he asked.

"Is it free?" Mickey asked.

"Yes," said the man, perplexed.

Mickey looked at the fridge and asked for a can of Foster's. Danny expected the man to ask for ID or simply turn him down, but he just handed over a can and when Danny was asked, he requested the same.

Danny had barely drunk alcohol before, lack of money being the primary barrier. During Euro '96, Mr Brown had let him have a couple of his small bottles of French beer that he'd brought back from holiday and occasionally, at his granny's, he'd tried to drink wine, but always found it repulsive and had forced it down because drinking alcohol felt adult. To admit to not actually liking it felt like admitting that you still quite liked *The Care Bears*.

Beer wasn't much better than wine in Danny's eyes, but being thought of as eighteen and being given free beer felt great, so Danny glugged mouthfuls, trying to ignore the taste. Before he'd finished, they were invited to go through into the theatre and when the other journalists carried their drinks in with them, Danny copied, clutching his rapidly warming can. Mickey had finished his and had asked for another which the man behind the bar seemed reluctant to hand over, but did anyway.

There were no adverts before the film. It simply opened with a screen revealing the film to be an 18: 'Includes graphic drug use, sex, violence and swearing.'

Mickey drained his second can of Foster's: "This is going to be good."

The opening scene burst onto the screen energetically, a shaven-headed man running through the streets while Iggy Pop's 'Lust for Life' jangled along in the background. Then it cut to a group of men playing five-aside football and then the shaven-headed man was collapsed on the floorboards of a sparse room, the voiceover announcing, "Who needs reasons when you've got heroin?"

Mickey let out a loud, "Yesss" and the three other members of the audience turned around. It was too dark to see their facial expressions, but it seemed obvious that they would be glaring at him.

The next hour and a half was like nothing Danny had ever experienced. The last film he'd seen at the cinema had been *Free Willy*. His dad had taken him and Simon and even though he'd felt like he was too old for it, he'd enjoyed Willy's leap for freedom at the end. Now, he was watching Renton disappear down a toilet in a heroin-induced high, the harrowing death of Sick Boy's baby and Begbie brutally beating a man to a pulp. Danny was overcome with the realness of the suffering unfolding in front of him and fixated by their lives, so far removed from his own, but not quite so far removed from Mickey's who was focused on how amazing those highs looked, ignoring how hideous the lows were. Mickey was inspired by Begbie's wanton violence, not put off by the destructive effect it had on his life and others.

The following day, Mickey was raving about the film, thanking Garth for letting him go, relaying all his favourite scenes. Bram tried to ask questions intended to get Mickey reflecting on the effects of the lifestyle portrayed in the film, but

Mickey batted them off, shouting, "I'm Mickey McMashup" and pounding his chest like a silverback if the questions ever pushed him in a direction he didn't want to go.

Although Mickey was full of praise for the film, it wasn't going to translate to a written review, and it was left to Danny to try and make sense of something that felt totally alien to him. He started by describing all that the characters had lost and tried to explain how the main character was really heroin, that it controlled everything about the characters' lives until they could break free.

He'd felt different, standing on the North Stand that evening. He knew the film was fiction, but it told what some people's lives were really like and perhaps, people with lives like that stood shoulder to shoulder with him on the terraces, or would addiction drive them away from everything else in their lives, drive them away from other joys like celebrating a goal amongst a mass of bodies?

Emerging from the cinema in the early hours of the morning and then walking the four miles home had left him feeling tired and disconnected from his surroundings. He'd walked past the Goldstone Ground at three o' clock in the morning, dragging a finger against the rough brick of the East Stand, peering in through the cracks at a dimly lit pitch. When he'd turned onto Old Shoreham Road and walked past the North Stand, he paused and looked at the blue wooden doors flecked with raindrops. He leant his forehead against the door and the moisture gathered and trickled down his nose and inexplicably, he gave the door a brief kiss before questioning his own sanity and walking on, past the row of shops, down past the fire station, climbing the hill past the cemetery until he was finally home.

He didn't tell Ethan or James about that moonlit romantic moment with the North Stand. He felt a little weird about it now that he was surrounded by people.

Exeter were a team within reach of Brighton that could possibly replace them at the foot of the football league and only one team plummeted to oblivion. During the first half of the season when wins were rarer than smiles on *Eastenders*, fans had accepted the substandard performances on the pitch, seeing them as a symptom of a diseased boardroom. Until the owners were removed, making a complaint about the quality of the football didn't feel like it was worthwhile. There was no point hoping that the team might actually win games because the victories would only mask the disintegration of the club. But now the team had started winning and the voices of fans had risen to a clamour, and maybe this turnaround in the form of the team was also a symptom, one that suggested that change was around the corner, that the talks that seemed to forever stumble and flounder would finally bear fruit. The fans no longer sang of relegation as an inevitability, but the demands for the board to go persisted. Not a ten minute period of a game would pass without a voice of protest tonelessly raised to be joined by hundreds and then thousands.

In amongst the anger, there was remembrance too. There were only seven more occasions when these people would stand in this spot, singing these songs.

"Johnny Crumplin, football genius," sprang forth.

Crumplin hadn't been at the club for three years, but in these last days, the fans' minds were wandering back through their memories as they watched the current team playing out the final football to be seen on this grass. Those men in blue and white were standing on the shoulders of those who had come before them. When Crumplin's genius had been celebrated, others joined, singing songs of their personal favourites and everyone, whether they'd seen the players play or not, joined in. Danny, Ethan and James had barely seen any of the names that they sung about play, but they were still heroes to them.

"One Garry Nelson, there's only one Garry Nelson…"

"He shot, he scored, it must be Peter Ward, Peter Ward, Peter Ward…"

"I'd go a million miles for one of your goals, oh Charlie…"

"No, no, no, no, no, no, no, no, no, no, no, no, no, no, Nogan…"

"Steve Foster, milord, Steve Foster…"

On and on it went, the match sweeping back and forth, the fans reminiscing, players of the past floating past like ghosts, scoring glorious goals, winning crunching tackles, saluting the North Stand after fighting for their joy.

The fans were woken from their reveries by the men of the present: Stuart Storer was surging down the right-wing, eating up the space in front of him. Delivering the ball into the box, both Craig Maskell and Ian Baird lunged for the ball, Baird getting the crucial touch and sending the ball into the back of the net. Thousands of times, the net had bulged and the fans in the North Stand had exploded and every time, it felt like the first time, an out-of-body experience, delirium contorting your limbs. James was once again pinned to the crash barrier, squealing in ecstatic pain, delighted and gasping.

Flowing football wasn't in evidence, but a gritty discipline was, Gary Hobson and Derek Allan winning every long ball that was knocked forward, Kerry Mayo scampering energetically through the midfield, sliding into challenges and thwarting danger, Denny Mundee calmly finding accurate passes under pressure. It was a performance that had rarely been seen. Desperate defending, hoping that a mixture of luck and poor finishing from the opposition might see you through had been the way, but Brighton were doing the simple things well. They didn't look like conceding and although the narrow scoreline made the final moments agonising, the victory seemed inevitable when it came.

The boys walked back to the Browns' house after the game, turning their faces away from the stinging oblique rain. With damp jeans leaving patches on the carpet, they sat gathered around Ethan's big hardback book about Brighton that detailed every season in the club's history.

"Look at this in '76-77," said Ethan. "Peter Ward scored thirty-six goals that season."

"They should have sung one for Nicky Rust," said James.

"He wasn't even playing," said Danny.

"Nicky, can I have your gloves?" said Ethan in the highest pitch he could muster.

The book was slid aside and James was dealt some friendly punches, simply because the adrenalin of a 1-0 win needed to be released.

11/02/97: Brighton 1-0 Exeter City (Baird)

15/02/97: Carlisle United 2-1 Brighton (Maskell)

22nd February 1997

Brighton & Hove Albion vs Swansea City

"I've only got two weeks left," said Mickey as Danny was trying to construct a crossword.

"How come?"

"You can only work here for six months and then they kick you out."

Danny stopped typing a clue for 'constipation' and looked at Mickey.

"What are you going to do next?"

"I don't know. Bram says I should get a skill."

"What kind of skill?"

"Like plumbing or bricklaying or something. I'm not going to work for a magazine, am I?"

Danny didn't want to confirm that it seemed unlikely that Mickey would ever be a journalist, considering he'd managed almost six months working for a magazine without actually writing an article, but he grunted affirmation that perhaps Mickey needed to think about other options.

"What do you want to do?"

"I don't know. I just want to be rich and have fun. What do you want to do?"

"I like doing this, writing articles and being a journalist. I don't know how I do that after leaving here though."

"This isn't real, is it? I mean, we don't really work for a magazine. No one would actually give me a job doing this. I don't even really do any work."

"If you did get a skill, you could probably get a lot more money."

"Yeah."

Mickey didn't sound convinced. *Sorted* offered a safe environment where failing was almost impossible, a weird sanctuary where it was both chaotic and safe. Huge mistakes like attacking a colleague were brushed over and everyone was fine about it the next day.

Bram came in and announced that there were some more free

tickets available, but before anything was decided about who would get the tickets, everyone needed to agree how they would react if they missed out. There was no need for such caution though. The tickets were to see Pulp at the Brighton Centre on Wednesday evening. Garth called them "soft-rock, spineless charlatans" - Danny was confused, thinking Garth was mixing his bands up. Mickey was only interested in "happy hardcore," music which he regularly tried to recreate with his mouth, spitting and spluttering at speed.

Danny had loved 'Common People' when it had come out the previous year. It had made him think of the kids at school strutting the corridors in dirty parkas, thinking they were Liam Gallagher. Being working class had become cool and Labour were riding that wave, but no one actually wanted the poverty. When Jarvis Cocker sang, "You'll never fail like common people, never watch your life slide out of view," Danny sang along, feeling a weird sense of pride that he did know what it was to fail, had felt like, as his school days ended, that he was sliding out of the education system and into an abyss. The blurry nothingness on the horizon had made him feel like that, but working at *Sorted* had changed that for him. Mickey, however, was still in that place, in the fog, not knowing or even really caring about his tomorrows.

With neither Garth nor Mickey wanting to go to the Pulp gig, both claiming they would prefer to do themselves an injury than attend, Danny was able to take both tickets.

When he told Ethan about the tickets, Ethan had other news. The Brighton Independent Supporters Association were hosting a meeting at the Concorde Lounge.

"Pulp probably won't come on until later in the evening," said Ethan who had been to see Radiohead the previous year and knew how gigs worked: lots of waiting around for the headline act to finally appear. "We'll be in town so we can go to both."

Danny wasn't so sure. He didn't want to miss the gig and have to confess the next morning in the *Sorted* office that he wouldn't be able to write a review. However, the meeting, now that he knew about it, felt like something he must attend, both as a Brighton fan and as a journalist.

Mr Brown drove the boys into town, dropping them off outside the blacked-out windows of the Concorde. People in Brighton shirts were milling around. Inside, it was a long narrow room with a stage at the far end. The walls were painted black and posters of gigs and club nights were plastered all over the walls. The room was buzzing with conversation between people gripping pints of lager in their hands. The boys shuffled their way through the crowd, hoping to find a seat, edging their way closer and closer to the front.

James knocked a woman's elbow, causing her pint to slop over the rim of her glass and dribble onto the floor, but they hurried on, thinking that once the meeting started, the closer to the front they were, the better.

Almost at the front, Danny heard a voice calling his name: "Danny."

He looked around to where the voice was coming from and there was Steve Gritt sat at a table just below the stage. He had the same broad smile he'd had when he opened the door to Danny at Sussex University. Danny walked over, followed by Ethan and James.

"Hello, Danny. Good to see you here. Are you going to look after me tonight? I might get some tough questions coming my way."

Danny nodded, not sure how else to respond. He had no idea how he could help Steve in this setting.

"Who are your friends?"

Danny introduced Ethan and James and Steve shook hands with the boys and then a loud shriek of feedback brought a hush to the room and the meeting started. The boys hadn't been able to find a seat and perched on top of a radiator at the edge of the room. There were lengthy descriptions of legal detail that none of the boys understood, articles, sub-sections and rules referenced that had apparently been broken and the man talking wanted to hold the board to account for these things. The meeting then seemed to veer from passionate outpourings from individuals who made broad emotive statements that got the whole room applauding and then people asking long-winded technical questions.

Steve Gritt was then announced to warm applause: "I

understand why you've all come here today. I understand that it's because you care deeply for this club and its future. I've come here today with Jeff" - he indicated his Assistant Manager who was sitting next to him - "to demonstrate that I know that this football club means everything to you. I manage the football side of things and I want to win games like you all do. Thank you for your support and for loving this club. I need you. The players need you."

The room applauded again, but then came questions. Two grey-haired women sitting at a table in the centre of the room peppered Steve and he kept telling them that he understood their point of view, understood why they were doing what they were doing, but that he was going to concentrate on the football. There were murmurs from some, but the feeling in the room was that he was a good man for putting himself in a vulnerable position by attending the meeting, that he clearly cared and that he was also in an impossible situation, at a meeting that was demanding the sacking of his employer.

Finally, the questions stopped and the final information of the evening was delivered, that all of the supporters' groups were united in wanting the same thing, that the consortium led by Dick Knight should be given full control of Brighton and Hove Albion and that they would continue to be creative in protesting against the current board until that happened.

Steve struggled to leave at the end. Everyone wanted a handshake, but as he made his way past the radiator that the boys were sitting on, he asked, "How did I do?"

"You did great, Steve," said James.

"Thanks, lads,"

Danny and Ethan fought their way back through the crowds and after saying goodbye to James, set off for the Brighton Centre at a run. They needn't have hurried though. People were still ordering pints of Snakebite, and they were able to join the keenest of fans, just four rows from the front. They hadn't even missed the support act who came and went, the crowd growing steadily, but also talking through their performance with only a few people bothering to give them applause between songs.

The lights went down and men wearing black clothes

shuffled around the stage, putting guitars on stands, rearranging the drum-kit and fiddling with amplifiers. A hush was beginning to fall across the arena with an occasional whoop of excitement after the men left the stage, leaving it shimmering in one thin spotlight. Figures emerged in the gloom, shouts from the audience growing and then the synthesiser starting pulsing, the start of *Do You Remember the First Time?* and then there was Jarvis, silhouetted by the spotlight, limbs spasming as he sang. The crowd surged forward, bodies leaping into one another. A figure passed overhead, Danny just about thwacking the trainer of the crowd-surfer to stop himself being kicked in the head. And then there was another Jarvis, two men, one an imposter, charging around the stage, two voices singing in unison as the guitar riff kicked in.

Danny and Ethan were mesmerised, glancing from one Jarvis to the other, not knowing which was the authentic frontman and as the song ended, one scuttled from the stage and the lights came up and there he was: tight jeans, a Mickey Mouse t-shirt and a smart suit jacket.

"Hello, Brighton," he said, but not emphatically, more like Badger greeting Mole late at night in *The Wind of the Willows*, curiously, inquisitively, as if he was slightly surprised to find himself in the company of others.

The songs were punctuated by anecdotes about vacuuming the house and visiting his great aunt and Danny and Ethan were transfixed throughout, loving the mosh-pits that felt like extended goal celebrations and feeling every poignant moment of the slower songs. When they played *Common People* during the encore, Danny sang every word even when he was flung to the floor by the moshing crowd, his right hand sticking to the beer-drenched floor until he was hauled to his feet by the strangers around him.

Out on the street afterwards, he was aware that he was soaking wet, sweat, much of it not his own, and sticky drinks, spilt and thrown all over him. The icy wind pinned his t-shirt to him, but after two hours throwing himself into others, the cold felt refreshing.

"That was amazing," said Ethan.

People were still pouring out of the doors of the Brighton

Centre onto the seafront, some singing, "Let's all meet up in the year, 2000…" Danny had been so jealous last summer when a group of boys from his tutor group had headed up to Knebworth to join a quarter of a million people watching Oasis. This had been minuscule in comparison, but being there seeing the music he loved performed in the flesh had been beautiful and made him feel part of something bigger than himself, not just a consumer, but someone taking part in life.

On Friday, when his dad called, Danny had felt like the gig was a huge thing to talk about and would get conversation flowing, but once he'd given the bare facts of attending a gig, there wasn't much more to say. His dad hadn't heard of Pulp, had asked what kind of music they played and Danny had said "guitar-rock," but that seemed such a broad term that it was no real description at all. Danny couldn't explain the atmosphere of the mosh-pits, the surging ecstatic feeling that had taken over him, how the lyrics, even when he didn't understand them, felt like they spoke about him - all he said was that it was really good and that he was writing an article about it.

The conversation continued as it always did, both Danny and his dad knowing that they were almost word-for-word having the same conversation they'd had for weeks. It was awkward, but strangely comforting as well.

Simon breezed through the conversations, going back to *Mariokart* as soon as he had finished speaking. It felt like his dad's absence didn't affect Simon at all after the initial week of tears. He'd settled into the phone-call routine as if that was how parenting worked. For Danny, the phone-calls were better than the months where there was no communication at all, but it wasn't really working. With every week, Danny didn't feel closer to his father, but further away, each conversation confirming that they were living separate lives and explaining the facts unemotionally on a weekly basis was in some ways, painfully futile, but it was also something that Danny clung to.

"Do you reckon Robbie Reinelt will start?" asked James as he put the finishing touches to his penis in the frost piece of art he'd created on the football pitch in Hove Park by dragging his heel through the spiky grass.

Brighton had delved into the transfer market, buying a player that had scored against them earlier in the season for Colchester United. It turned out not to be Ronny Rosenthal, but another forward with the same initials that was on Steve Gritt's radar. Ian Baird and Craig Maskell had formed a decent strike partnership, both of them scoring with some regularity, particularly at home and particularly since the arrival of Gritt, but every time either of them had been injured, Brighton had struggled. The boys had been excited by the signing of Nigerian striker, David Adekola, earlier in the season but he was released after just one game. Youngsters, Phil Andrews and Simon Fox had come into the team at times, but they had mustered a whole goal between them and always looked lightweight, a couple of years off being really ready for the physicality of men's football.

"They'll start Maskell and Baird," said Danny, "but we need another option if they get injured again."

Leaving the phallic artwork behind, the boys continued towards the ground, extolling the form of Kerry Mayo, a rare player out of the youth system thriving in the first team, and debating whether Mark Ormerod had proved himself to be superior to Nicky Rust in goal. James remained loyal to Rust, his first love, but recent clean sheets combined with meeting Ormerod at Hove Rec meant that Danny and Ethan firmly believed that Ormerod had the safer hands.

The North Stand was bustling before the game, the crowds growing with each win. Doncaster Rovers had been tumbling to within touching distance, having not won in their last six games and they were now just four points above Brighton.

The sight of Stuart Storer racing into the space behind defenders was becoming so beautifully familiar to the fans, a blue and white striped tiger lying in wait for the perfect moment to pounce and chase down his prey. Once he was in full flight, it seemed that no one could touch him and when he was released midway through the first half, the ball delivered tantalisingly into his path, he tore after it, jabbing the ball ten yards in front of him without breaking stride, knowing that he just needed to get to the edge of the box and deliver a cross. Puffing with the exertion of keeping up, Ian Baird arrived just in time to meet Storer's cross and send it beyond the keeper.

In the second half, it was Paul McDonald's turn. While Storer was all pace and power, McDonald was an artist, jinking, swerving, inviting the defender for a Latin dance lesson and when the defender floundered as he tried to match McDonald's hip motion, he was away and floating a ball into Baird's path for him to volley powerfully beyond the keeper.

Mark Ormerod came rushing off his line, getting marooned out of position and gifting Swansea a route back into the game, but Brighton reestablished their two-goal lead when a lofted high ball from Gary Hobson was chased down by Craig Maskell who finished low and powerfully past the keeper. There was an eruption of joy and relief in the crowd, Danny finding himself popped like a cork from beneath the crash barrier and celebrating in front of 'The Box' in a chasm created by fans surging forward with joy. A last-minute consolation goal was too late to give Swansea genuine hope and with Doncaster losing at Northampton, Brighton were now just one point behind them.

22/02/97: Brighton 3-2 Swansea City (Baird 2, Maskell)
01/03/97: Darlington 2-0 Brighton

4th March 1997

Brighton & Hove Albion vs Northampton Town

Mickey sat slumped across the desk, his face buried in his arms. Just a few hours remained of his time at *Sorted* and he'd spent the week veering between irritability and unhinged aggression. Garth, as always, was the victim of the aggression. There'd been nothing physical, but violent descriptions of what he would do if Garth didn't turn his music down were frequent. The arrival of the latest issue of the magazine had given Mickey and Garth the separation they both needed as Danny had joined Mickey and Garth had gone on a solo mission to shift as many magazines as he could.

Walking the streets, Mickey was transformed, the fresh air blowing the pugnacity away and he charmed the shopkeepers into accepting the magazine and seemed happy in Danny's presence.

Danny had never felt brave enough to ask Mickey what he'd been in prison for, but as they wandered the streets, Danny realised that this would be his last chance: "Mickey, what were you inside for?"

Mickey glanced towards Danny. It was a simple question, asked without judgement and Mickey accepted it.

"I was dealing drugs and this kid tried to mug me off, said he'd pay me at the end of the week and then he never turned up and I gave him a beating, put him in hospital and the next day, I was arrested and they searched my flat and found all my gear and the money I'd made. I was loaded and they took it all. I got done for drug-dealing and assaulting that little rat."

"Do you regret any of it?"

"I regret getting caught."

"Was the kid alright?"

"He looked okay in court. He shouldn't have messed with Mickey McMashup, should he?"

"Have you stopped all that... dealing?" asked Danny tentatively.

"Yeah, I'm watched now, aren't I? I've got to keep clean."

Danny didn't know what to say. He felt like he wanted to persuade Mickey that a life away from drug-dealing and violence was surely better. He understood how *Trainspotting* had appealed to Mickey, how he'd seen parts of his past magnified, taken to greater extremes, violence on a grander scale, drug-taking pushed further and Mickey had been enthralled by it all. Bram had indulged his desire to create a guide to drugs, surely with the hope that the more he researched, the more he would discover grim truths, but Mickey was blind to the downsides, a strange kind of optimist despite having gone to a youth detention centre as a sixteen-year-old and being rehabilitated during his time inside and then in his time outside, with *Sorted*.

"Thanks for telling me," Danny said.

He genuinely appreciated that Mickey trusted him. He didn't know what he'd done to earn his trust. He'd just spent time with him when Mickey had been open to that: fruit machines on the pier, occasional visits to the snooker hall, enjoying their Grubb's Burgers Christmas dinner, watching *Trainspotting* and shifting the magazine to newsagents.

The cloud of gloomy anger returned as soon as they were back in the office, chairs kicked, doors slammed and a dent punched into the toilet wall.

A few minutes before they were to break for lunch, Bram came through the door with two paper-bags bearing the sleepy, smiley face of the Grubb's Burger logo. He'd repeated their orders from Christmas and Mickey's head rose at the smell of the food and he silently accepted the gift.

"I thought your last day demanded a treat," said Bram. "I hope this has been a good place for you, Mickey. I've organised a placement for you with a friend of mine, a bricklayer. He's going to show you the basics over the next couple of weeks and if you think it's something you want to carry on with, you can sign up for a place at college to learn the trade."

Mickey didn't respond.

"There have been ups and downs," continued Bram, "but that is what life's about. Today might feel like a down, but it can be an up if you take what you've learnt here and let it help you to build a future."

Danny listened as Bram filled the awkward silence with attempts to encourage Mickey, to celebrate this moment and try and rid the office of the funereal atmosphere that Mickey was creating.

Once the burgers were finished, Mickey went back to his slumped position and the rest of the office tiptoed around him, keen for these last hours to pass in peace. When leaving time came, Mickey got up and walked out, not saying a word to anyone as they wished him the best and said goodbye.

Danny left the office a few minutes after Mickey and when he turned the corner onto St James' Street, Mickey was there, leaning against the window of the bakery.

"See you around, mate," he said and patted Danny's arm awkwardly.

"Yeah," said Danny and Mickey turned and walked off down the road, Danny thinking it unlikely that their paths would ever cross again.

That evening, Danny arrived home late from the Browns', having enjoyed being a guest for their Friday night Indian takeaway. Danny had been allowed to choose something from the menu and had gone for a Murgh Masala, excited by the idea of chicken and lamb within the same dish. It was a good choice, complimented on by Mr Brown who said he'd add it to his shortlist for when he made future choices. Danny had thought that the shortlist was a figure of speech, but Mr Brown had got a notebook out of a drawer and flicked through it, finding his list of curries and adding Danny's choice to the list.

Climbing onto the top bunk hours later with a bloated stomach, he heard a snuffling coming from the bottom bunk and paused.

"Are you okay?" he asked.

Simon didn't answer, but a stifled sob could be heard coming from beneath the blanket. Danny pulled the blanket back and Simon's bloodshot eyes and red puffy face looked back at him in the darkness, illuminated by the landing light shining through the crack in the door. Simon always demanded that a light be left on.

"What's the matter?" Danny asked.

Simon took a while to answer, shuffling up to a sitting position, his Power Rangers pyjamas riding up. He wiped his cheeks with the back of his right hand and Danny jumped to the floor and sat on the edge of the lower bunk.

"Matthew keeps punching me."

"Who's Matthew?"

"He's a big kid in my class."

"Where does he punch you?"

"On the arm." Simon rolled up his sleeve and showed his arm, revealing scattered purple bruises. "He says that if I tell anyone, he'll hit me harder."

"Why is he punching you?"

"I don't know."

"Have you told Mum?"

The tears came again. "Please don't tell her."

"Okay, okay. I won't tell her."

"What are you going to do?"

What was Danny going to do? What could he do? He had no idea how he was going to help his brother. He wanted to solve the situation, but how? He couldn't beat up a nine-year-old and he wasn't Simon's dad. He couldn't talk to the teacher for him, could he?

"Don't worry. I'll sort it," he said.

Simon reached out and clutched Danny around his waist. Danny awkwardly accepted the hug and when Simon lay back down, he tucked him in and sat on the edge of his bed wondering what he was going to do until Simon fell asleep.

Simon said nothing about it the next morning. The tears of the previous day had gone and he was back to being a carefree kid, confident that his brother's assurance that he would "sort it" was all that was needed.

Danny ran through scenarios in his head while watching Brighton's game on Ceefax, Brighton going 1-0, then 2-0 down to Darlington, a team that he was hoping would be dragged into the relegation battle. The glorious wins at home weren't being matched away from home. Steve Gritt hadn't managed a single away win and this was stalling their attempt to stay in the league, a step forward at home, a step backward away. With points to make up on their relegation rivals, they had to stop being so hopeless away from home.

On Monday, Danny decided to walk to school with Simon. He phoned the *Sorted* office and gave a vague explanation for being late on the answerphone. He couldn't just send Simon to another day of getting whacked after giving him big brotherly assurance. Danny's mum had been confused as to why Danny wanted to take on the task of walking Simon to school, but he said he needed to go that way anyway, the need being, to be his brother's rescuer.

They got to the school gate early and Danny told Simon to point Matthew out to him when he arrived. He'd decided that he was going to talk to the boy, make him aware that he knew what was happening, hoping that his presence alone would be enough to scare the bully off. He didn't know what he'd do if he was accompanied all the way to the school gate by a parent, but fortunately, like most of the children, the burly Matthew, with the build of a rugby prop, was freed from the shackles of his mother once the school was in sight.

Once Simon had pointed the boy out, he scuttled into the school to leave Danny to it. The miniature prop approached and when he got six yards from Danny, he said his name quietly, but sharply.

"Matthew!"

The boy turned to this stranger addressing him.

"I know what you're doing to my brother, Simon. It stops now," he said, trying to sound assertive and no-nonsense. He didn't want to veer into intimidation, but wanted this boy to know that what he was doing was known and to cause him to be too nervous to continue.

Matthew nodded, his lip wobbling as if he were about to break into tears. Danny walked away, doubtful that his words had achieved anything. He walked over to near where Matthew's mother was, a woman with a leopard-print fur coat. She was gathered with a group of mums, one of which Danny recognised.

"How's Matthew taking it?" he heard one of the women ask.

He came to a halt, turned his back to the women, pretending not to pay them any attention while trying to catch what they were saying.

"He's alright. It doesn't seem to bother him," responded Matthew's mum.

"I can't believe he just left you like that," said another mum.

"It's his loss," responded another.

"Fifteen years, I was with him," said Matthew's mum, "what a waste."

Danny walked on, down the lane leading away from the school, quick-marching past sluggish parents, aiming to get to the *Sorted* offices as quickly as possible.

At the end of the day, he walked through the front door to see Simon in his normal position, SNES controller in hand.

"How was your day?" he asked. "Any problems?"

"It was all fine," said Simon, distracted by the game.

"Do you want a game of *Mariokart*?"

"In a minute," Simon replied.

His words had been effective, at least for a day. It felt good that his brother was sitting there happily, steering Mario to victory.

"Robbie's got to be starting today," said James. "Baird's suspended, isn't he?"

"I love Bairdy and he just loves kicking defenders," said Ethan.

The boys walked around the side of the stadium to the club shop. James had turned thirteen during the week and he was intent on spending all £50 of his birthday money on Brighton merchandise. He selected the training top that Steve Gritt often wore on the touchline and a thin top with a black and white zigzag pattern, a club crest in the centre. To avoid having to carry his new purchases, he put both tops on over the top of the home shirt and blue Brighton sweatshirt that he was already wearing.

"Come on, Michelin Man, let's get into the ground," said Danny, jealous of and impatient with James.

The seesaw of home and away results meant that Brighton were still stuck to the foot of the table. Doncaster were again four points ahead of Brighton, but they weren't playing that evening, so a win would close the gap again to a solitary point.

The floodlights fizzed overhead, their light illuminating the pitch but casting anything beyond the ground into utter darkness. The night games had a more claustrophobic and intense atmosphere. It felt like you were in a bubble of light and that nothing else was happening in the world. The crowds were louder, the grass was greener, the blue and white shirts gleamed brighter. It felt like the dull claret of Northampton didn't stand a chance.

Robbie Reinelt was starting and he was eager to prove that he was a better option than Ronny Rosenthal, better even than Gritt's fantasy-purchase, Alan Shearer. Every pass was carefully executed and accurate, every tackle tenacious and full-blooded and every shot struck cleanly, pinging off his boot and arrowing towards the Northampton goal.

It was his head though that provided the first goal. A cross came in from Craig Maskell and he hung in the air and caressed the ball beyond the keeper, touching the ball just enough to redirect the cross goalwards. He ran to the North Stand and stood there, loving the chaos that he created as gleeful faces flowed back and forth in a sea of happiness.

In the second half, Jason Peake, who had disappointed since his £80,000 move from Rochdale, produced a rare moment of class, sending a beautiful arcing shot into the top corner from twenty-five yards out. Jimmy Case had played Peake regularly and he occasionally played an impressive pass, but he was largely anonymous in games and as Brighton got repetitively outrun in games, it was clear that Peake didn't have the tenacity that his manager had as a player. When Gritt had taken over, he had been used less and less frequently, but injuries and suspensions had given him a rare start and he had grabbed the opportunity, scoring his first goal, a glorious one.

As in the previous home game, Brighton gifted a late and inconsequential goal away with the whistle seconds away and as the fans exited, the short phrase, 'one point' was in every conversation, the gap to safety narrowed again. If they could win on Saturday, they might be off the bottom of the football league for the first time in months.

Danny walked into the darkness of his bedroom, dropped his clothes to the floor and got into bed.

"We are staying up, say, we are staying up," he whispered into the night.

04/03/97: Brighton 2-1 Northampton (Reinelt, Peake)

8th March 1997

Brighton & Hove Albion vs Leyton Orient

"You were good with Mickey," Bram said.

"Huh."

"You were good with Mickey. You were the only person that he seemed to be calm with, who he seemed to like."

"I just talked to him," said Danny.

"I think that was it," said Bram. "You accepted him, even when he did crazy things. You didn't say what he'd done was okay, didn't justify his actions, but you also didn't reject him because of those things."

Danny hadn't really thought about how he'd interacted with Mickey. He'd liked him and been, at times, a little scared of him, but with Garth living in a world of growled vocals screaming through his earphones, Mickey had been the only company since Tracey had left.

The office felt empty without Mickey, but new additions were on the way. On Wednesday, a girl called Emma started. Her tight black vest top revealed a poorly drawn tattoo of a smiley face at the top of her right boob. Her hair had been bleached months earlier and she piled it messily on top of her head. She didn't show any intention of doing any work, unwilling to even log into a computer. She just sat in the middle of the office chewing gum with loud smacks of her lips. She looked at Garth as if he were a puddle of vomit that someone had neglected to clear up and she treated Bram's suggestions that she might engage with an activity as a personal affront, but Danny managed to briefly bond with her when she said that she knew Jeff Minton, Brighton's enigmatic midfielder that promised so much, but delivered excellent performances only occasionally. Since Steve Gritt's arrival, he'd been dropped and handed in a transfer request, an act that felt like a betrayal with the problems the club was facing.

"I'll ask him for an autograph for you," she said

The next day, two more newcomers arrived - one a fourteen-year-old boy called Kyle with a bowl haircut who was going to have the day off school every Thursday to come and work in the office. The other newcomer would only last three hours, sent home when he was found snorting cocaine in the toilet.

Kyle was intent on becoming a DJ and at lunchtime, Danny accompanied him while he trawled around all the shops that sold second-hand CDs on St James' Street. Every now and then, he found one he wanted, but he had no money, so he hid the CDs at the bottom of the pile, hoping that they would go unfound until he could afford them. Each CD he wanted was a dance compilation, music that Danny had no interest in. As they tried to share their love of music with one another, they both led the other up repeated conversational cul-de-sacs, Danny having no clue who DJ Pulse or Dope Jam were and Kyle pulling a face like he'd just bitten into an anchovy-infused Snickers when Danny suggested Cast and Manic Street Preachers' albums.

Danny missed the fun that Mickey had brought to the office. Garth's constant attachment to his headphones, Emma's moody chewing and Kyle's music-obsession that allowed no space for conversation of any other kind were not entertaining and so Danny sat at his computer trying to write an article about whether aliens existed or not.

On Friday, the phone rang at its usual time. Danny walked to the television and turned down *TFI Friday* while Simon picked up the phone. Paul Merson was walking through the bar, greeting people to the Ocean Colour Scene riff. Simon chatted away happily. He'd never said anything to his dad about the punches from Matthew. Danny wondered whether it would have been different if his dad lived at home. Would Simon have gone to his dad or was this a task better suited to a big brother? The distance between Danny and Simon and their dad had made some aspects of their relationship defunct. So much of life was about being present and just didn't work as a conversation across counties. Danny couldn't even identify moments where he'd needed his dad, but he'd felt his absence, a dull ache that he sometimes dwelled on as he lay on his back on his bed and then, when he felt like the weight of the pain was too much, he'd roll over and face the wall and let the pain roll off him. Once, a tear rolled from his eye as he rolled over. He'd been unaware that his eye had slowly filled as he lay there and it surprised him when the tear had climbed the mountain of his nose and fallen onto his pillow. Eventually, he'd get up and decide whether Oasis' triumphalism or The Verve's melancholy was what he needed in that moment.

Danny remembered sitting by his dad's side in his parents' big double bed when he'd read him *Danny, the Champion of the World*. It has been the only book his dad had ever read him. The story of father and son pheasant-shooting had enthralled Danny and he'd remembered his dad telling him, after they'd read the last page, "Danny, you're my champion" and Danny had replayed that sentence over and over in his head, even when he felt childish revisiting that memory, but since his dad had gone, he'd blocked it out, forced his mind elsewhere if his mind ever strayed there. If his dad were still here, they'd be sharing life, not having to feel awkward and think about what to say; they'd just live life without realising how good it was. In his absence, awkward phone-calls were all they had. Danny knew it was better than nothing, but only marginally.

"Hi Danny, what have you been up to?"

Danny hated this broad opening question that Simon found so easy as a platform for inane wittering. He'd gone to work, gone to watch Brighton, kicked a ball around at the Rec, details that could be delivered in twenty seconds.

His dad tried, asked about the articles he was writing, asked whether Brighton were winning, asked him what his plans for the future were. He had no plans for the future, hadn't really thought that was something to think about. He was just living each day and seeing what happened, but, as he'd seen with Mickey, the position at *Sorted* was a short-term thing, something to kickstart him into doing something worthwhile instead of lying in bed most of the day and rising early once a week to collect JSA.

"Ryan's getting a bit worried about Hereford. They lost to, I think it was Exeter, last week and that was a big deal, apparently because they're down there as well."

"He doesn't need to worry. It's Doncaster we're chasing. Hopefully, we'll both be safe."

"I'll let him know. Thanks for being so good with him when he came down. He seemed to have a great time."

The conversation, as it always did, petered out and Danny's dad found an excuse to end the call, dinner being put out on the table, and the Friday routine was done, and Danny turned the volume back up on the TV as the Fun Lovin' Criminals started playing 'Scooby Snacks.'

It had gone three o' clock and the game still hadn't kicked off. Danny's chest was jammed against Barnet Bishop's back and every time the man next to him took a bite of his soggy burger, he elbowed Danny in the ribs. The match had been delayed to allow the bumper crowd to get through the turnstiles. Victories had bred hope and the turnstiles were busier than they'd been in years. Danny, Ethan and James were impatient for the game to start, having arrived an hour before kick-off. They'd watched the players warm-up, Danny and Ethan disappointed that Nicky Rust had been chosen over Mark Ormerod, but James was delighted and went running down to the front of the stand to ask, on repeat, whether Nicky might part with his gloves.

James rejoined them only when the players went back in the dressing rooms.

"Did he give you his gloves?" Ethan asked.

"No," said James grumpily.

"It's pretty harsh of him not to give you his gloves right before a football match," said Danny.

The North Stand pointed fingers towards an empty Directors' Box and ran through their anti-board repertoire, the simple, 'Sack the Board,' the melodic, 'Build a Bonfire' and the call-and-response, 'Archer Out.' There were no directors there to hear it, but the fans didn't want the board getting complacent and thinking that the fury had faded just because the team had started to win football matches.

Fans were still shuffling into place when the match kicked off and Brighton were kicking towards the North Stand in the first half, the Leyton Orient keeper ready to receive forty-five minutes of insults. It always disappointed the fans when Brighton kicked north in the first half as the North Standers wanted to suck the ball into the net in front of them during the game's denouement.

Brighton started brightly. A long kick by Rust was flicked

on in midfield and the bobbling, bouncing ball was latched onto by Craig Maskell who outpaced the defender and lifted the ball over the advancing goalkeeper and into the net. Maskell made it two, throwing himself at a Paul McDonald cross and sending the ball looping into the top corner. The larger crowd made it more of a battle to celebrate, each fan fighting for space to wildly convulse in. Five home wins in a row looked like becoming six. This didn't feel like watching a team at the foot of the league. Wins every fortnight - the home form made it feel like you were invincible, yet statistically, no one was worse.

The second half started chaotically, the ball given away repeatedly, and Leyton Orient scurried down the left wing and a low cross was prodded home. Brighton couldn't get a touch and a cross with the outside of the boot from the Orient right-winger was met by a glancing header and the ball trickled into the corner for Orient to equalise. And then the ball was bouncing across the edge of the Brighton box, the Brighton players statues as a swivelling Orient forward hit a powerful shot into the bottom corner.

The crowd exploded in anger. A win was desperately needed, perhaps lifting the Albion from the foot of the table and seemingly, the players had forgotten how to tackle, how to pass. A cacophony of swearing and incomprehensible instruction rained down on the players and somehow, they responded, Paul McDonald cutting back instead of crossing, sending the defender stuttering towards the touchline. His quick feet gave him space to send a cross to the back-post where a waiting Ian Baird stood, barely two yards from goal and all he had to do was make contact and Brighton were level again. His brow had done this countless times before and he didn't miss. 3-3.

Relief that the game was not utterly thrown away gave extra exuberance to the celebration and Danny hadn't retrieved his arms, one of which was trapped between two beer bellies, one of them exposed to the March sunshine by a tight football shirt that had ridden half way up the man's torso, when Orient kicked off, rolling the ball back to the experienced Ray Wilkins, seeing out his playing career in the fourth tier. He no longer had the legs to get around the pitch, but with the ball at his feet, he could still thread a pass through a pinprick of space, and, with seemingly no obvious player to pass to, he sent a ball arrowing towards the heart of the Brighton defence. An Orient forward let it run through his legs, fooling the Albion defence and the ball scuttled through to the penalty spot where four players, two from each team including Albion keeper, Rust, lunged for the ball. None of them got control of it and it popped free into Orient striker, Scott Mcleish's path just as Danny freed his arm by yanking it sharply so it slithered across the sweaty belly to freedom. Mcleish had the simple task of slotting the ball into the empty net and having done so, he ran to the North Stand and stood a few feet away, smiling and holding up four fingers, one for each goal Orient had scored. Brighton were going down and Mcleish was sending them to the Conference.

He turned and began a cartwheeling celebration, but the cruel snatching of a lead just seconds after Brighton had equalised, the gall of a man daring to enjoy his goal in front of the grief and anger of the fans was too much for some and over the barriers went one fan, who chased down the celebrating players, swinging a wild and inaccurate flying kick in their general direction before a luminous steward caught up and wrestled him to the ground. Over the barriers went another. He reached Wilkins first and as Wilkins raised a leg to defend himself, the balding man made a grab for his boot and dragged him to the floor. Orient players and stewards were one big scrum now and down tumbled the second man. Over the barriers went a third man, wearing a cream-coloured jacket, windmilling into the throng.

Danny watched on, amazed. Running on the pitch had been a thrill, a moment of righteous protest, but this was something very different: angry men who had lost all perspective. Thousands of players had scored goals against Brighton over the years and some had goaded the fans, but Danny had never seen anything like this before and he hated it, a sick taste in his mouth, the mindless violence making Brighton's fans look like hooligans, causing the protests of the past to be seen in a new light and feeding the narrative that brainless thugs were protesting about issues they did not understand.

The ruckus of fans, players, police and stewards took a while to clear, but eventually the game was happening again and with the atmosphere odd as if the thousands of decent fans were sharing a collective guilt for what had happened in their name, Brighton found their rhythm once again, finding space in behind the Orient defence while the opponents retreated, hoping to cling to the lead they'd gained.

Craig Maskell chased a pass into the box and just as he looked like he was going to reach the ball, he tangled with the chasing defender and tumbled, and the referee pointed to the spot.

The whistle went for Paul McDonald to take it, to snatch a point on this crazy afternoon, but as he approached, the whistle sounded again and he let his foot glide over the top of the ball and the referee brandished a red card to an argumentative Orient defender before McDonald finally dispatched the ball into the bottom corner.

Danny leapt back into the oblivion of celebration, but in the opposite direction of the bellies.

Back at the Browns' house after the game, the boys watched the news. Instead of showing the goals, the footage was of three fury-filled faces taking swipes at any Orient player they could reach. The interviews afterwards weren't about the football. Steve Gritt condemned the fans' actions and hoped that it wouldn't affect the progress that had been made. Leyton Orient Chairman, Barry Hearn was much stronger, demanding that the FA punish Brighton severely, reasoning that if this wasn't taken seriously, that there would be repeated acts of violence when fans were unhappy that a goal had gone in against them.

The news reporter announced gravely that there would be an investigation into what had happened, reminding viewers that Brighton had already had a two-point deduction for invading the pitch.

Brighton were still bottom, having matched Doncaster's draw and now, another points deduction hung over them and this one seemed almost certain. If they'd lost points for invading the pitch to protest against the board, surely, they would lose points for invading the pitch to whack Scott Mcleish.

08/03/97: Brighton 4-4 Leyton Orient (Maskell 2, Baird,

McDonald (pen))
15/03/97: Hull City 3-0 Brighton

22nd March 1997

Brighton & Hove Albion vs Cardiff City

"Mum, they've called an election," Danny called into the kitchen.

Neighbours had just ended, Lou Carpenter squabbling with Harold Bishop, an eternal struggle between the rivals for Madge's affection. *The Six O' Clock News* had followed and the first item on the agenda was the election, scheduled for May 1st.

Danny's mum walked into the front room, hands soapy. She crossed her arms and watched as Michael Heseltine and Tony Blair gave soundbites to the camera. Then, Nick Robinson stood outside Downing Street, explaining that John Major was with the Queen to officially dissolve parliament and was expected to make a statement shortly.

"Do you think Labour will win?" Danny asked.

"Surely, it's time," Danny's mum replied.

In which direction would the nation's affections swing? Would they fall into the familiar, constricting embrace of John Major or would their eyes be turned by the floppy hair of Blair?

The news rattled on about processes, campaigns and opinion polls.

"What will change if Labour win?" Danny asked.

"I hope the gap between the rich and the poor will shrink," said Danny's mum. "That's what a good Labour government should be judged on."

"How will they do that?"

"It's about who you protect and who you offer support to. There are people that are so rich that they don't need government support, but so often, the government seems to create rules and regulations that benefit the super-wealthy. They always say it's good for the economy. Then there are people that desperately need help."

"Us?"

Danny's mum paused and looked away from the TV and met Danny's eyes.

"Yes, us, but not just us and we're not the most in need, not by a long shot, but I hope Labour get in and I hope they make life better for ordinary people."

"What do you mean, you *hope* they make life better for ordinary people? Surely, they'll do that?"

"People disappoint you and powerful people have the power to disappoint the most."

Danny wondered whether his mum was talking about his dad. He wasn't a powerful man, not really, just an ordinary bloke, but he had disappointed Danny's mum and Danny. Probably Simon too, although he never showed it.

After a dinner of pepperoni pizza and chips, Danny walked over to the Browns' house. Walking up and out of the Knoll Estate onto Hangleton Road, a group of boys Danny recognised as kids from lower years at school steamed past him in a white Honda Accord, cheering and shaking their fists as they sped along the narrow roads. None of the boys were older than fifteen.

When he arrived at the Browns', he found that they had relatives visiting and Ethan came out onto the street to meet him.

"It's pretty boring in there," Ethan said. "My uncle has had too much to drink and is going on and on about the election. He loves Thatcher and he's arguing with my dad."

"Thatcher isn't even the leader of the Tories anymore," Danny said.

"I know, but he keeps saying, 'This wouldn't be happening under Maggie' and 'If Maggie were still in charge...'"

"Shall we go down to the ground?"

"Why?"

"It's something to do."

Danny and Ethan took the familiar walk towards the ground, knocking on James' bedroom window on the way. Danny asked them who they would vote for if they were old enough, but after dismissing the Liberal Democrats as the party of David Bellotti - he had briefly been an MP in the early '90s in Eastbourne - the conversation swerved, as it always did, to football. Why couldn't they just win an away game? Every weekend when Brighton played away, the boys refused to allow the failure of the past to dampen their enthusiasm and that weekend, they'd sat together in front of the Browns' TV watching Ceefax reveal a 1-0, 2-0, 3-

0 deficit against Hull, staying to watch until 'FT' revealed the game to be over.

The boys walked round to the derelict East Stand entrance, none of them suggesting that they climb in, but each of them knowing that now they'd arrived, it seemed like the obvious thing to do. Inside, they stayed in the shadows, wary of being seen by someone gazing down from a bedroom window in Goldstone Lane.

They clambered through the weeds sprouting through the concrete on the steps of the East terrace and then, onto the North Stand, sitting down in 'The Box', the place where they stood for each home match. They looked out over the pitch, dimly lit at the opposite end in front of the South Stand.

"I can't believe this will all be gone in six weeks," said Danny.

"It doesn't feel real, does it?" said Ethan.

"Do you think Nicky will give me his gloves after the last game?" asked James.

James was given a gentle shove by Ethan and he swayed away before bouncing back. They sat in silence, the gentle hum of traffic from the Old Shoreham Road in the background. Minutes passed, beauty and sadness dancing in the night air.

They looked out onto the pitch, a place where glory and anguish had walked hand in hand for the Seagulls. Brighton had played their first game on this turf back in 1902, defeating Southampton Wanderers 7-1 in their first ever match. Eight years later, Charles Webb had led the team to the Southern League title and then the Charity Shield: for the only time in Brighton's history, they were the best team in the land. For decades, fans flocked to watch men in blue and white kick heavy leather balls every fortnight until the Great War. A 1-0 victory against Crystal Palace was the last game to be played at the ground with players from both teams swapping football shirts for army uniforms soon after. Football returned when peace returned, but many players never did.

Years in the wilderness of the lower leagues were perhaps coming to an end when Brian Clough took the reins in 1973 after the ill-fated forty-four days at Leeds, but Clough without Taylor simply didn't work, an 8-2 defeat at home to Bristol Rovers encapsulating the forgotten chunk of his career. By the late '70s, the good times truly had come though, coinciding with Alan Mullery and Terry Venables' fall-out, birthing a rivalry with Crystal Palace. A game at the Goldstone was halted repeatedly as smoke bombs were launched from the crowd. By the end of the decade, the Seagulls and the Eagles had climbed into the top flight. Brighton did the double over European champions, Nottingham Forest in their first season and lasted four years at the top table, reaching the FA Cup final in 1983, the year they got relegated, the last Division 1 game at the Goldstone, a depressing 1-0 defeat to Manchester City.

In 1991, Dean Wilkins curled in a free-kick in the last minute in front of a delirious Goldstone, catapulting Brighton into the play-offs in a bid to return and if they had managed to dispatch Notts County at Wembley that day, their fate just six years later would surely have looked so different, but they lost 3-1 and had quickly tumbled through the divisions. So much had happened at the Goldstone, so much joy, so much sadness and the end was nigh.

"What's that?" asked James.

A fox had darted onto the pitch. It ran straight into the centre circle and sat motionless, silhouetted with the lights from the South Stand behind it. It seemed to be staring straight at the boys, but they couldn't see its eyes.

"What's it doing?" asked Ethan.

"This feels weird," said Danny.

The fox's ears twitched and then it darted off, disappearing under an advertising hoarding for Travis Perkins. The fox's departure felt like a signal for the boys to leave too. They reached up for the blue crash barriers and pulled themselves to their feet and made their way through the revolving metal gates which allowed an exit but not an entrance.

The following day, Bram greeted Danny with, "You know what your next article's going to be about."

Danny looked puzzled for a moment, the fox staring through the gloom still in his head; surely, Bram didn't know about his late-night excursion or want an article about Britain's wildlife and its relationship with football grounds, but then Danny realised that he was talking about the election-announcement.

"Politicians make politics so foggy, hiding their intentions with complicated words and deliberate distraction. People need something simple and clear, so they know what these parties really stand for," said Bram. "What d'you reckon? Can you write something like that?"

Danny took on the task, but quickly got distracted from understanding policies, instead looking at the celebrities backing each party. Labour had Ross Kemp and Alex Ferguson while Ginger Spice, Geri Halliwell had claimed that Margaret Thatcher was her hero, saying that Maggie was the first Spice Girl. Geri had grabbed centre stage at the Brit Awards the previous month with her Union Jack dress. John Major's sober screeds seemed as far away from Geri's pouting bravado as it was possible to be.

By lunch-time, he had a page of scribbled notes, with no ideas on how to form them into something worthwhile. He took his bag of chips to the seafront, taking the same route he had taken with Mickey the day he'd seen him pour his money fruitlessly into the fruit machines. Years earlier, he'd ventured onto the Palace Pier for the first time with his dad. He'd been given £2 to spend and had turned it all into 10ps, thinking that he could multiply his money by sending his money sliding into the machines loaded with 10ps ready to fall. He'd vowed that once he got to £3, he would then use the money to have three attempts on *Street Fighter 2*, but, like Mickey, his confidence in his ability to make a profit was misplaced and after feeding his cash into the machine, he'd walked away frustrated. His dad had given him one more pound and told him to spend it on a game he'd enjoy and he spent it on one solitary duel on *Street Fighter 2*, choosing to be Chun-li, never once managing a spinning-bird kick and getting quickly defeated by Blanka.

As he walked past the entrance to the pier, the smell of the doughnuts was both beautiful and financially elusive, Danny's money having to be carefully managed so that he could attend the Cardiff game on the Saturday.

Danny walked on and then sat on the stones. He watched the grey water drag the pebbles up the beach with a crackle before tumbling them forth again. Some small children with wellies were chasing the retreating water, then running screaming as it chased them back up the beach. A fat seagull chick stood ten yards from him, eyeing his chips and waiting for a moment's inattention. It took flight when Danny clambered to his feet and scrunched up the greasy paper.

Walking back up onto the promenade, Danny paused to allow a man to jog onwards without breaking stride, but the man stopped as he reached him.

"Danny!" exclaimed the man.

Danny hadn't properly taken in the man, but when he looked at his face, he realised it was Steve Gritt.

"Danny, how are you doing?" asked Steve.

"I'm, er, I'm okay," he said.

"I'd love to see the article you wrote."

"Oh. I could get you a copy."

"Yes, that would be great. If you drop it into the ticket office, they'll get it to me. Are you coming on Saturday?"

"Yes. I'll bring it then."

"Good lad. I'll see you on Saturday. If you chant for a wave, I'll send one your way," and he was off, running along the promenade.

Danny walked back to the office, unable to keep the smile off his face. Just to be remembered felt amazing. When he got to the office, he got a magazine from a huge pile and put it into a brown envelope. He wrote a brief note, saying he hoped that he enjoyed the article and then wrote Steve's name on the envelope.

On Saturday, he got to the ground with Ethan and James an hour earlier than usual to complete the one-minute task of delivering the magazine to the ticket office. He hoped that the woman working behind the desk realised the close connection that he obviously had with the manager. It was so early that the turnstiles weren't even open yet and the boys sat on a wall, watching the other early arrivals mill around: programme and fanzine sellers, officials in suits and smatterings of Cardiff fans.

The boys were the first through the North Stand turnstiles and onto the terrace, and they sat on the steps that looked out on to the empty turf, waiting for the goalkeepers to warm up. James thought it a perfect opportunity to try and gain Nicky Rust's gloves, so when Mark Ormerod emerged to warm up, Danny and Ethan laughed while James sulked, calling it a "stupid decision that would get us relegated."

Seeing the ground gradually fill felt like such a satisfying experience to Danny, the grey concrete disappearing beneath the swathes of people, the blue and white seats of the South Stand disappearing and once again, other than the abandoned North-east terracing, the ground was full, fans gathering in numbers to witness the accelerating death throes of the Goldstone Ground.

Doncaster had beaten Hereford the previous evening and a flurry of good results had seen them climb seven points away from Brighton and above Hereford, Ryan's team slipping closer to the drop zone. Meanwhile, Hartlepool hadn't won since their 5-0 humbling at the Goldstone and they were now the team closest to Brighton, five points above the Albion. A win today and Hartlepool and Hereford would feel Brighton's salty seaside breath on the back of their necks.

The fear of faltering was tangible in the air, a desperation for success causing frustration at misplaced passes, the groans of impatience, high-pitched and fraught. But relief came, a Cardiff defender wrestled Ian Baird off the ball with too much aggression and the referee pointed to the spot and Paul McDonald showed composure that none of the crowd possessed, hitting the ball hard and low into the bottom corner.

And then Stuart Storer was off, racing into the space, the refrain of the season, seats in the expensive stands clacking as expectation propelled people off their seats and the North Stand roared its appreciation as he raced after the ball while defenders seemed to trudge through sludge. Storer's pace always bought him space and time, and with this freedom, he drilled the ball across the six-yard box and the sliding Ian Baird connected, knocking the ball in and fans who hadn't even realised that they had been holding their breath, exhaled and cavorted extravagantly.

As the fans exited, quick sums were being done. Hartlepool had lost and the gap was down to two points, those two points that had been docked by the FA. Equations and permutations were interrupted as the boys emerged from the North Stand by a sea of Cardiff fans turning the corner at the top of Goldstone Lane and onto the Old Shoreham Road. Police officers scuttled between the aggressive horde of Cardiff fans and the exiting Brighton fans from the North Stand.

Danny, Ethan and James hurried across the road and onto the safe grass of Hove Park, but most stood their ground, feeling the threat and choosing to stand and fight instead of a seagull's flight. When the boys turned, a ten-foot gap, a no man's land had formed with police, but too few of them, performing the charade of holding back men who wanted the appearance of tough men up for fight, but had no desire to actually exchange punches with a stranger. Not everyone was there simply to maintain the pretence; some wanted to deal with the pain of their lives by inflicting pain on another. The busted nose of a Cardiff fan would provide a cathartic thrill that would last until the darkness of night descended. Those with a thirst for violence sensed the opportunity and charged forward and for a brief moment, wild fists swung and the fluorescent coats of the police swam into the crashing waves, swinging batons and hauling men apart.

Danny's heart thumped, feeling like it wanted to escape his ribcage. He didn't want to see any of this, wanted to look away, walk away, but his eyes were transfixed and his feet static. Ethan and James were in the same state of paralysed absorption.

Sirens blared and reinforcements had arrived and as the police tumbled out of vans, men backed away, ambled around as if none of this had anything to do with them and what moments ago had been a scene of violence and tension was a miraculous calm, men switching from machismo to nonchalant disinterest, playing the role demanded of them by their own crazed logic.

Danny realised that his leg was shaking. He'd always hated violence, feeling his stomach constrict when it approached. At school, kids had run to watch as boys slugged at each other or girls tore at each other's faces, but Danny always walked away, shaken by the thought of what was happening in the middle of the crowd. Once, he'd been the first on the scene of a fight and seen a boy's nose erupt, blood squirting into the air and those three seconds had replayed in his head thousands of times, the familiar squirming in his stomach accompanying each time.

The clashes between the Cardiff and Brighton fans had been

concealed by a mass of bodies and even though Danny had watched on, he had seen nothing but arms swinging and bodies squashed against one another.

The boys turned and walked away, Danny and Ethan silent, their emotions overpowering their ability to speak.

Eventually, James broke the silence: "Nicky would have kept a clean sheet too."

22/03/97: Brighton 2-0 Cardiff City (McDonald (pen), Baird)
29/03/97: Chester City 2-1 Brighton (Minton)

1st April 1997

Brighton & Hove Albion vs Barnet

"Danny, I'd love to see you again. Do you think you're ready for that?"

The conversation had been going the same awkward direction it always did, Danny fumbling to extend his answers, but finding his mouth empty, sentences starting but with no real idea how they would end. His dad's question had not caught him completely off-guard. Hereford had continued to stutter, drawing their previous three games and the possibility that Brighton's final-day trip to Hereford could be crucial seemed increasingly likely, and if it was, Danny had to be there and that meant being in the city that his dad lived in.

"Next month, Brighton are playing Hereford. I'd like to come up for that. Maybe, I could see you then."

Danny uttered the words, thinking only of being there at the climax of the season, but as the words left his mouth, he realised the enormity of them. It had been over a year since he'd seen his dad and now Steve Gritt was taking him through the North Wessex Downs to his dad's door.

"When is the game?"

"May, the third," Danny replied.

Danny could hear scrabbling down the phone-line, before his dad replied, "Yes, that will work."

As simple as that - football had provided a pretext and this event, that made Danny's stomach feel like it was grinding rocks, was happening. Brighton just needed to make it worthwhile. He didn't know if he could face travelling to Hereford, knowing that Brighton were already relegated. If that happened, he'd have to create an excuse.

Danny visited the library on Monday morning after Bram had told him that the political parties had published manifestos and that they would have copies in the library. He sat at a huge wooden table with three hefty documents, one for the Conservative Party, one for Labour and one for the Liberal

Democrats. He scribbled phrases down as he flicked through the pages, but much of it was bewildering, every idea sounding like a good one. He struggled to find the differences between what they claimed to want to do, and he distrusted whether the words on the pages meant what they claimed.

When he got back to the office, Bram said, "The important thing is what they don't say, not what they do say," but Danny had no idea how to read something, trying to figure out what it didn't say.

After lunch, Bram called Danny into the small office where they'd first met.

"Danny, we need to talk about what's next for you. You've done so well, but you're getting close to the end of your time here. You're always welcome to write articles for *Sorted*, but we need to think about the next step. Have you got any ideas about what you want to do next?"

"I'd like to carry on with journalism."

"I'm so pleased, Danny. As you can probably tell, not everyone here decides to pursue journalism. Do you know how to take what you've done here further?"

"Not really."

"You write really great articles, but journalists need training and if you're serious about this, you need to look at college courses. I've got prospectuses for the colleges in Brighton. You should have a look through them and see which courses have links to journalism."

Bram went to a shelf and pulled down a bunch of prospectuses and gave them to Danny. He'd hated the idea of going back to education, but that was when it was painful and pointless. Doing a course that might lead somewhere, might give him the opportunity to do what he loved and earn a proper wage felt exciting and purposeful.

"Bram, I have a favour to ask," Danny said.

"Go on."

"On Monday, the tickets for the last ever game at the Goldstone go on sale and you have to turn up at the ground in person for tickets. I reckon that I'll probably have to queue for a while. Is it okay to have some time off that morning?"

"Danny, I really appreciate that you've asked and not just

done what a lot of people would have done and phoned in sick. Of course you can go. Oh, and there's a film I think you'll enjoy reviewing. It's called *Fever Pitch*."

On Monday morning, Danny, Ethan and James were in the queue an hour before the ticket office opened and it still stretched all the way up Newtown Road. Bleary-eyed fans, a few clutching cans of Red Bull, were waiting in an orderly line. Ethan and James had their school uniforms on under their coats and had needed to do a lot of negotiation with their parents to convince them to let them miss the beginning of the day. The rain started to drizzle down and Ethan and James pulled their hoods up, but Danny only had a thin orange Adidas tracksuit top which was rapidly absorbing the rain and beginning to cling to his body.

At nine o' clock, the queue began to inch forward. Ethan and James were happy with the sluggishness of the queue - the longer the wait, the more of school they would miss. Danny would have felt exactly the same a year ago, every extra minute in bed clung to, every opportunity for procrastination taken, but now, he wanted to get on with his day. Last night's news on TV had been all about sleaze, a broad term that seemed to be sticking to the Tories. Danny wanted to get his head around what this meant for his article. The news had talked about 'cash for questions' before showing footage from the last Prime Minister's Question Time, a cacophony of jeering and insults traded back and forth. The whole conversation seemed so childish, a playground argument where two angry toddlers were accusing each other of the same thing. Danny wanted to know what these questions were and who was paying for them to be asked, but it seemed like the closing of parliament meant that the investigation had to be halted with ten MPs going forward into the election without the public knowing whether they were guilty or not. It seemed unlikely that these Tory candidates were going to be trusted by their constituencies.

The boys had taken gradual pigeon-steps forward every minute or so and when they were in the shadow of the West Stand, one of the windows opened and the queue turned to look up to see who would emerge. The first thought was that David Bellotti would poke his head through the gap to face derision, but the head that emerged was a loved one: Steve Gritt. His brief appearance was met with cheers and he responded with a warm wave. Danny wondered whether he'd read his article yet.

Finally, they were inside the Ticket Office - they knew that they would be able to get tickets, but the fear was that the North Stand might sell out, that they might have to find a new home for this last game, but their early arrival had ensured that they would be in their usual place for the last ever game. With the square tickets in their hands, the end felt so much closer.

With neither Emma, Garth or Kyle showing any interest in a midnight showing of *Fever Pitch*, Danny took Ethan along and this time, Ethan following Danny's lead when he asked for a can of Foster's from the tiny bar as they waited to be invited into the theatre.

The film started with a scene in a restaurant, a father with two children - a boy and a girl - having an intensely awkward conversation, the children unable to respond with more than a single-word response to their father's questions. Danny immediately thought of his Friday night phone-calls and the upcoming visit to Hereford. Was his dad going to try and take him to a restaurant and try and keep a conversation going? The longest conversation between them had been six minutes, fourteen seconds. The idea of actually spending time with his dad for a prolonged period filled him with dread.

The film then jumped forward, telling the story of Arsenal-obsessed English teacher, Paul. The opening scene had been him as a child and his dad had found football to be a language that they could understand, a platform for a relationship between a boy and a departed dad. The film jumped between the man's love life and Arsenal's attempts to win the First Division after going eighteen years without topping the table. For both Danny and Ethan, the relationship parts of the film dragged, both boys eager for the film to get back to the football: life was like that sometimes.

Eighty minutes into the film, the climactic Liverpool versus Arsenal title decider began, a game which Arsenal needed to win by two goals to win the league, the film flitting from footage of the match to Paul's pessimism. The way the fixtures had fallen that season had been perfect, the two title-contenders facing each other with everything at stake. So many seasons fizzled out with one team marching to an emphatic victory and in the final few weeks, many results didn't seem to matter at all, but in 1989, the fixture computer had provided a delicious scenario.

Danny remembered watching this game at his granny's house in Devon. He preferred the red of Liverpool to the yellow of Arsenal and had chosen the reds as the team he wanted to lift the trophy, but if the match had been reversed and Arsenal had been the home side in red, his allegiance would have switched. The film turned you into an Arsenal fan while within the dreamlike confines of the cinema. Alan Smith headed Arsenal into a 1-0 lead and then, in the last moment of the game, Michael Thomas broke through the Liverpool defence and lifted the ball over Bruce Grobbelaar. As the film replayed the goal eight years on, Danny felt a rush of adrenalin and a shiver as the hairs on the back of his neck stood on end. Thomas' celebration was a gloriously uncontrolled one; at one point, he seemed to have flipped himself up off the ground with his head.

"Maybe our season will end like that," said Ethan as they walked out of the cinema.

Liverpool and Arsenal battling it out at the top of the football league could be mirrored by Brighton and Hereford battling it out at the foot of the football league if results went that way.

This possibility of Brighton taking it to the final day was made more likely on Friday when the FA made the surprising announcement that Brighton would not face any punishment for the pitch invasion and attack of Leyton Orient players. A further points deduction had seemed like a certainty, Brighton fans believing that the FA cared nothing for clubs in the lower leagues, demonstrated by their lack of action in the mismanagement of the club. Here, however, the FA had given them a reprieve, a chance of survival if they could keep the results coming, but the results continued to disappoint away from home, yet another defeat, this time, 2-1 to Chester City the next day, Danny, Ethan and James watching on Ceefax. Hartlepool had finally ended their winless streak, winning 1-0 and Hereford had drawn 0-0 with Fulham. The gap that had narrowed by the weeks was widening again.

A win on Tuesday was essential, the last night-game at the Goldstone, the last opportunity for the otherworldly atmosphere that the floodlights created.

Danny had gone straight from the *Sorted* offices to the Browns' house where Mrs Brown had created a beef casserole with dumplings for all three boys as a pre-match meal.

"There is nothing better than a night game," said Ethan as he used the last dumpling to mop up the remaining juices on his plate.

After dinner, the boys slowly got ready for battle, scarves looped once around the neck and tucked neatly into tracksuit tops, hats pulled snugly onto heads. Ethan was in his dad's 1983 beanie hat; James had gone for a blue and white bobble hat while Danny had noticed that the toilet roll cover that his granny had knitted was a perfect Brighton hat. It had a chaotic blue and white pattern and on the top was a crocheted seagull. It was extremely tight, his head substantially wider than a toilet roll, but with a few sharp yanks, it passed as a bespoke hat, even if his nan had made it without even thinking about how its colour scheme and bird-choice matched Brighton and Hove Albion.

The boys walked through the darkness of Hove Park, the floodlights bright and welcoming on the horizon. Shining inwards onto the pitch, everything around the stadium was in darkness and the boys found that they strayed from the footpath and onto the grass, only realising when their feet squelched in the mud.

The fans had so much to carry: anxiety over potential relegation, anger at the board, encouragement for the players who seemed to be drinking the fervour of the terraces and turning it into incredible performances. It made the atmosphere both electric and confusing as a roar of encouragement was followed by a bellow of protest and then tension hung like a cloud in the air until encouragement or anger blew it away, but only until the end of the song.

Stuart Storer, the man who was so desperately needed to stretch the Barnet defence, leapt into action just before half-time when, after several failed attempts, he was finally let loose, racing towards the North Stand like a lover towards an embrace. You could almost hear the thudding of his feet as he galloped across the green, cutting the ball back across the face of goal when he approached the touchline. The ball eluded the goalkeeper, launching himself fruitlessly towards the fizzing ball. Across the face of the goal the ball went and at the back post, there was Ian Baird, off balance, puffing, and he just threw his whole body forward, bringing his chest crashing into the ball and sending it and himself into the net and the crowd exploded.

Barnet kicked towards the North Stand in the second half and the anxiety cloud hovered above, but every attack was repelled, every cross headed to safety and when a Barnet player was shown a red card for crunching through Jeff Minton, the cloud shrunk and Brighton got their foot on the ball and passed their way to the end of the match. Hartlepool had lost and Hereford had drawn and the gap had closed up again, both teams within two points.

01/04/97: Brighton 1-0 Barnet (Baird)
05/04/97: Scunthorpe United 1-0 Brighton

12th April 1997

Brighton & Hove Albion vs Wigan Athletic

On Saturday, Danny, Ethan and James were once again on the Browns' sofa munching nervously on Wotsits as the results scrolled through. They knew the narrative, knew that away matches only ended one way. Brighton lost 1-0 at Scunthorpe while Hartlepool and Hereford were finding form at exactly the right time, both recording wins. The gap between Brighton and the Hs was now five points and only four games remained. Brighton were on their way to being relegated, and in fury, Ethan threw his remote control out through the sliding glass doors; it spun in the air before landing with a plop in the fish pond. The boys had watched Brighton pick up twenty-three points from twenty-seven at home since Steve Gritt's arrival. It had felt like they were watching world-beaters - "Just like watching Brazil" the fans sang - yet still, they were rooted to the foot of the league, the trapdoor of non-league beckoning them down into its murky depths.

Every day, *The Argus* seemed to deliver the same news about the potential takeover: talks were stalling. Dick Knight wanted sole control and Bill Archer wasn't budging. If the club remained in the hands of Archer and Bellotti, no one believed the club would last much longer, disappearing off to Gillingham to slowly disintegrate and never return. There were reasons to hope though - Knight's continued efforts to get his foot in the door seemed to go hand in hand with the team's performances; the home wins felt like goals for Knight, his bald head rising above Archer's flailing glove to nod into an empty net, but the away losses felt like equalisers for Archer - Bellotti supplying an angled pass for Archer to scramble the ball in at the far post. Negotiations between these middle-aged men were the key to Brighton's future.

On Monday, Danny suggested to Bram that he go onto the streets of Brighton to interview teenagers about what they thought about the upcoming election for his article. He was frustrated with the waffle of political manifestos and politicians' hollow soundbites delivered to journalists. He wanted some normal voices, so he took his Dictaphone and walked down into town and into the North Laines' narrow streets, packed with unusual shops. Danny looked longingly into shop windows, wishing he had the money to buy the brown corduroy flairs, the customised orange and green Reebok classics and the six-foot poster of Oasis that gazed back at him.

There were plenty of people milling around, but approaching them and asking them to talk about politics felt weird, somehow invasive, and Danny feared their reactions. He plucked up the courage and started to approach individuals who looked bored and seemed to just be waiting around. Most said that they didn't want to talk, but some were happy to be asked questions. People seemed to be split between distrusting all politicians and thinking that nothing any old bloke in a suit said would make any difference to their lives, and those that hoped for change, hoped that Blair's Labour would make life fairer for people. Not one person supported the Tories, but one lone voice said that he'd vote for the Referendum Party if he was old enough, that he thought that people should be allowed to vote on individual issues and have a voice. Danny hadn't really considered the Referendum Party. There was a bloke up the road from him who had covered his mobility scooter in flags and stickers in support of them, but the party seemed like an obscure irrelevance, so Danny was surprised that they were the only party other than Labour that anyone spoke of positively.

He'd meandered his way through the Laines and was almost beyond the shops when a voice called out shrilly, *"Big Issue."*

Danny looked towards the voice to see a girl of about his age with a shaven head, a long flowery dress and a leather jacket.

"Tracey?"

The girl looked at Danny with dawning recognition and then replied, "Danny, what are you doing here?" as if walking through the city he lived in was an unusual place to be.

"I'm... I'm still working at *Sorted* and I'm doing some interviews with people about the election? How are you?" he asked.

It felt like the wrong question to ask someone who was

selling the *Big Issue* on the street. The last time he'd seen her had been when she'd walked out of the *Sorted* office, the violence between Mickey and her housemate's boyfriend creating an atmosphere that she could no longer abide. In the few months since her departure, her look had changed from teenage conformity to punk chaos.

"Yeah, I'm good," said Tracey.

It was difficult to believe that Tracey was simply 'good,' that life had been on an upward trajectory since she'd left *Sorted*. Danny knew nothing of Tracey's life, how she'd ended up in a safe house, and now, how she'd ended up selling *The Big Issue*. He saw the scars on her scalp and felt miserable about how she must have suffered.

"Can I buy a *Big Issue*?" Danny asked. He wanted to support her, wanted to show that he cared.

"You don't have to."

"No, it's okay. I want to. How much are they?"

"80p."

Danny opened his wallet and took out a pound coin and handed it over.

"Don't worry about the change."

She put a damp magazine in his hands. On the front cover, the rapper, Tricky looked out at him. On the back cover was an advert for the Supergrass album that had been released that day, *In it for the Money*, an album Danny desperately wanted, but he'd just halved his lunch money by handing a pound over to Tracey. *In it for the Money* was going to have to wait.

Danny held the magazine and searched for something else to say. He didn't feel like he could ask Tracey about her life, didn't want to talk about *Sorted* and remind her of the way it had ended for her.

"Are you interested in the election?" he asked. "Will you be old enough to vote?"

"What election?" Tracey asked.

"Next month, there's a general election. I'm asking young people about it so I can write an article about it."

"Why would I care about that?" Tracey asked.

Danny looked at her. Would a change in the government make any difference to Tracey? Would her suffering decrease?

"I don't know," said Danny.

A silence lingered while people bustled around them. Danny searched again for words, but nothing came and all he could think of was, "Bye, Tracey," and he walked away, hearing her pleading, "*Big Issue*" at people who pretended she didn't exist.

Danny walked on and saw a tower block rising in front of him. As he got closer, he read a sign saying, 'Brighton College of Technology' and he remembered that this was one of the places Bram had given him a prospectus for. He'd flicked through it and circled a course titled, 'National Diploma in Media with Journalism.' He arched his head backwards and gazed up, the bricks climbing high into the sky. Students came in and out of the doors and Danny imagined himself walking through those doors each day. It didn't look or feel like a school, students in baggy flairs or tracksuits with poppers or tight leather trousers walking in groups, laughing and chatting. This didn't seem to be a place of relentless cruelty. A man with a huge grey beard swaggered out and climbed onto the back of a motorbike, squashed his beard inside a helmet and roared down the road.

Back at the office, Bram handed him a card, saying that it had been delivered through his letterbox the previous day. It was a pledge card, detailing Labour's five election pledges. Danny read through the bullet points that promised smaller class sizes for infant school students, the cutting of NHS waiting lists, no rise in income tax, reduced unemployment, and fast-track punishment for young offenders. The first four sounded like obviously positive things, but Danny wondered what the last pledge would mean for people like Mickey. Fast-track punishment sounded good when it was a stranger you didn't know, but it felt brutal and thoughtless when Danny considered Mickey.

Danny sat down and tried to gather together what he had: the mixture of indifference and engagement of the young people Danny had spoken to in the Laines, Labour's pledges and how they affected young offenders and whether any of this was relevant to the poorest in society, the homeless, Tracey. He wanted to get this article finished so that he could get on with his review of *Fever Pitch*.

On Friday night, plans for Danny's visit to Hereford made the conversation with his dad easier: what he wanted to eat, what he needed to bring replacing the litany of questions that normally struggled to fill an amount of time that didn't feel inappropriately short. Danny had been tempted to find an excuse to cancel the trip, believing that survival was going to be too much for Brighton and seeing his dad was going to be too much for him, but a morsel of hope remained for both. Brighton might just stay up and seeing his dad again might just be okay. Okay was where his optimism peaked.

The next day, Danny, Ethan and James were back in 'The Box', back on the North Stand. The crowd size had more than doubled since the start of the season, the hope that glimmered within Danny returning to fans across the town. The stands were packed again for the visit of Wigan and like the game before and the game before that and the game before that, a win felt absolutely essential. Anything less felt like guaranteeing relegation and this time, they were facing the league leaders. Promotion already seemed assured for them, but the league title was still being hotly contested with Fulham and Carlisle.

Barnet Bishop seemed apoplectic with the rest of the fans for failing to travel to Scunthorpe, delivering his mantra, "If you all went to Scunthorpe, all went to Scunthorpe, all went to Scunthorpe, clap your hands," on his own while eyeballing everyone around, spitting the first syllable of Scunthorpe and then clapping directly into people's faces as a demonstration of his loyalty and their betrayal to the cause by failing to make the journey. Danny dared to whisper to Ethan that he wished he'd stayed in Scunthorpe.

In the first half, Wigan showed why they were the team on top of the pile, the Spanish pair, Roberto Martinez and Isidro Diaz creating neat passing patterns, bamboozling the Brighton midfield as Kerry Mayo scampered back and forth like a terrier, never quite arriving in time to nick the ball, but as Wigan poured forward, the Brighton defence stood firm, Mark Morris, a colossus, throwing himself into challenges, climbing higher than the Wigan strikers to head clear. Wigan's Graeme Jones had already scored twenty-nine goals including the winner when Brighton had lost away, but Morris was an impenetrable wall.

In the second half, Brighton started to exert a little bit of pressure, mainly through long hopeful balls forward. Danny looked high into the sky repeatedly to see the ball hanging there momentarily at its highest point before sailing back down into a jostling mass of players. Time and again, the ball pinged chaotically away from danger, but finally, one of Mark Ormerod's punts upfield evaded the players who were more intent on each other than the ball. With the ball squirming to freedom, it was nudged out onto the left wing where Kerry Mayo was waiting. He swung the ball into the box and Craig Maskell connected, sending a header rocketing into the top corner.

The crowd contorted in relief, exhilaration coursing through every body, the tension of an hour transformed into an explosion of joy.

"1-0 to the Albion…"

It was all that was needed, a single goal bringing a precious three points if they could keep it solid at the back. It was back to the Marks, Morris the warrior, getting up to fight time and time again, and Ormerod, reaching for crosses and blocking shots with fingers, legs, a thigh. In front of the North Stand, the players repelled the opposition and the fans roared every moment, a toe diverting the ball to safety feeling like it was all that mattered in the world.

Football gives you that: a world within a world, a world that doesn't matter and means everything, a place where the pain of life fades for ninety minutes as the world shrinks to a rectangle of grass where Mark Ormerod's fingertips and Craig Maskell's forehead decide whether misery or joy will define eight-thousand people's existence. Then the whistle goes and you march or trudge back onto the street where the world you put on pause restarts.

Mr Brown had bought a new remote control and when Ethan had promised that he wouldn't throw it into the fishpond if he didn't like the results, he typed in page 306 and the page scrolled through to reveal that Hartlepool had lost, and Hereford had drawn. Brighton's 1-0 win meant that they were both back within reach.

12/04/97: Brighton 1-0 Wigan (Maskell)
19/04/97: Cambridge United 1-1 Brighton (Reinelt)

Brighton & Hove Albion vs Doncaster Rovers

"What do you think about this?" Danny asked.

He pointed to the National Diploma he'd circled in Brighton College of Technology's prospectus.

Bram picked it up and took his time reading through the details.

"It sounds great, Danny. Are you going to apply?"

"I think so. The only thing is, you're meant to have five GCSEs and I've only got three."

"You've got loads of experience with journalism working here. If you make that clear on your application form, maybe include some of your articles, I reckon they'd be a fool to turn you down. Listen, why don't you apply and see what happens. If you get in, you know you've got a really great option for next year if you want to take it."

"Okay."

"Let's photocopy the application form and then, you can have a go at it. I'll have a look at it with you once it's complete."

Danny had been delaying taking action, happy at *Sorted*, not wanting to commit to the next step, but he knew he only had a few weeks left and Bram's words propelled him into action. By lunchtime, he'd completed a second draft of the form with Bram and with encouragement, was on his way to the college to hand it in.

He walked back past the spot where he'd seen Tracey the week before, but she wasn't there. He didn't want to acknowledge the fact that he felt relieved. He hadn't wanted another conversation, but he wouldn't have ignored her had she been there. He wondered whether going to the college would mean that passing her would be a regular routine, an uncomfortable moment where the directions their lives had gone in since leaving *Sorted* was too abundantly obvious. He thought about Mickey too and feared that without the stability of *Sorted*, he may not be making the wisest of life choices.

Danny walked into the foyer of the college and took the

envelope with the application form to the desk and handed it over. It was in, delivered, an effort to grasp at the future. He'd never done that before, just let the days churn on and bring what they would bring, little hope that life would bring anything good, but now, with Bram's prompting, he was living life rather than simply existing.

Back at the office, he started to write his review of *Fever Pitch*, trying to capture the thrill of Michael Thomas' dramatic goal in the opening sentence.

On Saturday, Danny, Ethan and James were back to watching Ceefax roll through its pages, desperate for scores to shift in their favour. Brighton's point, gained through a 1-1 draw at Cambridge United kept hope alive. Hartlepool had beaten Darlington to pull away, but Hereford were held at home to Torquay and three points separated the sides with two games to play. If Brighton could win both, they would stay up; the trip to Hereford was looking increasingly meaningful.

Every day, a pronouncement from John Major or Tony Blair was grabbing the headlines. Major seemed intent on waffling on about the single European currency, apparently, "the biggest decision of our lifetimes." He wanted to "negotiate and decide" which didn't really seem to give any indication of what voting for him even meant. Danny didn't really care, didn't understand the economic quandary. The strongest arguments against adopting the Euro just sounded like meaningless nationalism. Major's biggest opponents seemed to be coming from within his own party, presenting Britain with a squabbling disunited mess of a party as the election loomed. Blair was quick to take advantage of the obvious discord: "The Conservatives are disintegrating before our eyes." The opinion polls agreed, the Conservative vote dwindling while support for Labour continued to rise.

It was a different shift of power in the local news, a shift of power that meant more to Danny than any election win. The news greeted Danny when he arrived in the Browns' close on Tuesday. He hadn't seen any news, hadn't popped into a shop to scan the back page of *The Argus* as he regularly did, so was unprepared for the impromptu street celebration. What greeted him was Ethan and James wearing every piece of Brighton merchandise they owned, swinging scarves around their neck, singing, "Dick Knight's blue and white army" on repeat.

"What? What's happened?" asked Danny.

"It's happened!" exclaimed Ethan.

"Archer's gone. Dick Knight's in charge," said James.

"Dick Knight's blue and white army," they sang, thrusting a screwed up newspaper into Danny's hand.

He struggled to read it as they jumped all over him, but it was true, mostly. The talks and the negotiations that felt like they were forever breaking down had finally borne fruit and Dick Knight was the Chairman of Brighton. It wasn't quite as simple as Knight in, Archer out, as James had claimed. Bill Archer was still part of the setup, something that had been a non-negotiable in the past, but he wasn't the one in charge. He'd finally been deposed and even if he was there, as long as Knight wielded the power, surely, this was the new dawn the club so desperately needed. Ethan and James didn't want to know the minutiae - they just wanted to celebrate the hope that this moment brought and Danny wanted that too. He hauled his t-shirt up and over his head, clambered as high up the nearest lamppost as he could and joined the song that thousands would sing that Saturday, "Dick Knight's blue and white army!" while waving his t-shirt like a flag to the bewilderment of the pensioner looking out of her window at number six.

On Saturday, Danny, Ethan and James enjoyed Mrs Brown's chicken pie although each of them scalded their tongues in their haste to eat it. They then embarked on their last ever walk to the Goldstone Ground. It felt both colossal and normal as they walked through Hove Park. Rain spat down upon them, tears from above that would join the many shed that day.

"We'll never do this again," said Danny.

Ethan and James looked at him, not knowing how to deal with the loss. They wanted to treasure this last moment doing what they loved, but the normal excitement of the walk to the ground was dampened by knowing they would never take these steps again, and by the agonising nerves they felt, so desperate were they for a result.

193

"What will we do without this?" asked Ethan.

Their friendship had been wrapped tightly around their football club and they each knew that trips to Gillingham were going to come at a cost, one that they would be unlikely to be able to afford. The rhythm of their life was being violently disrupted, a CD stuttering on a scratch before malfunctioning altogether.

They pulled their tickets from their pockets and entered through the North Stand for one last time, the turnstile creaking as they were admitted. They were early, but many others had chosen to do the same thing, to spend as much time savouring this day as they could.

On the pitch, players were warming up, jogging slowly and then breaking into a sprint. Afterwards, they stood in a circle, drilling passes to one another. Mark Ormerod was leaping to save shot after shot, bouncing to his feet as quickly as he could between each one. The feeling of colossal normality swept over the boys once again. This is what they always did. This is what they'd never do again.

Before the game started, the boys looked over to the Directors' Box - it had only held owners of visiting away teams for the last few games, but now, it was full again and sitting in the middle of it all, Dick Knight. He rose magisterially and humbly, and waved, smiling broadly as the fans sang his name. A man who had stood on the North Stand supporting his local team for decades was now the man in the Directors' Box. It was the way it should be, a fan who wants the best for the club, not a moneyman who lives miles away and never attends games.

A sense of empowerment flooded the stadium. Every individual had stood up for something they believed in, had felt powerless and ineffectual at times, but had joined together with other voices and those voices had grown, drawing in supporters from across the globe, and those voices had tumbled a powerful man. Every voice had been vital, every voice, one more added to the throng, the voice of Danny, the voice of Ethan, the voice of James, the voice of Ryan, travelling down from Hereford to say that this was bigger than loyalty to your local team. As the teams continued to warm up, two Doncaster players carried a banner around the perimeter of the pitch: 'DONCASTER PLAYERS

SALUTE BRIGHTON FANS.' Rapturous applause met them in every stand. Their simple statement reinforced the support Brighton had garnered from across the football community. The fans had started with fury, chaos and disruption, a desperate cry for help, but the protests had evolved: marches, walk-outs, poetry, whistles, meetings, hand-cuffs and that glorious gathering of the football community for Fans United, and every moment had chipped a fragment of rock away from a seemingly immovable boulder until it had finally been destroyed.

The ground was fuller than Danny had ever seen. Outside the ground, every vantage point was crammed with people. The gardens on Goldstone Lane were packed. In the gap between the East Stand and the South Stand, there was a mass of people standing in the middle of the road, a spot you could see a fragment of the pitch from. On the roofs of shops and offices, people stood, desperate to see this last ever game at the Goldstone.

A lone bugler walked out onto the pitch and the crowd fell silent as he played 'The Last Post'. This was real. This was never happening again. In 'The Box', Barnet Bishop collapsed against the crash barrier and wept. Dick Knight's arrival was a glorious new beginning, but he couldn't stop this brutal ending. The ground had been sold and there was no reversal.

When the players finally emerged for the game, it was almost a surprise, as if the fact that the reason they were all here - to watch a game of football - had been forgotten, but the reality that Brighton could be relegated today was back at the forefront of the fans' minds. Once again, a win was vital. Hereford were travelling to Leyton Orient and it was accepted as fact that Orient would let them win as an act of petty revenge for the attack on their players when they'd visited the Goldstone.

11,341 voices got behind the twenty-two men on the pitch, although the small section of Doncaster fans squeezed into one corner of the South Stand were pretty much drowned out. Without a board to protest against, the support for the team was constant, one chant rolling into another and another. Every fan wanted to savour this last day and sing every song that was sung.

"We are Brighton, we are Brighton, super Brighton from the South; we are Brighton, we are Brighton, super Brighton from the South."

The atmosphere was charged, every tackle full-blooded, every sprint lung-busting. When Ian Baird and Doncaster's Darren Moore tangled near the touchline in what seemed to be an innocuous moment, suddenly punches were flying, both players swinging wildly while team-mates waded in to both separate and create further conflict. Red cards were swiftly brandished and both players, still seething, marched away to their dressing rooms. Brighton had lost one of their biggest goal-threats, but Doncaster's loss of the mountainous defender was perhaps a greater loss for them.

With both teams reduced to ten men, the match continued at a frenetic pace, devoid of quality but not of passion. Danny's eyes flitted from the game to the stands, inhaling the last breaths of Goldstone air: stale cigarettes and glory. A dishevelled man in a tatty parka was clambering over the club-shop roof to get a better view. People on nearby rooftops were helping others to join them, the masses that hadn't been able to get tickets gaining whatever view they could.

At half-time, the boys sat down on the cool concrete steps for one last time. They listened to the half-time scores. Crystal Palace were winning at Swindon, so there was no last rousing cheer at their expense, but the score they were really waiting for was Hereford's. If Hereford bettered Brighton's result, Brighton would be relegated, but like Brighton, they were goalless, at Leyton Orient.

The teams hadn't long kicked off though when news of a goal at Orient rippled through the crowd.

"Orient have taken the lead."

"Orient are 1-0 up."

"1-0, ORIENT!" bellowed a voice from the back of the North Stand.

"We are staying up, say we are staying up!"

It was the loudest chant Danny had ever heard. You couldn't hear your own voice joining the throng, but just had to trust that you were part of this tumult. For minutes, the chant swept through the whole stadium and just as it abated, pockets of squeals were heard again from people clutching radios to their ears.

"It's 2-0!"

Seventy-five miles away, in a match that was immaterial to them, Leyton Orient were doing Brighton a massive favour.

All that was needed was for Brighton to score and they would be off the foot of the football league for the first time in months.

They pressed forward and a Doncaster defender bundled the ball out of play for a corner. Jeff Minton jogged over, spun the ball in his hands and placed it carefully down. Down in the south-west corner, corner-takers had to run up a slope before delivering a set piece and Minton stepped carefully back before lofting the ball high towards the back post. Mark Morris tussled with his man, getting his head to the ball and heading back towards the front post where Stuart Storer was waiting. Storer got his head to the ball, sending it looping towards the goal. There was never enough on the header to trouble the goal-keeper, but Craig Maskell jumped with the keeper, dragging him backwards towards the net and all he could manage was a flimsy punch to the ball, sending it back towards Morris while Maskell and the keeper collapsed into the goal. The net was gaping and Morris climbed again, sending his header ricocheting against the bar and back to Storer who jabbed at the ball sending it crashing, finally, into the top corner. The celebrations in the North Stand had stuttered with each attempt, but when the net bulged for the very last time, limbs were everywhere, delirium taking over every body. Danny lost a shoe; Ethan was on the floor with people tumbling over him and onto him, and James was squashed against the crash barrier in ecstatic agony.

For the last twenty minutes, there was endless chanting; the louder they sang, the more they could ignore their nerves. As full-time approached, Danny, Ethan and James climbed the barriers at the side of the pitch with many others and stood with their toes on the touchline, willing the thing they loved to come to an end because it was so important that it end with a win. The ball was played down the line and if Danny had reached out a foot, he could have brought the ball under control. There was no way the ball could leave the pitch unless it was launched over the heads of the fans who had made a fence with their bodies on the touchline, and then it came, a final blast of the whistle and as the referee and the players ran for the tunnel, the fans poured onto the pitch.

Danny sprinted into the centre circle and fell to his knees, the wet turf seeping through his jeans. Excitement and sorrow combined in every face, the result titanic. Hereford had pulled one back, but had lost 2-1 and Brighton were off the bottom of the league and if they could draw at Hereford next week, they would still be a member of the football league. But no football would ever be kicked on this pitch again. No goal would ever be celebrated in the North Stand again. In a few months, the whole place would be flattened and people would be selecting their groceries on the spot where Stuart Storer had volleyed in the last ever goal. How could something so soulless as potato-selection replace what the boys had just witnessed?

Danny dug his fingers into the turf as deep as he could and then wrenched a sod free. All around, people were doing the same. In the far corner, the giant stadium clock was being removed. A hammering sound could be heard as seats were smashed free of their stands. People carried huge advertising hoardings across the pitch.

James ran to where Danny was.

"Come and get a bit of the net," he said.

Danny walked back towards the North Stand. A member of the St John's Ambulance team was cutting squares of netting and handing them out to fans. Danny joined the small crowd gathered around him and waited until his hand was the next one reaching out to take a piece. Behind the goal, he pulled a peg from the ground and put it into his back pocket. He wanted to take everything, take the whole ground and rebuild it in his back garden, but he was limited by how much he could carry.

With his pockets and hands full and having found Ethan, the boys made their way back to the centre of the pitch. On the abandoned East Stand, one man had climbed up the terracing and pulled his trousers down to face the crowd. He gyrated his hips, while stumbling over his trousers and pants that were around his ankles. A poignant moment had become oddly farcical as fans cheered him on, a man finding a moment of exhibitionism the way to cope with loss.

Danny, Ethan and James joined with fans who stood and

sang for a while and then aimlessly wandered around the pitch, wanting to cover every inch of turf. They walked up to the goal in front of the South Stand. The netting had gone, but the posts remained. Danny stood on the spot Storer had scored from and swiped his leg through the air, recreating the moment, visualising the ball flying unerringly into the back of the net.

It felt impossible to leave, but the crowd was thinning and people were dragging themselves away, saying goodbye, doing what they knew had to be done. The boys walked back up the steps of the North Stand, wanting to leave the way they did after every match, through the gates that opened to allow the crowd to depart en masse. Daubed on the back wall of the North Stand was fresh paint, reading 'My Home, 77-97.' Beneath the paint, a man slumped forward, head bowed, hands clasped in front of him.

On the way out, Danny gave the frame of the gate a tap, a goodbye gesture. Bubbles of rusty blue paint chipped off at his touch and fluttered to the floor, the stadium already crumbling. He put one arm around Ethan's shoulder and one around James'. Affection was usually only ever communicated through punches, but the moment felt bigger than something a dead arm could express and they walked across Old Shoreham Road and into Hove Park.

26/04/97: Brighton 1-0 Doncaster Rovers (Storer)

3rd May 1997

Hereford United vs Brighton & Hove Albion

During the week, Danny walked past the Goldstone on the way home from work every day and each time he picked up more debris. On Monday, he carried a sink that had been smashed off the wall of a toilet all the way back along the Old Shoreham Road. On Tuesday, a row of metal spikes that had fallen from the top of a wall was carried home. When he'd arrived home, there was a letter from Brighton College of Technology telling him that his application had been accepted. He'd expected rejection, thought that his lack of GCSEs would be frowned upon, but the letter simply said that he'd been accepted and that he was invited to come into the college to meet the course leader in two weeks' time.

On Wednesday, he was back at the Goldstone, unscrewing a lightbulb from within one of the turnstiles which he then screwed into the light fitting in his bedroom when he got home. On Thursday, as the nation took to the polling stations, Danny carried home two seats, a wooden one from the West Stand and a plastic one from the South.

He was a year off being able to vote, but when he got home, his mum had waited for him and asked if he wanted to come to the polling station with her. They took the short walk to St Richard's Community Hall. When they arrived, Ivor Caplin was outside. Danny had seen his picture in *The Argus* regularly and had heard his name sung from the terraces of the North Stand when he'd opposed the Brighton board and spoken of his love for the Albion and his desire to work for their future, but this was the first time he'd seen him in person.

"Can I count on your vote?" he asked as Danny and his mum approached.

"You can," Danny's mum replied. "Do a good job for us."

Ivor Caplin looked into Danny's mum's eyes, caught off-guard by her words.

"I'll do my best," he said.

Danny followed his mum into the polling station where she

picked up a card. She showed Danny the list of names and they walked to the voting area, an area where you could place your X anonymously. Danny watched as she cast her vote before folding it in half and putting it into the box. For twenty-four years, Labour candidates had tried to oust the Conservative candidate, Tim Sainsbury - son of a Baron, Eton-educated, fabulously wealthy because of the success of the supermarket chain. No Labour candidate had even got more than half the votes that Sainsbury had accrued, but he'd stepped aside and Ivor Caplin was facing Robert Guy instead. The Tories' plummeting popularity combined with Caplin's energy and admired support for the Albion meant that this Tory safe seat was very much, under threat.

Later that evening, Danny sat in the green armchair that had the best view of the TV. He rubbed his fingers back and forward on the armrest, feeling the friction of the velvet before stroking it back into place. Simon had grumbled when he'd been told that he wasn't allowed to finish his game of *Donkey Kong Country*, but Danny had demanded that they see the start of the election coverage.

Danny's mum took her seat as self-important music was played over a montage of the white cliffs of Dover, green fields, London streets, Big Ben and Downing Street and then David Dimbleby was strolling round a busy studio talking about the "biggest upset since 1945." Exit polls were declared to be predicting a sizeable Labour majority, but actual results were slow to come; preamble, interviews and various complicated graphics were shown, all of it making a victory for Tony Blair sound absolutely guaranteed.

"They can't be wrong," said Danny. "They're all saying Labour are going to win."

"Let's just wait," said his mum and she disappeared into the kitchen to make a cup of tea.

The TV showed people charging around in Sunderland South, rapidly carrying boxes of voting slips while people at desks flicked through votes. It still took close to an hour to actually declare though and Labour were 1-0 up, but David Dimbleby explained that this seat was a safe one for Labour and one that you couldn't read too much into. The camera cut to Peter

Snow who explained that although the Sunderland seat was safe, it still indicated a swing of votes towards Labour and although it was too early to get the champagne out, the voting in Sunderland suggested that the exit polls were accurate.

Results continued to be slow to come, all of them matching the prediction of a Labour victory. Danny felt his eyes closing. He convinced himself that he'd listen with his eyes closed and open them for each announced seat, but quickly, his head was resting against the back of the chair and he was fast asleep.

A few hours later, he woke with a start.

"What's going on?"

"David Mellor's just lost his seat. I think it's happening."

All Danny knew about David Mellor was that he'd been on the front cover of the tabloids. Apparently, he'd had an affair and worn his Chelsea kit in the bedroom during his indiscretions.

Danny tried to pay attention and lasted another fifteen minutes, every seat announced, even those won by the Conservatives, seemingly making the victory for Labour seem inevitable.

The next time Danny awoke, he looked blearily over to his mum. She was sitting on the sofa, her cheeks damp, but a smile on her face. On the television, Michael Portillo was making a speech, another Tory faller.

"It's happened," his mum said. She was certain now.

His mum got up and walked over to him, bent down and wrapped her arms tightly around his neck. It reminded him of when he was a little boy and he'd called her name from his bedroom and then told her that he'd had a bad dream. She'd sat with him, held his hand and then hugged him, telling him it would be alright. Now she hugged him again, like when he was scared and little. He could feel the dampness of her cheeks against his own. He felt awkward, but he put his arm around his mum.

"I love you, Danny," she said and then pulled away, wiping her cheeks and smiling.

"I love you too," he mumbled back, wanting to say the words, but finding them so hard to utter.

She walked back to the sofa and sat down. Danny was wide awake now. Everyone in the studio was saying that this was the moment; Portillo going had to mean that Labour had won the election and by the time Danny got out of bed at ten o' clock the next morning, it was confirmed. Labour had won. Ivor Caplin had won. It felt like new beginnings were happening everywhere: Dick Knight, acceptance into college, but later today, he was going back to the past, back to his dad, back to those painful memories.

He'd taken the day off work to travel to Hereford the day before the match that would either secure Brighton's league status or send them crashing into non-league. The train left at 11:13am and he needed to walk to Hove Station to begin the journey, a journey on his own, the first time he had gone to a game without Ethan and James, but his dad had only got tickets for himself, Ryan and Danny. The idea of sitting in the Hereford stand had felt hideous, but he had to be there, had to be present for this moment and sitting in the wrong stand was better than not going at all. He didn't have the money to fund the travel and the ticket, so the only way to attend had been to accept his dad's gift.

Danny headed down the Old Shoreham Road, thinking that he'd walk past the Goldstone Ground on his way to the station. He chucked a few clothes, including his Brighton shirt, into the backpack that he'd used for school. He almost forgot to take any toiletries, but he turned back at the garden gate and re-entered the house and grabbed a can of Lynx and his toothbrush and just as he was about to leave again, he thought he'd take a book and climbed the stairs, three at a time and looked at his sparse collection on the bottom shelf. Most of them were part of the Narnia series or Roald Dahl books (books from his younger days), but there was one he hadn't read, a copy of *Great Expectations* by Charles Dickens. On his last day of school, his form tutor had given a book to everyone in the group, all of them cheap classics. In the front of the book was a message, a simple, 'All the best for the future, Ms Perkins.' He'd never been tempted to pick the book up before - the cover had an unappealing and uninspiring brown tinge and featured men in top hats and women in bonnets, but with nothing else to choose, he thought he'd give it a go to pass the time on the train journey.

Checking the time, he broke into a jog to ensure that he

didn't arrive at the train station late. He jogged down the hill past the cemetery and then up the hill on the other side, his back getting slick and slippery as his backpack bounced up and down with every step. Once he'd ascended the hill, he felt confident that he was back on track and when he reached the Sackville Road junction, he realised that he actually had plenty of time to spare and stopped off in the newsagent that sold cups of tea in polystyrene cups for 20p. He asked for three sugars and walked towards the Goldstone Ground, sipping the sweet, scalding liquid.

When he arrived at the plundered Goldstone Ground, the gates into the North-west terrace were wide open and cars were parked in a neat row in the small car park. Danny walked in and looked out onto the pockmarked pitch and was amazed to see a group of men playing football in front of the South Stand. There were the unmistakable dreadlocks of Peter Smith and the tufty spiky hair of Ian Baird and the carefully constructed centre parting of Mark Ormerod. It was the Brighton team in training, risking broken ankles as they charged around the cratered surface, the missing chunks of soil and grass scattered across homes in the town. Steve Gritt was stood in the middle in baggy shorts and white football socks rolled down to the ankle, pointing, shouting, gesturing. Danny wished he could just stand there and watch the players prepare for the biggest match of their lives, but he couldn't be late for the train and he dragged himself away, gulping down the last of the quickly cooling tea and then breaking into a jog once more, down the hill to Hove Station.

He made it to the station with four minutes to spare, the first leg of the journey taking him to Fratton Station. He didn't like the idea of travelling to the station next to Portsmouth's Fratton Park, his first thought being that this had almost been the journey that Brighton fans would have been forced to make next season if they wanted to see 'home' games, although there had been constant chants of "We'll never go to Pompey" when *The Argus* had broken the plan secretly concocted in the Brighton boardroom.

Danny looked out of the window, enjoying watching the world whizz by for the first half hour. He liked pushing his forehead against the cold glass, eyes adjusting from the blur of close-up details that could barely be discerned to vast open fields trundling past. With his eyes occupied, his mind emptied, a mindless peace flooded him. When he leant back in his chair, his mind sprang back to life: his dad, the match and that this was life with Labour in charge.

He pulled *Great Expectations* out of his bag, read of a young boy meeting an escaped convict in a graveyard. He was surprised at how interested he was, how he felt nervous for the boy, Pip, having to steal food from his physically and verbally abusive sister to feed the convict who threatened to murder him if he failed. He read the first two chapters, but could feel his eyes closing as he started the third and he allowed himself to succumb, waking up in a panic a little later, convinced that he had been asleep for ages and had missed the stop, but the next announcement revealed that Fratton was still to come.

At Fratton, he changed for Newport. He didn't understand why the journey was taking him into Wales when Hereford was in England, but his dad had given him the instructions and he was following them, not having a clue what he would do if any of the connections failed. He tucked the piece of paper with the details of the three trains he needed to catch inside the page of *Great Expectations* that he'd got to.

When he got on the train to Newport, he picked up the book again, reading of Pip's successful snaffling of a pie, brandy and a file and delivering his haul to the convict who was softer and a little grateful on the second meeting. By the time he'd got to Newport, Pip had received a strange invitation to an old woman's house after the convict had been found and arrested.

From Newport, it was only forty-nine minutes to Hereford. Danny hadn't thought about packing any food and it was well into the afternoon. A trolley with chocolate bars and crisps had repeatedly passed him, but when he'd seen someone buying a Boost for 60p, he couldn't bring himself to pay double the normal price for any food and he decided he'd wait until he arrived in Hereford, hoping that his dad might provide him with something. He couldn't concentrate on reading any longer. Just hearing the word 'Hereford' announced made Danny feel sick with nerves for what might happen the next day. As soon as he brought his emotions under control about the match, he started thinking about what he'd say to his dad. He didn't want to fake an emotional reunion like on *Surprise, Surprise*, but he also didn't want to appear moody and he knew that his emotional awkwardness was often interpreted that way.

He couldn't settle on a phrase which captured the middle-ground between a willingness to forgive his dad and move on whilst also wanting his dad to know that he didn't absolve him. It felt like a contradiction, but he knew that what he felt was right: that people do wrong and horrible things, but that there's no point in holding onto it forever and letting bitterness coil inside you like a snake. There were conversations that they'd never had and while Danny hated the thought of talking about the hurt he had felt, still felt, he knew that it was important that his dad know and understand the impact that his choice had on him.

It was a complex labyrinth of emotions, one that would be hard to navigate by two emotionally illiterate people like Danny and his dad.

The meeting was further complicated, when it came, by Ryan's presence. Danny didn't mind Ryan being there, didn't blame him for any of this. He'd been annoyed that his dad hadn't thought that this would have been better with just the two of them, but Danny was also glad that after a brief and awkward greeting, Ryan released the tension when he launched into football chat, starting by bemoaning the fact that the league table was ordered by goals scored rather than goal difference when teams were level on points. If goal difference were the measure, Brighton would still be rooted to the bottom of the football league. Danny pointed out that Brighton should never have been deducted two points and if that injustice hadn't happened, then Hereford would be bottom of the league and after friendly bickering about who was most deserving of being bottom on the car ride back to Danny's dad's house, they agreed that it was incredibly annoying that Hartlepool had started winning. It would have been far better if Brighton and Hereford fans had been able to celebrate survival together at Hartlepool's expense. They regretted that this beautiful moment was not a mathematical possibility anymore and tomorrow, one of the boys would be celebrating while the other grieved.

The football chat went back and forth as they walked

through the front door. Danny hadn't prepared himself for meeting Ryan's mum, Sharon, the woman that his dad left his mum for, and when she interrupted Ryan's fulsome praise of Hereford striker, Tony Agana, Danny felt like he'd been ambushed.

"You must be Danny," she said.

"Er, yes."

"It's so lovely to finally meet you."

This was the opposite of lovely. He hadn't even thought about the fact that he would be meeting her and the suddenness of being confronted by her was horrible, but it only showed in clipped short answers and a lack of eye contact on Danny's part.

"Do you want to play SWOS?" asked Ryan.

Danny grabbed the opportunity to escape and Ryan led the way to his bedroom, switched his computer on and soon, *Sensible World of Soccer*'s title sequence was scrolling up the screen.

"Do you want to make a custom Brighton team? I've got a Hereford team with all our greatest players," said Ryan.

The only name Danny recognised was Ronnie Radford. Danny made quick work of creating his Brighton team, a few of the current players included: Stuart Storer and Paul McDonald on the wings, Jeff Minton in central midfield and Peter Smith at right-back, but he filled the rest of the team with his favourites from the past: John Keeley, Ian Chapman, Steve Foster, Paul McCarthy, Dean Wilkins, Kurt Nogan and Peter Ward, the last, the only player he'd never seen play, but the regular renditions of his name on the North Stand made him impossible to leave out.

Danny wasn't used to the joystick that Ryan handed over and his performance was clumsy, losing 8-1, Ronnie Radford scoring a screamer from forty yards to complete the thrashing.

"That's what's happening tomorrow," said Ryan, dancing around the room in celebration. "We are staying up, say, we are staying up."

Danny didn't believe in omens, but he didn't like the fact that less than an hour into his time in Hereford, he'd let Brighton down badly already.

They carried on playing, choosing to take turns playing half a match each on career mode, managing Neuchatel Xamax in the Swiss league to avoid a quarrel about whether Brighton or Hereford would be selected.

They only stopped playing when a pizza delivery arrived. Danny didn't think his dad had ever ordered a takeaway when they lived together, but he wasn't complaining. He hadn't eaten since the bowl of Weetos he'd had in Brighton ten hours earlier. They sat around a small circular table in the kitchen, plucking slices of pizza from their cardboard boxes. Danny's dad asked him the same questions he usually asked on his Friday phone-calls, but Ryan made conversation much easier, probing further, wanting to know about *Sorted* magazine and getting excited when he told him about his interview with Steve Gritt.

"That must have been incredible. I would absolutely love to interview Graham Turner."

Once they'd eaten, they went into the living room. Danny had hoped that he'd be able to escape up to Ryan's bedroom and continue their career as player-coaches in the Swiss league, but he hadn't wanted to suggest it, realising that his dad would want to spend time with him. However, the TV was switched on and conversation centred around what they were watching. It was *TFI Friday* and Sean Bean was being interviewed about the election. He hadn't voted, said he was too tired to, but he would have voted Labour if he had which got a cheer from the crowd at the bar.

"Did you vote, Dad?" Danny asked.

"Of course. I voted Liberal Democrats. I would have voted Labour, but no one round here votes for Labour. Voting for the Lib Dems was a tactical vote. I was pleased that Labour won overall. Did you vote?"

"I'm not old enough, Dad."

"Oh, yes, sorry son."

"Did the Lib Dems win round here?"

"They did. Fellas at my work were saying that the Tories have been in power here since the war, but not anymore."

The Foo Fighters had started playing on *TFI Friday* and conversation subsided other than Sharon's comment that they were a "bloody racket."

The evening passed with intermittent conversation,

comments on what they were watching and at ten o' clock, Danny pretended that he was tired and went upstairs, followed by Ryan. They played three more hours of SWOS, winning the Swiss league comfortably and then beating Barcelona home and away in the group stages of the Champions' League.

In the early hours, Ryan got into his bed - he offered it to Danny, but Danny said that the blow-up mattress on the floor was fine - and they got back to talking about Brighton and Hereford.

"That match I came to watch at your place, when you thrashed Hartlepool: it's those goals that mean you're above us."

Danny remembered Ryan celebrating with him in the North Stand, a beautiful communal moment and now here he was, realising that those goals had hurt Hereford, could spell the end of their league existence. They tried to construct a joint Brighton and Hereford side, going through the positions and selecting who was the better player, but it was impossible as neither of them had any knowledge of the other team, having only seen them play once this season and that had been the match when the fans had walked out early.

Danny woke early the following morning and he was instantly alert and wired. He squeezed his fists and released and clenched them repeatedly and then got back onto Ryan's computer to continue playing while Ryan slept on. Still Ryan slept on and Danny pulled *Great Expectations* out of his bag and read about Pip's visit to Miss Havisham's, a weird swerve in the story where the young boy telling his story was face to face with an old woman in a dirty, yellowing wedding dress.

At breakfast, Danny's dad announced that he had a special treat for the boys. Danny thought that his dad had forgotten that he was talking to sixteen-year-old boys and not children half that age. The treat was a visit to The Black and White House Museum, an idea that Ryan groaned at, and Danny understood why when an hour later, they were wandering through what was essentially, just an old house. All Danny and Ryan could think about was the football match and they tried to hurry Danny's dad around, but he insisted on drawing them back to plaques of information.

They finally escaped to have lunch in McDonald's, Big Mac

meals all round. Danny and Ryan inhaled their meals as if kick-off was three seconds away rather than three hours away and drummed their fingers on the table while Danny's dad went to get more napkins at the end of the meal and then revisited the counter for a cup of coffee.

"There are hours to go until kick-off," he said, sensing their impatience when they emerged onto the high street. "Do you want to see the cathedral, Danny?"

"Dad, can we just go to the ground?" he replied, realising that in all the phone-calls, he had never expressed frustration with his dad. It felt normal to be back, griping at his dad and finding him utterly annoying.

"Really, already?" his dad asked.

"Yes," chorused both boys who started walking in the direction of the car park.

They arrived at Edgar Street with two hours to go before kick-off, but there were already hundreds of fans milling around. Danny's Brighton shirt was hidden beneath his orange Adidas tracksuit top, zipped right up under his chin. He wanted to feel the clingy polyester on his skin, the seagull crest resting against his rapidly beating heart even if the shirt remained hidden in the home end.

The turnstiles weren't yet open and they wandered around the ground, Ryan describing each stand, the Meadow End where he normally stood on match-days, the Len Weston Stand named after a now-deceased chairman who came to the club's rescue time and time again, the Blackfriars Street End where the Brighton fans would be and the Merton Stand where Danny's dad had bought tickets, a stand that would be shared with the directors of both clubs, both of them desperate to not face the financial stranglehold of non-league football.

As they stood outside, longing for a torturous ninety minutes to begin, Danny spotted a face he recognised walking towards him, head bowed, trying to avoid attention: David Bellotti. What was he doing here? *The Argus* had declared that although Bill Archer was still part-owner, David Bellotti would no longer be at the club, but here he was, at this pivotal moment, hoping to avoid any Brighton fans. His wife was with him and they approached a steward and were ushered in. Danny hoped his appearance would go unnoticed by other Brighton fans. At Doncaster, the fans had celebrated the new hope that a new board brought to the club. Bellotti hadn't been seen scuttling into the Directors' Box at the Goldstone for months, his presence inciting unrest and the potential for violence on his final appearances. If the Brighton fans realised he was in the stands, things could turn ugly, particularly if things weren't going their way on the pitch.

When the turnstiles opened, Danny, his dad and Ryan were some of the first of the crowd in and they took their seats. Danny rubbed his cheeks vigorously with the palms of his hands, curled his toes up inside his shoes, leaned as far forward as he could, resting his face on his thighs.

"Are you alright, son?" his dad asked.

It was unbearable. Ryan was going through similar contortions, neither boy able to contain the tension that tingled through their bodies. Around them, anxiety was written across every face, Danny's dad the anomaly amongst a crowd of people that had spent weeks obsessing over this game, knowing that this final fixture was bound to define their season, their future. Relegation from the Second Division to the Third Division meant nothing really. Teams bounced up and down between them all the time, but only one team fell out of the football league each year and often, they never returned. There was the additional complication that you could only get promoted into the football league if your ground met the requirements of league football and Brighton didn't even have a ground.

The players appearing from the tunnel brought a welcome distraction and Danny and Ryan looked to opposite ends of the pitch to see who had made the starting line-ups. Mark Ormerod or Nicky Rust in goal was the biggest question and if James were here, he would have been disappointed to see Ormerod warming up. The experience of John Humphrey was preferred to the pace of Peter Smith. Kerry Mayo's energy was partnered with Jeff Minton's guile in the centre of the park. There was no space for Robbie Reinelt who had become a more regular goal-scorer in recent weeks. Ian Baird and Craig Maskell would lead the line.

As the Brighton fans broke into song, Danny mouthed the words, silently yearning for Brighton to do enough. As the game grew closer, a huge bull was paraded around the perimeter of the pitch, slowly waddling along the touchline. As it toddled on legs that looked too thin to carry its massive bulk, the Brighton fans burst into a song celebrating Burger King, the bull walking by having heard it all before.

It felt like they'd been in the ground for hours when the game finally started, Brighton taking the kick-off and promptly hammering the ball straight out of play. Both teams were attempting a direct style, sending the ball sailing into the opposition half at every opportunity. For Brighton, the ball just came straight back whereas for Hereford, they were managing to win the loose balls and find their wingers, but the crosses were poor, either under-hit and easily cleared at the front post or sailing harmlessly over the strikers in the box.

When Hereford gained a corner though, their crossing was more accurate and when one corner was scrambled clear to the edge of the Brighton box, Hereford had the first effort of the match that seriously threatened the Brighton goal, a volley that sailed just wide of the post and everyone around Danny leapt to their feet and held their heads in their hands when the ball ended up in amongst the Brighton fans instead of nestling in the back of the net.

Hereford were desperately pouring forward, knowing only a win was good enough for them. Striker, Tony Agana was once part of the Leeds United squad that had won the top flight the year before it became the Premiership. He was showing his quality, jinking past Brighton defenders before going tumbling on the edge of the box. Again, the crowd were on their feet, howling for a penalty. Danny desperately hoped that the foul was outside the box. Agana had clearly been crudely chopped down, but the referee showed the striker a yellow card for diving and Brighton were awarded the free-kick. Danny hid a smile in his collar while impotent fury surrounded him. Ryan punched the chair in front of him so hard that the plastic splintered. Danny's dad looked around in confusion, having no idea what the fuss was about, but he was wise enough to keep quiet and mimic the crowd's stand-up, sit-down routine, following fractionally later, sometimes understanding that what was happening on the pitch excited them, but often, not really being sure how what happened on the turf related to the crowd's movement. Danny also stood up with the Hereford fans, not wanting to out himself as an infiltrator and also not wanting to miss a moment, even if it was a Hereford shot.

The pressure kept coming and Agana was at the centre of it again, attempting an acrobatic finish as the ball came towards him in the box. He mistimed his leap and didn't make contact with the ball and Ormerod rushed out to dive at his feet, but Agana was back to his feet and sent the ball squirming past the onrushing Ormerod and across the edge of the six-yard box. Hereford and Brighton players charged towards the ball: the flame-haired Kerry Mayo sliding through the box was the first there, but his touch sent the ball flying up and into the top corner of the net. The Brighton fans were stationary behind the goal, Mayo flat on his back with his head in his hands, but everywhere else was bedlam; Danny's dad knocked into Danny who chose to let himself fall to the floor and let the agony of the moment take him. On hands and knees on the concrete, he stayed, a wounded animal, a bullet ripping through his flesh, leaving him gasping and stunned.

No one noticed this one boy. They were too distracted by their own joy.

"The Whites are staying up," they sang, "the whites are staying up, and now you're gonna believe us, and now you're gonna believe us, and now you're gonna believe us, the Whites are staying up."

Arrowed fingers were pointing at the Brighton fans. They stood and took it for a moment, but they'd been bashed and kicked so many times this season, by businessmen and other teams, that even the horrific tragedy of the local teenager accidentally inflicting a catastrophic wound to the team was not enough to defeat them and the shout of "Seagulls" from a few was quickly joined by thousands who knew that their voices would lift the players, would stir their souls to fight.

Kerry Mayo hauled himself to his feet and the Brighton players forced their bodies back into the battle, to fight for every ball, but still it was Hereford who were calmer and could find passes in the final third of the pitch. Agana raced clear, but at an angle, smashed the ball into the side netting. Again, Agana raced through, skipping past Ormerod, but he was forced wide by a heavy touch and forced to cross instead of shoot and after a moment's mayhem in a crowded penalty box, the referee blew the whistle and Brighton were given a reprieve, a free-kick for a trip on Minton.

Brighton only once managed to shoot at the Hereford goal in the first half, Paul McDonald jinking off the left touchline and advancing towards the area. With a defender approaching, he attempted a shot from range that was so weak that the goalkeeper waited as it piddled towards him, bending to one knee to pick up the ball that barely reached him.

When the half-time whistle went, Danny was relieved that Brighton were only one goal behind, that there was still some hope, but only if they managed to get hold of the ball.

Danny turned his legs sideways to allow Ryan to shuffle past to go to the toilet. It was the first time he had been alone with his dad since he had arrived in Hereford.

"There's something I need to tell you," his dad said.

Danny turned to his dad.

"I'm going to get married again, to Sharon." He left the sentence hanging in the air and looked at his son.

"You're still married to Mum."

"Yes, I know that. We need to sort out the divorce first, but once that's sorted, we're going to get married. I haven't told Ryan or Simon yet. I wanted to tell you first."

"Okay."

"What do you think? Are you alright with it?"

None of what his dad had done over the last year and a half had been alright. He wasn't alright with his dad marrying Sharon, but it was the rotten cherry on top of a rotten cake. What was the point in complaining about the cherry when the whole thing would make you sick? The first moment of betrayal was what hurt. Everything from then on had just been the collateral damage from that moment.

Danny looked ahead, the turf waiting for players to emerge. He could feel tears pricking his eyes. He didn't want to deal with this now, but he had no choice. His dad had chosen this brief interval to seek his approval, to squash the guilt that he surely felt.

"It hurts," said Danny, fighting to be honest, "but it's okay," accepting that he didn't get to choose what his dad did, and he could fight it or accept it.

Ryan returned and Danny's dad whispered, "Thank you, sorry," and patted him awkwardly on the back.

"Forty-five minutes to ensure survival," said Ryan, rubbing his hands together.

The mood in the Merton Stand was still nervous, but not at the same level that it had been at the start of the match. Hereford's good performance in the first half and Brighton's inability to threaten the goal in any way had birthed a confidence in the Hereford fans.

Ten minutes into the second half, Paul McDonald went down clutching his leg after a heavy challenge. Every challenge had been heavy that afternoon and it was inevitable that someone was going to get injured. He hobbled to his feet, limped to the sidelines and was replaced by number twelve, Robbie Reinelt.

Hereford were still looking the more likely team to score and when Adrian Foster dispossessed a ponderous Mark Morris, he looked like he was racing through on goal. Ross Johnson darted across and collapsed onto the ground in front of him, bringing him tumbling down. Inexplicably, the referee waved play on and for the second time in the game, Hereford fans were furious, telling the referee that he didn't know what he was doing and much worse.

Brighton were getting increasingly desperate and Stuart Tuck shot from thirty-five yards, hopelessly wide, the Albion fans behind the goal groaning in agony as the goalkeeper retrieved the ball and set it down for a goal-kick. He'd been launching goal-kicks high into the sky and into the Brighton half all game, but this time, he scuffed the kick, sending it fizzing along the floor. A Hereford defender reached a leg out and scooped it into the centre circle where Jeff Minton was waiting, and he hooked the ball back up and over the now disorganised defence. Ian Baird chased it down, but got a hefty shove in the back and the ball was back with Hereford, but again, they failed to clear their lines, shanking a clearance up into the air to the edge of the area. The Hereford defence had been so solid all game, hammering the ball clear, but one poor goal-kick had spread panic. Craig Maskell met the poor clearance with a volley which arced towards the far corner of the net, the keeper launching himself across the goal. Instead of finding the net, the ball pinged off the post, back out into open play and there was Robbie Reinelt, only on the pitch for a few minutes, drawing back his left foot and then drilling the ball back across the scrambling keeper and into the bottom corner.

Danny gasped, squeezed his thighs tight with his fingers and then pulled his tracksuit collar up and into his mouth to stifle a scream of delight. He'd never had to suppress a celebration before, had always been in the home end, letting delirium control his body and now with the most important goal he had ever seen, he was having to fight himself to avoid getting a beating. Reinelt was in front of the Brighton fans, other players leaping all over him. The Brighton fans were a churning tempest of ecstasy and Danny wished he were in there, swept up in it all, but at least he was in the ground, seeing this moment.

"What's the time?" he asked his dad.

He had no idea how much time had passed, and he hoped that the game was almost over, but it was only quarter past four. There was still half an hour to go.

Straight from the kick-off, Hereford were on the attack, again and again and again, a volley looping just wide, Ormerod missing a punch and Agana heading just past the post, a long range drive that Ormerod tipped to safety.

Brighton occasionally got the ball forward, but the players seemed intent on sending the ball flying into the Brighton fans behind the goal instead of the back of the net. Each time, the Brighton fans would refuse to give the ball back and a few precious seconds were wasted while a fresh new ball was supplied.

The challenges were becoming more and more reckless, the players fearlessly putting their bodies in danger to gain an advantage. A three-way slide tackle left Jeff Minton, Stuart Storer and a Hereford player clutching their shins in agony and Storer left the pitch to be replaced by Gary Hobson. The collision had given Hereford a free-kick on the edge of the Brighton box and another chance came Hereford's way, this time a snatched shot smashed over the bar.

"What's the time?" Danny asked for the fourteenth time

since Reinelt's goal had gone in.

"It's twenty to five," replied his dad. "Do you want to leave now to beat the traffic?"

"No," chorused Danny and Ryan, their hearts tugging in opposite directions.

Hereford had stopped trying to defend, desperately seeking a winner to keep them in the league and with no one back, an aimless clearance sent Maskell racing in on goal, but his blasted shot was tipped wide by the goal-keeper.

"What's the time?" Danny asked.

"Quarter to five," his dad replied.

It should be over. The game should be over, but still it went on. A long ball bounced high and over the tired Brighton defenders and Adrian Foster was clean through on goal, Ormerod racing out to meet him. Time seemed to stand still. This kick would relegate Brighton, would send those Hereford fans pouring onto the pitch like they'd done when Ronnie Radford had scored his thunderbolt, but Foster was not to be the hero. He scooped the ball straight into Ormerod's arms and the fans around Danny howled while he felt like his heart was going to burst out of his chest.

It was the final chance. The final whistle went and Danny hid his face in his hands, silently screaming his delight. On the other side of his dad, Ryan covered his face with his hands to hide the tears that were flowing. They would be brothers soon and here they were, sharing this moment: joy and agony side by side.

The Brighton players ran to the Brighton fans, arms aloft, shirts thrown. Several hundred Hereford fans ran onto the pitch, met by riot police with huge circular shields stretched across the halfway line, but the fans weren't looking for trouble. They were surrounding distraught Hereford players, hugging them, lifting them to their feet, thanking them for giving their all. Police Officers with Alsatians were pouring out of the tunnel onto the pitch, but there was only peaceful sorrow in the face of delirious joy. No one wanted to fight.

Danny's eyes sparkled with joy as he watched the Brighton fans celebrate. Dick Knight was now strolling onto the pitch, arms above his head, applauding the fans. His instalment as

Chairman felt complete with this survival. Brighton could build from this, but they would have to start by doing it without a ground, playing their home games at Gillingham.

Danny's dad suggested they leave three times before the boys were ready to depart, Ryan wanting to linger in his sadness, Danny, not wanting to leave the party.

That night, as he lay on his back watching the Reinelt goal replaying again and again in his mind, he whispered to a sleeping Ryan, who had faded into a miserable sleep hours earlier facing the wall, "We're going to be brothers. I wouldn't choose what's happened, but you're going to be a good brother."

The next morning, Danny's dad drove him back to the station, Radio 2 switched on to distract them from the awkwardness they both felt when they were alone together.

"Thank you for coming," his dad said.

Danny looked at him as they sat waiting for a red light to turn green. "That's okay," he replied.

"You're welcome any time," and Danny knew that he was and that this visit would be repeated, always bringing connection and pain, a relationship being slowly built again on fragile foundations.

As they said goodbye at the station, neither of them knew quite how to act, a hug too much, a handshake too formal. Danny's dad put his hand on Danny's shoulder. Danny could feel the warmth and weight of it and it was still there as he gazed out of the window, the train speeding back to Brighton, through villages, towns and cities, his dad left behind with his new life and new family. Now and then, he picked up *Great Expectations*, but found it difficult to concentrate, a surge of euphoria tingling through him as his mind drifted from the book to Robbie Reinelt's goal. In just a few days, Labour had ousted the Tories, Dick Knight had ousted Bellotti and Archer, he'd met his dad for the first time in seventeen months and Brighton had pulled off a miraculous escape from relegation out of the football league. In a few months' time, he'd be starting college. There were so many hurdles that had been overcome, so many moments where he could have fallen, the club could have fallen, but he was still standing, the club was still standing. Things, somehow, seemed to be going right. But, his dad still lived hundreds of miles away and the Goldstone Ground was no more. These were things that weren't changing.

When the train pulled into Brighton Station, Danny hoisted his backpack up onto his back and walked towards the concourse. Two boys stood the other side of the ticket barrier, holding scarves aloft, standing, waiting for their friend. When Danny saw them, he broke into a run.

03/05/97: Hereford United 1-1 Brighton (Reinelt)

Football League, Third Division: 1996-1997

	P	W	D	L	F	A	Pts
1. Wigan Athletic	46	26	9	11	84	51	87
2. Fulham	46	25	12	9	72	38	87
3. Carlisle United	46	24	12	10	67	44	84
4. Northampton Town	46	20	12	14	67	44	72
5. Swansea City	46	21	8	17	62	58	71
6. Chester City	46	18	16	12	55	43	70
7. Cardiff City	46	20	9	17	56	54	69
8. Colchester United	46	17	17	12	62	51	68
9. Lincoln City	46	18	12	16	70	69	66
10. Cambridge United	46	18	11	17	53	59	65
11. Mansfield Town	46	16	16	14	47	45	64
12. Scarborough	46	16	15	15	65	68	63
13. Scunthorpe United	46	18	9	19	59	62	63
14. Rochdale	46	14	16	16	58	58	58
15. Barnet	46	14	16	16	46	51	58
16. Leyton Orient	46	15	12	19	50	58	57
17. Hull City	46	13	18	15	44	50	57
18. Darlington	46	14	10	22	64	78	52
19. Doncaster Rovers	46	14	10	22	52	66	52
20. Hartlepool United	46	14	9	23	53	66	51
21. Torquay United	46	13	11	22	46	62	50
22. Exeter City	46	12	12	22	48	73	48
23. Brighton & HA	46	13	10	23	53	70	47*
24. Hereford United	46	11	14	21	50	65	47

*	Brighton deducted two points for pitch invasions in their home match vs Lincoln City, October 1st 1996

If teams were level on points, league position was decided by goals scored. Brighton's goal difference was inferior to Hereford's, but they had scored three more goals.

Acknowledgements

Helen, thank you for your patience while I obsessively got lost in my writing. I appreciate you sitting and listening as I read the book aloud to you. Ned and Jarvis, I love doing this all over again with you, but you get to see a Premier League team that I never thought was possible. Ed and Jon - what glorious memories of standing on the North Stand together. Thank you for sharing the experience of being fans and being massive encouragers of me while I wrote. Ed, thank you for your work on the front cover. Jethro and Sian, thank you for your meticulous proof-reading. Your advice helped me to craft and shape the book. Steve, you were so generous with your time. It was such a pleasure to sit with you as you recounted those wonderful times at the Goldstone. You are a hero to all Brighton fans and I'm grateful for what you did all those years ago and your generosity in sharing it with me. Julia, thank you for your detective work. Anton, thank you for your encouragement and championing of me, and for all those dinners in the '90s.